St. Abient Run

by

Jeana Kendrick

Panther Creek Press

Spring, Texas

Published by Panther Creek Press
SAN 253-8520
116 Tree Crest
P.O. Box 130233 Panther Creek Station
Spring, TX 77393-0233

Cover photograph by Jeff Kendrick
Photo image used with permission of Paul Popov
Cover design by Pamela Copus
Sonic Media, Inc.
Plano, TX

Manufactured in the United States of America
Printed and bound by Data Duplicators, Inc.
Houston, TX

1 2 3 4 5 6 7 8 9 10

Library of Congress Cataloguing in Publication Data

Kendrick, Jeana

I. St. abient run   II. Fiction

For my husband Jeff; fellow writer, editor, publisher and friend Guida Jackson; Ruby Tolliver; and family and friends for their encouragement and support.

St. Abient Run could not have been written without the assistance of a number of people. My gratitude is endless to my editor and publisher Dr. Guida Jackson who is a joy to work with and a treasured friend. Special thanks to Bill Laufer and Joyce Harlow who worked behind the scenes, and to Pamela Copus, who designed the book cover. Thanks to Ann Nelson for proofing the German contained herein and to Ann Andersen, Jack Crumpler, Ruby Tollivier, Kathryn, Jim and Elaine Kendrick, Sharon Davis and Rhonda Mayfield who shared a fountain of insight. Lastly, thanks to my husband Jeff for his help throughout this process.

1

Susan Pardue dropped into the worn leather chair across from her managing editor. "Jerry, you're not sending me to France again?"

He leaned forward as if impatient, his hands grazing a stack of papers on the walnut desk. "Sorry, but someone has to go."

Susan stared out at the blue skies and line of forest greenery, a backdrop for Houston's surrealistic skyline. Another backwater assignment, she thought. Since her Andersen feature had boomeranged she'd been forced to eat her story on the oil tycoon, almost word for word. An informant she'd relied on turned out to be an undercover plant from a competing company. Not entirely her fault, but as she was learning, in this competitive business, one mistake could downshift a promising career into neutral.

When Andersen threatened to sue, she'd been on the verge of being fired until Jerry went to the top honcho on her behalf. Reluctant as she was to stir up sentiments she'd been trying to put behind her, she must take this assignment.

Jerry handed her a file with an enclosed brief. "There's more to this than you imagine. I want you to delve deep on this one."

She skimmed the pages.

St. Abient, northern France: French author and pastor, John Volar, established a Christian Center, popular for retreats, conferences and training programs throughout Europe. Reliable off-the-record sources allege the Center may be a cover-up for illegal activities including drug trafficking.

Her breath caught at the mention of drugs. She forced herself to continue reading, knowing that to give into the guilt would leave her paralyzed within. Forgiveness was the marrow of the new life she sought.

On June 10, a banquet will commemorate the Center's twentieth anniversary. Influential church leaders and donors from across Europe are expected to attend. A member of the Trudeau family, the chateau's former owners, will present the award of excellence. Volar is a popular author in Christian circles throughout Europe and has a small but growing audience in America.

Susan wondered if her friend Gayle would be attending. Shortly after her transfer to Paris, Gayle began seeing Dominic Trudeau. The connection might prove helpful. Beyond the air-conditioned walls of *Random World's* three-story glass building, the thick and humid heat of early June was already unbearably sticky. France, at least, would be cooler. She looked at her boss. "Tell me what this is really about."

Jerry's smile didn't quite reach his eyes. "The word is, an international drug ring may be operating out of the place."

The image of her brother Matthew's slow, easy smile and soft, bright eyes flashed before her. She tried to remain calm. "So talk to the DEA or an investigative reporter who's more fluent in French than I am."

"We can't call in the authorities on hearsay. Besides it's best to keep this quiet. Volar and his associates have wined and dined some of our board members. The pressure is on for the magazine to endorse him. If there is any chance these reports are true," he paused, "the last thing we need is another scandal. Fortunately, we have an inside track, Mark Ashley."

Ashley was one of the big bosses at Random World who seldom came within her orbit. Winning brownie points with him could be terribly beneficial to her career. This might be an opportunity to make the upper echelon aware of her and regain some of the ground she'd lost. Feeling more sanguine, she said, "What's the board's position?"

"Most of them can't see past Volar's facade. To be frank, if Mark hadn't confided his concerns, I'd never have bought into an investigation."

"Has the board agreed?"

"They don't know. Mark refuses to tell them until the rumors can be substantiated. It wasn't easy convincing him to bring you in."

Why did he? she wanted to ask but Jerry didn't give her a chance.

"Mark has a young cousin who dropped out of college to join Volar's discipleship program. Since then, his behavior has been erratic; he disappears periodically. He's cashed in thousands in certificates of deposit, part of an inheritance from his grandmother, and won't say why. The family is worried he might be on drugs."

Susan couldn't help thinking out loud, "It seems not only out of character but unnecessary for someone with Mark Ashley's resources to take such a hands-on approach."

Jerry winced. "Let's just say Mark is both arrogant and concerned enough to believe no one else can do as good a job as he can."

She felt the scrutiny of Jerry's gaze, probing, as if reassessing his choice of her one last time.

Her thoughts turned inward, the familiar ache surfacing. Matt, oh

Matt, she thought, twisting a curl around her forefinger in agitation. Outside, a siren split the air, a succession of horns blaring in the aftermath. "Susan, this info is off the record. Take tomorrow off to pack and tie up any loose ends." He gave her the tickets. "Your flight leaves Wednesday at four P.M. First stop is Amsterdam." His upheld hands halted any further questions. "Don't ask why; Mark will fill you in when he's ready. For the next two weeks you will be his assistant." Jerry gave her a sympathetic smile as he opened his office door ending their discussion.

Two days later at Houston's Bush Intercontinental Airport, Susan waited for the last boarding call for her flight to Amsterdam. Jerry had said Mark Ashley would contact her but so far she hadn't heard a word. She craned her neck, searching for a man with penetrating blue-green eyes, who stood a head above the crowd. Snatches of Spanish and German conversation flew by her. Two seedy-looking middle-eastern businessmen gave her a wary smile. But her employer was nowhere in sight.

The office had made her hotel reservations in Amsterdam. Maybe he would contact her there or better yet meet her at Schipol, where her flight landed. Years of traveling abroad had taught her to take things in stride.

Susan boarded the KLM 747 with a stream of other passengers and maneuvered down the aisle to stow her carry-on bag and trench coat in an overhead compartment.

"Here, let me." From behind a long arm seized her belongings.

She turned to find herself standing a hair's breadth from Mark Ashley. "Thanks."

"Glad to be of help." He fitted her things inside and then waved to two young men in football jerseys across the way, before disappearing up the aisle. It seemed he hadn't recognized her.

As the plane lifted, Susan leaned back and closed her eyes, whispering a prayer. When the overhead light clicked on, she brought out her laptop, settled it on the tray, booted up and opened the file on St. Abient Center and Volar. Susan scanned through the notes she'd made, typed in a few more, then glanced up startled as a flight attendant handed her a message, explaining it was from a passenger in first class.

Susan opened the memo.

Miss Pardue,
Meet me at the Red Baron tomorrow, 7:00 P.M. The business details of another venture make an earlier time unlikely. If necessary reach me at the Sheraton.
M. Ashley

On the bright side, he could have left her hanging longer. Feature stories were her normal line. When they met she planned to get the specifics of this assignment up front. Criminal investigations might not be her forte, but the accumulated bills from her mother's last hospital stay made it impossible for Susan to turn down any assignment without fear of losing her job, especially in the wake of the Andersen fiasco.

Ten hours later Susan rushed down the jetway and began the long trek to customs and baggage. Her back ached and she wished it weren't 7:30 in the morning.

The ease with which she passed through customs in Amsterdam always puzzled her. It was a well-known center for international drug traffic and a haven for druggies and lowlife. She guessed economics was the key, another concession to the tourist trade. Probably, luggage from places like Turkey and Pakistan, where drugs were known to be readily obtained, was examined more thoroughly.

Susan trudged by a string of boutiques and rode the escalator to the ground floor, purchasing a train ticket and tram card. By now she imagined Mark Ashley in a limousine on his way to the Sheraton. Never mind, she told herself as she boarded the train. The sky, an ominous grey, further depressed her flagging spirits. A fine drizzle obscured the grassy flat land and the windmills she glimpsed in the distance, both solitary contrasts to the nearby city.

As the train pulled into Central Station she shook off a sense of growing unease about her assignment. Susan hurried to the tram, dodging bikes, cars and pedestrians on the damp, cobbled road. She shifted her Delsey suitcase from her right hand to her left, juggling it between her laptop and tote, as she tried to squeeze past a very broad woman carrying two shopping bags.

The woman veered to the right, forcing Susan into the doorway of a small antique jewelry shop to avoid a collision.

"Careful," Susan called, but the woman never heard. Neither did the stranger who rushed out of the shop and into Susan. Her purse was jarred from her shoulder and she saw it slide down her arm, drape itself over her suitcase and twist itself around the man's legs.

"What the— " He caught the metallic frames sliding off his nose, looked at Susan an instant, then down at his legs. He grabbed her purse and for a minute Susan thought he meant to run with it. Instead he untwined himself, held the purse out to her and muttering an apology, turned stepping into the street.

Seconds later, a slow-moving car brushed against him, knocking him to the ground. The man struggled to his feet, apparently unhurt, and looking rather ill and embarrassed, walked rapidly on down the street. It was then Susan noticed a small package lying where he'd fallen. She darted over and scooping it up, followed the man down the street and around the corner. With her bags weighing her down, it was impossible to keep up as he disappeared into the crowd. Weary, she traced her way back to the antique jewelry shop he'd left; she held the box out to the swarthy dealer behind the counter. "A man wearing metallic frame glasses who just left here dropped this. He was—"

"Yes," the dealer interrupted, his hands closing greedily around the tiny box. "I recognize the parcel and will see it is delivered at once." He thanked her and set it under the counter.

Relieved, she stepped outside and breathed in a whiff of tangy sea air. Three-story, white-gabled, dark brick houses and storefronts flanked the streets overlooking the tangled web of canals winding through the megalopolis by the North Sea. She stepped over a pile of dog litter, wrinkling her nose. Someone jostled her and she cast a cautious glance over her shoulder as two punk rockers with green and purple hair, dressed in motorcycle leathers, strode past. Again she felt a little uneasy but scanning the crowd she detected nothing unusual. Had Jerry's suspicions made her jumpy? Colored her perceptions? Or was it just that she was in Amsterdam on her own.

Jet lag setting in, she threaded her way across the lobby of the Red Baron, pulling her battered grey Delsey. Susan registered, then upstairs in her room, slipped on a gown and tumbled into the bed too tired to worry anymore.

When the alarm shrilled, Susan struggled out from the covers. The two-hour nap had done little to relieve her jet lag. Come night she would be glad she hadn't slept more, but at the moment wakening was agony. A hot shower revived her enough to prepare for the meeting with her boss. She booted up her computer and went on-line, digging up more past newspaper and magazine articles on Volar and the Center so she would be well-versed.

Susan dressed for the evening in her favorite royal-blue shirtwaist, adding a delicate hand-painted Delft porcelain necklace and earrings set in sterling. She ran a brush through shoulder-length black curls and glancing in the mirror, realized she'd lost a few pounds which boosted her spirits.

The phone rang as she slipped on a pair of matching pumps. It was Ashley, asking if she minded switching their meeting place to his hotel. It didn't matter to Susan where they met. She called the front desk to arrange for a taxi, then peered out the window, idly scanning the people below. There was something vaguely familiar about the man standing beneath, looking up. She shrugged off the feeling. It was time to leave.

On the ride to the hotel, her insecurities surfaced at the thought of meeting Mark Ashley away from the usual business venue. Their backgrounds and education were universes apart and class barriers were not merely a thing of the past.

While she had worked her way through the University of Houston on a partial scholarship, Mark had attended Groton and Harvard. He then tried a brief career in his father's hotel conglomerate, whereas her first and only prior position was with an overseas mission.

As the cab eased to a halt in front of the Sheraton, Susan smoothed her hair and stepped out into the brisk night air.

She spotted him as soon as she entered the hotel lobby. His brief start of surprise told her he had not recognized her on the plane. He smiled into her eyes and led her into the dining room, insisting they start out on a first name basis.

After they were seated, Susan picked up the menu, aware of Mark Ashley leaning back in his chair, studying her. He motioned toward a folder on the table. "You've been with *Random World* two years?"

She nodded. "I responded to an advertisement you ran in the French edition." Intrigued and weary of living permanently abroad, and wanting to escape a painful relationship, Susan had dashed off a resume as soon as she saw the ad.

He opened her file. "I see you were with Interaid Relief four years before that. Your responsibilities included...?" He gave her a questioning look.

Her resume was in front of him, and from what Jerry had told her, he had checked her out. But she answered, "I wrote for an in-house publication as well as a second magazine geared to solicit public support."

"With a specialty in Third World development?"

"That and communications."

"Working with us must seem frivolous in comparison," he said.

"Not at all. I find it challenging. Feature writing, though, is more my forte. I like doing interviews and getting people to open up." She winced, realizing she'd probably reminded him of the Andersen fiasco.

"Your success is impressive," he said dryly, closing the folder.

She felt the tension drain away as the interview ended. She hadn't expected that at this late date. Maybe this was his way of getting to know his employees. Layers of bureaucracy and management separated him from most of the staff. Jerry had recommended her for this assignment. She could almost hear him. "The lady's honest, dependable and can she ever wield a pen."

They ordered and Mark came straight to the point. "I realize this is an unusual assignment for you. Jerry confided personal aspects of your background which could be useful in my investigation."

Susan tensed, hoping she was mistaken. Surely Jerry hadn't told him about her brother Matthew. Her private life had nothing to do with *Random World*. Jerry and his wife had stood by her when her parents divorced and when her father died and her irrepressible, younger brother came to live with her. Vulnerable and mixed up, Matthew fell constantly in and out of scrapes.

As if he sensed her discomfort, Mark said, "In a last ditch effort to convince me to take you on this trip, Jerry reluctantly told me of your brother's addiction."

She felt a shaft of pain. Unbidden, a picture of Matthew, tall and gangly with his eager brown eyes and crooked smile rose before her.

"I hesitate to involve you in an investigation which may be dangerous," he said.

Susan watched him refold his napkin, creasing the fold with his left hand. Mark's hands were large with a few soft callouses near the edge of his palm. She tried to quell the rising tide of turmoil Matthew's memory brought and forced herself to concentrate on Mark's words.

"I believe Jerry has explained our family's concern for my cousin Benjamin. Since he dropped out of college to join Volar's discipleship program, he's cashed in thousands in certificates of deposit, part of an inheritance from his grandmother, and won't say why. We're worried he might be on drugs. It's only fair to warn you we could be dealing with hardened criminals."

Susan swallowed. She was too warm. But the room temperature had little to do with it. Even though it had been years since Matthew's death, she felt again the onslaught of guilt and shame, the fallout of her failure to reach him in time. And Susan's mother still blamed her for Matthew's death. It had been so easy to paint the world black and white and demand her brother accept responsibility or bear the consequences. Too late she realized he had to learn his own lessons.

She had bought him a car, given him a place to live and got him a job. She had encouraged him to attend church and read the Bible, hoping to separate him from the friends accelerating his demise. Unwittingly, she had woven a web of responsibility and expectations he rejected as a trap. He had left. His accusations still rang in her ear, "I can't be lily-white and perfect like you. I tried but I'm not good enough." He plunged back into the drug culture, dealing drugs with his foolhardy friends. In a matter of weeks he was dead. There would be no more chances to help Matthew.

Mark's expression was sympathetic. "This investigation must be done without the board's knowledge. Aside from the one assignment in Saint Abient, you'll be seen as vacationing with me."

Susan started to speak, then stopped as the waiter came to ask if they'd like dessert. When they were alone again, she said, "I want to make it clear, I've no experience as an investigative reporter."

"I'm aware of that."

"Also what exactly do you mean vacationing?"

His gaze revealed his uneasiness. "Don't worry. For all practical purposes we'll enjoy a holiday in Europe, travelling together as friends with separate rooms. How others will see us is another matter. My chief concern is what we'll encounter at Volar's Center."

"Is there truly a risk?"

"I don't know but the possibility exists."

"And you feel the circumstances warrant the chance we'll be taking?"

"That's a decision you'll have to make for yourself. But tell me, if Matthew were still alive and involved, would you hesitate to help?"

Her shoulders dropped as she acknowledged the hit, reminded yet again of her fruitless efforts to help her brother.

"Kids are dying every year, manipulated by drug lords. Most of us steer clear of the problem, until it strikes home and we're affected personally." He looked down at his napkin, smoothing the edges, before lifting his troubled gaze to meet hers. "If we can stop one death, break up one ring, it's worth it to me. My sister Julie died at sixteen. Her first exposure to drugs was an overdose. It killed her." His voice was stilted, bitter.

"I'm sorry." She felt the rush of raw pain that accompanied his words and realized that he had been hurt, too.

"I don't even know if you can help." His face reflected his embarrassment and uncertainty. "But if people think we have a romantic interest in one another it might make our prolonged stay more plausible and deflect some of the heat off our investigation."

Despite the high stakes, she suddenly knew she had to do this for Matthew and for herself. There was no question of turning back and walking away.

"When do we start?" she said.

2

Susan spent the next day alone in Amsterdam, trying not to resent the high-handed way in which Mark Ashley had arranged events. Apparently, he didn't trust her enough to accompany him. She doubted if he would bother revealing anything he learned. Well, why not investigate on her own? she decided, flagging down a taxi.

Her first stop was the library. On the way up the steps she happened to glance back; there was that man again with the metallic frames who'd dropped the package. Their gazes locked and for a second she felt as if a searchlight scorched her. Troubled, she quickened her pace. Inside, she located the information desk by the large-lettered sign marked *Auskunft*. Although Susan didn't speak Dutch, she was fluent in German and there was enough similarity between the two for her to identify some words.

"Excuse me, please, could you direct me to the reference section?" she said to the lanky young man behind the desk.

"Third floor, turn to your right."

Upstairs Susan flashed her press card for extra leverage, when she requested English material on international drug trafficking. Within minutes she was surrounded with sufficient newspaper and magazine clippings to keep her occupied the rest of the day. She refused to leave her fate in the hands of Mark Ashley.

At his high-rise Brussels office, Peter Frazier stared moodily out the window as the onslaught of another migraine threatened to ruin his day. His secretary rang and he pressed the speaker button.

"Your wife's holding on line one, sir."

His wife's hesitant voice came over the line. "Are we still on for lunch? I've arranged a sitter for the boys. It's been ages since we've done anything like this together."

Peter swallowed, hating to say the words he'd said to her so many times before. "Sorry. Something's come up. I can't make it."

"Of course, I understand." Her flat response told him she didn't. How could she, when he'd made a career of missing dinners, anniversaries and birthdays? But this was one appointment he'd wanted to keep.

"Go on without me. Do a little shopping. It'll be good for you."

Her small voice told him she'd shrunk into herself once again. It had taken him so long to coax her out for lunch. He cursed his partner, blaming him, wishing they'd never met. But they had and forged a bond when Peter's twin sister died. Peter's family had paid the price and they were still paying.

As he hung up the phone, his partner burst into his office, seething over what he called Peter's bumbling naivete! Peter braced himself, realizing there would be a reckoning regarding the journalist, despite his attempts to cover up the matter.

As if on cue, his partner demanded, "Tell me again what happened. Don't leave anything out."

Peter lowered his gaze, concealing his thoughts as he wondered how long the fear within him had been growing. He answered as convincingly as he could. "It was nothing. I dropped a package, she returned it inside to the dealer, end of story."

"You fool, the girl is a reporter on her way to the Center, stirring up all kinds of dust. She's got to be killed."

Peter felt the blood drain from his face. "I won't be a party to murder."

"If you haven't the stomach for it, Karl does. You forgot to mention the diamonds were in that package. Why else would you follow the girl?"

Peter thought back to the day the dealer had brought the package to his hotel and told him the girl had found it. As soon as he left, Peter cursed and tore open the package. How could he have dropped three million dollars worth of diamonds? He had checked his pockets after the run-in with the woman but the jet lag and stomach flu had taken its toll.

He held his aching head. His partner had insisted he make the pick up to ensure supply lines were running well. They both knew someone in his position shouldn't go near the gems. But tired from the long flight and weakened by the biological war going on in his body, he'd agreed.

He counted the glittering white, blue and yellow stones, making sure none was missing. He was especially relieved to find the five karat canary yellow diamond hadn't been lifted. What if the woman knew? Impossible—maybe not, though the gem dealer insisted she hadn't been out of his sight long enough to examine the package.

Still, one could never be too sure. She might have.... His pulse raced at the possibilities.

He grabbed his jacket and headed for the door. He'd have to check her out, have to do it himself to keep his partner from knowing. Their relationship was strained enough without his learning of this. He drew out the gem dealer's card, reading the woman's name and address scribbled on the flip side, as he climbed into the taxi.

The driver shifted into gear. "Where to?"

He leaned back, trying to visualize the woman he'd bumped into earlier. Was he making too much of this? Should he just let it go?He stared at the back of the driver's head. "The Red Baron Hotel." He couldn't ignore the threat the woman represented.

It had been two days since their first encounter. He'd made a point of watching her since then and now his partner had found out. Now Peter faced his partner, fists clenched as he raked the borders of his patience. "One of these days, you're going to push me too far." For years Peter had lived in the shadow of his partner's powerful charisma, mesmerized by his uncanny ability to draw people and manipulate events. Take how he used the Center for his own gain but came off saintly. If it weren't for his sister's memory, he might have seen the truth sooner.

His partner snapped, "Then do as you're told and let's have an end to this." His face softened abruptly as he took in Frazier's sister's picture and lifted it off the desk top. He ran a finger gently down her cheek. "We were good together. I've never told anyone but you, how when she died I thought I'd go insane. For her sake, I've cut you some slack but don't challenge me again." Tenderness erased, the amalgamation of sludge and steel he'd become stood before Peter for one moment unmasked.

Peter looked away, uncomfortable at sharing his sister's memory with the man his partner had become. He heard the office door slam and felt weighted with the knowledge that he could do nothing to stop him.

Ewald Lauter made his way to the Wigam's Financial Group's annual luncheon. He entered the Paris Ritz and looked about expectantly.

From a seat nearby, Dominic Trudeau rose to greet him. "Good, I'm glad you're early. Let's go in and order."

The exclusive dining room Dominic led him to held about five hundred of Europe's wealthiest investors. Today he was to be the keynote speaker and honored as the most astute businessman of the year. Ewald could hear the murmurs as they walked past to the head table.

"That's him—Lauter, the genius with money."

He shot Dominic a self-deprecating look. It was impossible to tune out the many remarks as they proceeded through the room.

"They say his personality's positively magnetic."

"He gave more than two million for cancer research."

A group of businessmen broke apart as they passed, their comments too loud not to be overheard. "Yeah, a nice guy with looks that most of the women in this room would kill for—and money to boot."

"Who's that with him? He's no slouch either."

"Dominic Trudeau. Filthy rich. Old money there."

"The old and the new joining hands, interesting."

Ewald sat and exchanged an amused look with Dominic. He'd never particularly tried to impress people but the newspapers and his associates were continually running on about his generous gifts to charity. He gave the waiter his order, then turned to Dom. "I suppose we have the newspapers to blame for making such a big deal over every little thing."

"I wouldn't call giving ten million to your charities small, Ewald." He looked up surprised. "Now where did you hear that?" He shrugged. "Never mind. It doesn't matter. It's easy enough to tally the sums printed. Disgusting isn't it, this lack of privacy."

The waiter arrived with their food and they devoted their attention to the steaks both men had ordered before continuing their conversation. Ewald speared a bite of asparagus and said, "Where were we?"

"The annoying media." Dom smiled. "Enjoy your popularity while it lasts. Reporters can be dreadfully fickle."

Ewald washed down the steak with coffee then said, "You're thinking of that young fellow, Nick Sarb. Maybe it'll be the making of him. New money, you know, has a different feel to it than old."

Dom chuckled, buttering a roll. "Touché. But mentioning Nick reminds me of a favorite charity of mine that could use some of your philanthropy. How about cutting in Reverend John Volar's Center?"

Ewald hesitated. "One can never be too careful what philanthropic endeavors one funds. I've heard two Americans are investigating the Center. If there's anything phony going on, as a legitimate philanthropist, I'd like to help them uncover it. And if we don't find anything, I'll feel better about contributing."

Dom stiffened, pushing aside his dessert. "Despite the rumors making the grist meal, I'm willing to personally vouch for both Volar and the Center's integrity."

Ewald threw him an apologetic look. "Sorry, I didn't mean to step on any toes. It slipped my mind that you're actually on the board there. Still, why not send these Americans to me. I've already told my lieutenant Karl to see if there is any way we can be of assistance. If there's nothing there, you'll be rid of them that much faster."

"You're interfering in something that's none of your business."

"The reputation of philanthropy in this city is very much my business. But to show my good faith, have the Reverend's Center forward a grant proposal to my staff and I'll have them fast track the evaluation for my consideration."

Dom seemed to relax. "Fair enough."

"Now if you don't mind, I think I'll take a moment to look over my notes. They'll be calling me to speak any minute."

"Go ahead, but you could have this crowd in the palm of your hand blindfolded if you chose."

Ewald shook his head. "Why do I get the feeling people think I'm so much more than I am? You of all people shouldn't tease me with this passing popularity thing the media has pounced on."

Dom laughed. "I suppose it's now my turn to apologize, even though I've only spoken the truth."

Ewald held up a hand in protest, as the MC took his place behind the microphone. "Well, that's my cue. Up I go."

Another overcast day, Mark noted from where he waited in front of the American Embassy for his old college roommate Zach Towers. Three years had passed since he last saw Zach, but they had always been close. Ever since the day Mark had come across a group of upperclassmen seriously beating up the new freshman football star and had waded in on Zach's behalf their friendship had been sealed.

Mark knew he often came across as arrogant and unfeeling, and his temper flared too easily. He was too much like his dad. Family and close friends accused them both of being suckers for loss causes. His mother always said they were like hard candies with soft centers, hard to penetrate but once you did, they'd do anything they could for you. He hated to see unfair odds. He supposed that's what had drawn him to Zach.

After graduation they had toured Europe on Eurail passes. Their belongings stuffed into backpacks, they slept in youth hostels. At the end of that year, Zach signed on with the CIA, moving from post to post up the ladder of rank, while Mark accepted a junior position in his father's hotel conglomerate, his rise to the top assured. But after five years, he quit. His dad understood his need to test his abilities. His sole request was that Mark retain his position on the board of directors of the chain he would one day inherit. Mark invested his savings, doubling and eventually tripling their value.

Meanwhile, he began writing freelance for business publications, gradually expanding his market to comprise a wider range of topics. In an attempt to help several friends seeking publication, he'd acted as their agent. Before long Mark established his own agency and found himself submerged in editorial reviews and sales. When a friend offered him a chance to buy into *Random World*, he didn't hesitate to put up one-third of the funds, but he made sure it included one-third control.

The magazine specialized in travel features, but included political analysis, sketches of prominent personalities, as well as cultural, geographical and historical tidbits. They had banked on the average traveler having broad interests, and *Random World's* overnight success verified this. That was four years ago.

Now, Mark glanced at his watch, wondering why Zach was late. He was counting on his buddy to give him some answers, providing his reticence to speak of government affairs could be overcome.

17

Zach raced up, panting, and clasped Mark's shoulders. "You old dog, what are you doing in Amsterdam?"

Mark grinned. "You haven't changed much, still the same old bloodhound."

Zach gave him an affronted look and they walked down the street to a little café around the corner. Zach ordered coffee before sending an inquiring glance Mark's way. "So, what's up?"

"What do you know about John Volar?"

"Only that he's a French author who has a Center in Saint Abient. Why the interest?"

Mark felt tenseness behind his friend's casual question, aware that Zach sensed the same in himself. He hesitated, unwilling to tip Zach off to any information that could rebound on his cousin. Ultimately, he decided to drop a few facts and see where they led. "Some rumors have been circulating about the Center's connection with the drug trade."

Zach's mouth firmed into a thin line. "You and I both know that's unlikely. I'd like to know who's been talking and why?"

"Remember Ed Blinders?"

"Yeah, with the CIA," Zach interrupted. "Take it from me the questions you're asking are way over your head."

"But you admit it's more than a rumor."

Zach frowned. "Why the preoccupation with the Center? It's not like you to hit up an old friend for a headline."

"Relax. It's not a story I'm after. My cousin Benjamin's there and the family's concerned."

After learning the press wasn't gunning to blow the agency's investigation sky high, Zach loosened up. "Volar and the Center are under investigation. It's one of the quietest in the whole department, high level and strictly hands off for outsiders," he warned.

Mark wasn't displeased at the outcome of their talk. Although Zach was unwilling to share details, he had confirmed that the State Department had sufficient grounds to consider Volar suspect. Mark returned to his hotel and booked an evening flight to Paris with overnight accommodations. He checked out of the Sheraton and caught a taxi, hoping a storm wasn't brewing. The sky had turned charcoal grey.

Minutes later, he stepped from a drenching rain into the Red Baron's crowded lobby and had the clerk ring Susan's room. There was no answer and she'd left no message. Worried about Benjamin and irritated by her absence, Mark turned away from the desk, wondering where she was.

He found an empty chair and settled his briefcase on his lap, but instead of catching up on paper work he stared out at the chilling rain, hoping this was not a portent of what he could expect in the days ahead.

3

Susan strolled into her hotel in a much better mood than when she had left that morning, to find Mark Ashley worriedly pacing the lobby. "You're early," she said. "I hope you haven't been waiting long."

Annoyance chased his fleeting look of relief at seeing her. "It would be helpful if in the future you'd leave a message at the front desk where you'll be or get word to me somehow."

"Good idea. I'll feel a lot better knowing how to reach you as well."

He looked disconcerted for a brief moment, then continued. "We're booked on an evening flight to Paris. Can you be ready to leave by seven?"

"Sure. Has something happened?"

Mark frowned at his watch. "No. I want to get an early start tomorrow. You'll need to hurry if we're not going to miss our plane."

Susan nodded and headed for the elevator, resolving not to let his curtness affect her. She hadn't expected to leave until morning and wondered if they would travel straight from Paris to St. Abient by car or train. Since she had only unpacked the essentials, she was able to arrive in the lobby with minutes to spare. Her boss darted a glance at his watch but failed to comment until later when they boarded the plane.

"Sorry for the brusqueness back there," Mark said. "But this is the last flight of the day to Paris." His blue-green eyes narrowed as he led her to the first class cabin and motioned her to the seat beside him. "From here on, assume we are being watched."

She fastened her seat belt. As the plane sped down the runway for takeoff, Mark leaned close, a lock of sable-brown hair falling across his forehead. "Remember we're supposedly on holiday. Smile."

Susan swallowed, the required smile in place. She searched his face, taking in its contours, the jut of his chin, the dimple to the right and the aloof reserve which seemed to characterize him.

Their eyes skidded together for a nanosecond, then awkwardly apart. It was beginning to sink in that Mark Ashley was not going to be easy to deal with. For the remainder of the flight, he buried himself in paper work. She worked on drafting an article on a prominent TV personality she'd interviewed earlier that month. Back at the hotel that morning, she'd spoken to Jerry briefly and promised to e-mail it ASAP. She finished just as the pilot requested everyone to be seated for landing.

As the plane touched ground, she wondered, what they'd find in Paris. Mark had unbent enough to explain that they would probably spend two days there.

On the ride to the hotel, the fast-paced traffic, the crescendo of horns blaring, and the throngs of people, somehow felt menacing. Their taxi driver maneuvered through the confusion with typical French savoir-faire, until they reached a roundabout near the Arc de Triomphe. A young man aimed a pistol at their cab. Susan's heart pounded. Blood-red liquid squirted from the gun, splattering the window. Her pulse rate slowed, relief warring with horror at the childish prank. The culprit doubled over with raucous laughter, reducing their driver to shouting angry threats. Abruptly, the crisp Paris air seemed to scream danger.

Later, in the privacy of her hotel room, Susan booted up her laptop, checked her e-mail and sent her story off to Jerry, then typed up a report of her findings. Her research had not been riveting, but there was growing evidence that drug traffickers from South America, Southeast Asia and Europe were uniting in order to widen distribution and increase profits.

While cocaine consumption had dropped in the United States under the present administration, it had increased worldwide. Until recently, she learned, cocaine was mainly in the Americas and Europe, but in the last decade cocaine and heroin use had spread further into Africa, the Near and Middle East, Southeast Asia and the South Pacific.

It was quite an operation. Could Volar be involved? Had he traveled lately to South America or Africa? If so, what did he do there? One paper reported that the South American traffickers backed by European smugglers were selling cocaine in major cities across Africa. Cocaine farmers from South America were being flown in to train the natives to grow coca plants. Already, Nigeria, Cameroon, Egypt, Kenya, Morocco and the Sudan were raising crops of coca and opium poppies, the raw materials from which cocaine and heroin are made.

How did it all fit together? Was it simply an underground drug operation greedy for money? Or did the worldwide network have a deeper motive with political ramifications? Susan shook her head, more determined than ever to uncover the truth.

Also troubling was her close friend Gayle's involvement with Dominic Trudeau and Susan's discovery of his close connection to the Center. Too often he was cited in the clippings she'd studied. Of course, his philanthropy could be entirely above board.

With a sigh she set her travel alarm for seven and climbed into bed. She was barely asleep when the dream about her brother Matthew came.

An older man, one she had never seen before, was quarreling with Matthew in the parking lot of an apartment complex. His scarred face was jaded and twisted with hate.

"Matt, Matt! He has a gun. Run!" Susan screamed soundlessly.

Frozen, unable to save him, she watched helplessly. Friends gaped as the gunman fired a shot and Matthew collapsed.

But the man didn't stop; the shooter kept firing. He bent over Matthew and cruelly grabbing his arms, dragged him across the asphalt to his car. Ignoring the gushing blood, he thrust Matthew into the back seat.

"Call an ambulance," someone yelled.

The car started and was rammed into drive, the tires squealing as it careened across the lot. The vehicle lurched to the left, and then plowed into a nearby field, disappearing from sight.

People were running and shouting. "Help! He's going to die!" someone cried. "Call the police, hurry, quick. Someone follow that car."

Susan tossed and turned; whimpering she woke with a start. "Matt, oh Matt," she cried. Tears streamed down her face. "Why, oh why, God? Did he have to be murdered?" she sobbed, anguish tearing her apart.

Mark had not been able to sleep. With a copy of a New York Times best seller in hand, he tried to relax with a cold drink, but he was too uptight. He paced the room. The connecting door brought Susan to mind. She hadn't fussed about the adjoining rooms which their arrival a day early had forced them to accept. Later, he realized it might actually help bolster their cover. How much should he tell her? He had to put together some kind of a plan.

Mark heard what sounded like muffled sobs coming from her room. He quickly crossed the floor, placing his ear against the connecting door, just as a low moan penetrated the wall between them. Without knocking he rushed into her suite, expecting to find an intruder. Instead he found Susan alone, huddled on the edge of the bed, weeping.

He stiffened, his astonishment turning to compassion at the depth of her despair. In a rush, he was beside her. He gathered her into his arms, awkwardly patting the tangle of silky locks. "Shh.... It's okay," he murmured. "It was just a dream."

"But it wasn't," she protested, sitting up straight. "Matthew's really dead." She wiped her tears with the back of her hand.

And it was true. There weren't any words that could bring him back, Mark reflected, remembering his own sister Julie's death. He squeezed her hand. "Do you think you can sleep now?"

She nodded. "I spent the day at the library, reading a lot of clippings. I guess that brought the past back."

"Well, try to get some rest. And Susan, it's not too late to bail out," he said as he closed the door.

4

The next morning Susan awoke to the memory of herself in a clingy, cotton gown sobbing on Mark's shoulder. She cringed at her lack of professionalism and eyed the connecting door with embarrassment. How could she have forgotten to lock it? Scenes from last night's nightmare tumbled through her head.

She was amazed at how patient and gentle Mark had been. No doubt the circumstances of his own sister's death prompted his empathy. An empathy which could turn to contempt if he learned of her past. Perhaps he had already left and it wouldn't be necessary to face him again until dinner.

Susan donned a grey pantsuit, applied her makeup with a light touch, then brushed her hair, drawing it back with a pearl clasp. Encouraged at the thought of a temporary reprieve, she descended to the lobby in search of breakfast. Her gaze fell on Mark as she entered and he signaled for her to join him.

She sat facing him, determined to apologize at once. "I'm sorry about last night. Believe me, nightmares and emotional scenes are not part of my normal repertoire," she said with an attempt at lightness. "I don't know what came over me."

"There's nothing to apologize for, but I am glad to see you've recovered," he said, as he took in her appearance. "Have you given any thought to bailing out?"

"No, I'm not a quitter. Unless...that is...you'd rather I leave. So far, my assistance hasn't amounted to much."

"Your presence does mask my inquiries to some extent."

"Have you had any success?"

"Somewhat. I've been able to confirm that the state department is investigating Volar. I hope to dig up more today."

While they ate, she filled him in on the details of her research, most of which he was already aware of. Still, she couldn't help commenting, "Volar's past itineraries could prove a definite connection between him and the drug trade. Once we reach Saint Abient, the anniversary story will give me the perfect cover to question his associates and help us gain access to his office and home."

"Susan, I'm willing to level with you and share information on the condition that you don't act without my say-so." He reached across the table, placing his hand on hers. "If what we suspect is true, the least hint of suspicion could be fatal. Are we agreed?"

She nodded and withdrew her hand, realizing the futility of arguing and accepting that she was rowing in uncharted waters. "What have you planned for today?"

"There are a few leads I need to follow up on and I'm lunching with an old family friend who happens to be the Paris Correspondent for the *US Daily*."

He gave her an inquiring look, no doubt expecting a verbal blow-by-blow description of her activities as if every moment was on company time.

She sighed. "There's not really much I can do. I'd like to visit an old friend who transferred here last year." She didn't want to explain about Gayle and Dom unless it was truly relevant. She'd know more after speaking with Gayle.

"Fine. Just leave me an address and phone number in case I need to reach you."

"Okay." Susan pushed back her plate and glanced briefly around the restaurant, her gaze colliding with the man she had come to think of as the stranger with the package. He sat at a table near the door eating breakfast. From the looks of it he traveled frequently in his line of business as well. She hoped that's all it was. Yesterday, Amsterdam, today Paris. She rather thought the odds were against four random run-ins so close together. Still she'd wait and see, if it kept up, then she'd have to tell Mark.

5

From the hotel, Susan hailed a taxi to her friend, Gayle Regan's, pausing outside to admire the charm of the old weathered saffron building. It was then she noticed a beefy lumbering sort of man staring at her. Surely, she had seen him the night before at the airport in Amsterdam and again in Paris. She climbed to her friend's third floor apartment with a feeling akin to panic, struggling to shake off her fears. First, the stranger with metallic frames and now this man kept reappearing. Why would anyone follow her? Did someone think Mark knew something he had confided to her?

Gayle greeted her with an exuberant hug that helped to calm her. Susan made an effort to set aside her apprehension. There was no sense worrying Gayle too. Inside, she barely recognized the scruffy antiques they had scoured the city for earlier that year. "You've done a marvelous job refinishing," she said. A creamy gold tapestry rug set off the heavy, dark furniture and a shimmering autumn landscape hung over the fireplace. It was a perfect backdrop for Gayle's gorgeous red hair, creamy skin and the high-fashion model's figure Susan had always envied.

Gayle motioned her to a seat and set a tray with coffee and chocolate-filled croissants on the table between them. Susan groaned at the thought of the extra walking she'd have to do, "It's treacherous to tempt me so."

"Pretend they're fat-free. You'll enjoy them more."

"Just what I need, encouragement." Susan bit into a flaky *petit pain au chocolat*, savoring the delicate trace of chocolate in the center. "Umm...this is what I come to France for. And I leave to avoid the same temptations. How do you stay slim with pastries like this in the house?"

"The secret," Gayle said with an elegant wave of her hand, "is to buy them fresh for unsuspecting guests and insist they eat every morsel."

Susan laughed, her gaze meeting Gayle's with warm affection. They'd been the best of friends since grade school. "How's the new job?"

"Wonderful. I was positively terrified when they offered me the supervisory position here in Paris with a foreign airline. Now I'm so glad I accepted. How about you? Is your Mom any better?"

"A little, but we still don't talk." Susan winced at the series of events leading up to her mother's heart attack last fall. Nothing about them had been easy. Her brother's death loomed between them like a festering sore neither dared to touch.

"Susan, you're not still blaming yourself, are you? Matthew made his choices. You didn't make them for him."

"If he had never followed me that day he might be alive."

"It wouldn't have changed things. Matthew was looking for trouble."

"He was searching for a way to prove himself. I led him into trouble."

"You were only seventeen. And you tried to get him to turn around."

That was the summer Susan learned her parents were not the perfect people she believed them to be. The late night fights...explosive, angry words...whiskey on her dad's breath...his funny smile and the slurred words, as he hugged her goodnight, "Daddy loves his little girl."

When had they changed? A confused and bewildered teenager, she began hanging out with a different set. She even smoked marijuana and snorted cocaine.

How lucky she was to have come out of it alive and sane. It had taken her six months to realize she was hurting no one but herself. To this day she was thankful for the jealousy which prompted one of her "new friends" to plant a bag of marijuana in her purse and then report her to the dean. The incident had ended her bout of rebellion and brought her parents closer for a period. And it was then that her relationship with Christ had been sealed.

Unfortunately, Matthew had been one of the casualties of that phase of her life. He had followed her to a party one night, despite her protests and there he tried drugs for the first time. Her mother had never forgiven her. Susan expelled a weary sigh. "I've gone over it a thousand times in my mind."

"You did everything you could to stop him." Gayle frowned in concern. "There were years in between the day he followed you and his death."

"That helps. But in any case, he did what he guessed I was doing. Let's not talk about it. Please."

"All right. Tell me about the story you're covering."

Susan gave her a grateful smile. "It's the anniversary of a Christian Center in Saint Abient. You've heard of Pastor John Volar?"

"Mmm. He's popular and among more than just the evangelicals. Will you be interviewing him?"

"Him and anyone else I can."

Gayle shifted in her seat, stretching her long legs out in front of her and crossing them at the ankles. "You know that I've been dating Dom Trudeau, but were you aware that he'll be presenting the awards for the anniversary ceremonies?"

"I wondered if Dominic was involved when I saw the Trudeau's mentioned in my brief. But I've forgotten how did you two meet?"

"At a company party for some of our larger accounts. Dom often flies with Transway and several of his holding companies ship with our airline as well."

"Sounds interesting. Anything serious?"

"No, we're friends." Gayle smiled wryly. "My main attraction is that I'm not scheming to marry him."

Susan had uncovered enough information from old magazine articles to know that Dominic Trudeau had been involved in the Center from the beginning. For Gayle's sake, she hoped he wasn't involved in any drug deals. Since he too was scheduled to attend the anniversary celebrations, they were bound to meet. If he was legit, he might be able to shed some light on the recent rumors. And if not, the sooner she learned it, the better for everyone's sake, especially Gayle's. "I'd love to meet him. Why don't you and Dominic join us for dinner?"

"Us? As in the mysterious boss you're suddenly traveling with?"

"Who else?"

"You haven't said a word about him."

Susan said, "He's rather arrogant. A bit of a chauvinist at times, but, he does have his nice moments," she admitted, and remembering their supposed romance added quickly, "I rather like him. Call Dominic, then you can both meet him tonight."

While Gayle phoned, Susan rose and walked over to the window. Her breath hitched as she glimpsed the burly man standing below. She took out her notebook and quickly jotted down his description and the times and places she'd seen him. Then going on intuition, recorded her run-ins with the stranger who wore the metallic frames as well.

"Is something wrong?" Gayle said, as she replaced the receiver.

"No," Susan said, willing it to be the truth. "Just anxious to meet Dom to help round out my feature on the Center. Is dinner set?"

At Gayle's nod, Susan felt the stiffness in her shoulders loosen. An early interview with Trudeau could be the break they were looking for.

6

That same day, Mark entered *La Vigne* looking through a haze of smoke for his friend. Tables set with starched white linens filled the oblong room. At a loss, he turned to the hostess, gesturing toward the crowded tables with a questioning shrug. *"Excusez-moi, mademoiselle, Monsieur* Bob Chandler?"

"Oui, monsieur." She led him to a quiet corner in the back.

Mark and Bob grew up next door to each other in Houston's prestigious River Oaks. The Chandlers' fortune dated back to the 1800s and it lasted until the 1986 oil recession when, with hundreds of other Texas companies, Chandler Refineries was forced to file for bankruptcy.

Mark grinned at his old friend, who appeared to have taken the financial reversal in stride. Perhaps his greyish-brown hair was greyer than it should have been at thirty-six, the eyes a little colder and his short compact frame thinner, but his smile was the same Mark had always known.

Mark ordered *coq au vin* and Bob *boeuf bourguignon*. While they ate, they hashed over old times. With a trace of humor, Mark pointed to the faded scar on his forehead. "You owe me one."

Bob grimaced. "Are you still trying to trade on that?"

It was a friendly jest. When Mark needed Bob's help, the scar became his bargaining point. It referred back to a golf game in their thirteenth summer, when Bob had slammed his club into Mark's forehead. The result—ten stitches and a reluctance on Mark's part to play with his friend the rest of the summer. Bob's nature was generally amiable, but he had a fierce temper which could be cruel when unleashed.

"What is it this time?" Bob said, his interest clearly kindled.

"Heard any rumors of an underground operation involving the Reverend John Volar?"

Bob's expression turned guarded. "What's this about?"

Mark ignored the warning bells going off in his head. This was Bob, his lifelong friend. "Last November my cousin signed on for a year at Volar's place in Saint Abient. Now eight months later, he's a different person and I don't mean religious. He's moody, unpredictable and avoids any communication with the family." Mark went on to voice his suspicions regarding Volar and the Center.

"I don't know," Bob said. "Simply because the kid's on drugs doesn't mean the Center's involved. Drug usage is on the rise across the continent.

Haven't heard a sniff about Volar." He hesitated. "I wrote a series of articles on him for *US Daily*. His sincerity impressed me."

Maybe he was mistaken, Mark thought. Maybe there were no drugs and Benjamin was all right...merely asserting his independence. His gut feeling though, wouldn't let up. He felt Bob was holding back. Something was wrong and Volar was involved. He'd bet on it.

Bob cleared his throat. "Look, I have this friend, Nick Sarb, who manages a string of bars across Paris. Occasionally, he sells me information."

"Can you trust him?"

"Sure. A few personal hangups...bitter, but who wouldn't be? His father left his entire fortune to the city for museum upkeep. A case of the aristocratic heir reduced to working in bars to support his mother and sister." Bob's laugh rang hollow.

Bob appeared more affected by his family's reversal than he let on. It couldn't have been easy. Mark paid the bill and they left for Nick's.

At Henri's Bistro beyond the showcase walnut bar, couples enjoyed their drinks at small tables arranged for intimate conversation. Nick Sarb's office was in a back room. He flashed them a cordial smile, his dark eyes assessing as he rose from behind the desk to shake hands. The grey silk suit molded to his medium build was well cut, but worn. The jet-black hair curling along the collar needed a trim. Mark liked him instantly.

But when Bob offered him money, Nick drew back, his expression enigmatic. "Sorry, there is nothing to tell."

"Come on," Bob said. "Your sister Danielle attends there. Think how you'd feel. He's worried about his cousin."

Nick said, "Okay, there has been some talk, but don't ask me what. It takes a lot of *francs* to keep that Center open and fund Volar's travels and charities. Just a hint, find out who's supplying the capital and why?" He refused to say more.

Discouraged, Mark returned to the hotel restaurant and waited for Susan. It had been a long day and he wasn't in the best of moods. Nick's innuendos pointing toward Volar's backers told him nothing. It was time to leave for Saint Abient. A week remained before the anniversary celebrations and following that event they would be hard pressed for an excuse to extend their visit.

From a corner table he watched Susan enter with another couple in tow. Tired, hungry and worried, Mark was not looking forward to an evening spent in company.

Mark and Susan exchanged veiled glances as she greeted him and introduced her friends. He gave her high marks for managing to snag one of Volar's backers so fast.

Almost before Mark could cover his surprise, she was seated between him and the Frenchman, gazing at Trudeau with wide-eyed interest. "Have you always lived in Paris, *Monsieur* Trudeau?"

"Dom, please, and may I call you Susan?"

She flashed him a shy smile. "Of course."

They were interrupted as a rather distinguished gentleman in a black suit seated at the next table rose to greet Dom. "I have been sitting here envious and quite alone for a full five minutes."

Dom threw the group an amused look. "Whatever you do, don't believe him. My friend, Ewald Lauter here, is currently all the rage in Paris' financial circles."

After he was introduced around, the gentleman smiled at Susan, admiration in his gaze. "What brings you to Paris?"

Gayle broke in, "Susan and Mark are journalists with *Random World*. They're here to cover Pastor Volar's Anniversary celebrations out at the Center."

Mark nodded. "Just so."

Ewald returned his attention to Susan. "If I can be of service during your visit, please, don't hesitate to call." He slipped a card into her hand.

Susan thanked him and then joined the chorus of goodbyes as he took his leave. After his departure, her focus returned to Dom.

It left Mark a bit uncomfortable to see Susan monopolizing Trudeau. Still, Mark chatted with Gayle in an effort both to reassure her and discover how she had come to know Trudeau. But she was clearly torn between answering his questions and listening to Susan and Dom.

Eventually, Mark rose, pulling Susan up beside him. "Excuse us a moment, there's an important phone call we need to make." He led her toward the foyer, stopping when they were out of sight. "Susan, this isn't a game. You're being a bit too obvious. I thought we had a deal."

"This is an ideal opportunity for me to find out about Dom. He's dating my best friend and he could be the mastermind behind the entire drug operation. Who would suspect someone with his impeccable lineage to be involved?"

"Motive, Susan—you need motive. Trudeau isn't Volar's sole contributor. We're leaving for Saint Abient first thing in the morning to learn everything possible about Volar and his backers. Meanwhile, please try for a little subtlety. Don't blow holes in the single cover we have."

Mark sat back down feeling as if the day had gone from inauspicious to rotten. All he wanted was for it to end. His hopes were set on Saint Abient and finding a cooperative Benjamin to help resolve the case.

7

Gayle didn't have much to say to Dom on the drive back to her apartment. But she did have a lot on her mind. Why was Susan so intent on Dom? Why so insistent to meet him? If an interview was what she wanted, why hadn't she asked for one? Something was wrong, that much was clear, something Susan wasn't confiding. At her apartment door Dom gave her the usual farewell kiss on the cheek.

The warmth of his touch lingered against her face. "I'll call you later, *cherie*. Why not drive up to Saint Abient with me next weekend for the celebrations?" His gaze gently mocked her. "It would be a chance to see Susan."

"Could we make the trip in a day?"

"Better plan on the weekend. Let's leave early Friday." One hand caressed her shoulder. "*Au revoir, mon petite*." He blew her a kiss and left.

From her upstairs bedroom window she watched him climb into his Porsche. She had been tempted to voice her suspicions concerning Susan's sudden interest in him. But a childish fear that he might think her jealous had kept her silent. And was she? Dom's attentiveness to Susan had caused her to reconsider their relationship. Unlike most women, she was not impressed by his family's wealth and background. Until tonight she had thought herself immune to his devastating good looks.

She judged people by what they were on their own merit. Her indifference, she supposed had initially presented a challenge to someone as confident as Dom. But soon enough they became friends, enjoying each other's company. Perhaps she had grown complacent, taking his presence as her due. Did she want more?

Gayle turned from the window and pausing caught a glimpse of herself in the mirror. Curly, red hair and blue eyes, inherited from her Irish father, stared back at her. The pert nose, generous mouth and curvaceous five-feet-ten figure came from her English mother. She smiled at her reflection. No one had called her petite since early adolescence. Impulsively, Gayle decided to accompany Dom to Saint Abient. It was an opportunity not only to be with him, but to discover what Susan was hiding.

8

Later that same evening Bob Chandler phoned Volar and related the gist of his old friend Mark's concern for his cousin.

Volar's reaction was not encouraging. "Ridiculous. It is impossible to maintain a close watch on each of our students."

"Any idea how the rumors of a drug connection got started?" Bob said.

Volar hesitated. "Where do rumors ever start? Misunderstandings, malicious gossip...who knows? I'm not even convinced this so-called government investigation is not pure supposition."

Far from satisfied with the results of their conversation, Bob called Mark next, leaving a message for the call to be returned. While he waited, his gaze roved around his small efficiency apartment. He hated it. Every day he told himself it was temporary. One day there would be a break and when it came he'd take it and leave the *US Daily* behind.

At least he needn't struggle to support his family, like Nick Sarb with his mother and Danielle. Poor old Nick, reduced to managing bars instead of his late father's fortune. He knew Nick feared for his mother. The shock of her husband's death, followed by such a harsh will from a man who had seemed devoted to his family, was shattering and incomprehensible. One might even say suspicious, considering Volar's chief backer profited the most from Nick's father's will.

The phone rang, breaking into his musings. "Mark, I wanted you to know I spoke with Volar this evening."

"You what?"

"A direct approach was worth a try."

"I spoke to you in confidence."

"Relax. Volar promised to help with Benjamin. He's as perplexed as we are about your cousin's behavior, and I'm not surprised—"

"You had no business talking to—"

Bob interrupted, trying to calm him, "There's no reason to be upset."

"Let's hope you're right, Chandler." Mark went off the line.

9

Susan and Mark left the next morning for Saint Abient in a rented silver Mercedes. She relaxed as they edged out of the city. The car hugged the curves along Highway Two as Susan drank in the beauty of hillsides, checkerboarded with spring wheat and golden chamomile.

Near the small town of Marle, Mark slammed on the brakes as a bent old man hobbled into the road, trailed by a flock of squawking chickens. Susan bit back a scream, then let out a breath of relief. The old man had made it safely to the other side, though two chickens didn't.

"That was close," Mark said, as they drove on.

The drab, stucco homes lining the thoroughfare reminded her more of Romania than Paris or the Riviera. In the provinces, the French sometimes deliberately made the exterior of their homes unattractive in order to lower their property taxes.

Susan glanced at Mark, aware of the strength emanating from him. But it was more than his broad shoulders and lean physique. She sensed a subtle confidence in the way he spoke and moved; integrity etched within his eyes and features. They were more at ease with one another now.

"Did I forget to shave this morning?" he said.

"No." She lowered her gaze, disconcerted to be caught studying him.

"We're halfway there. How about a cup of coffee?" he said, pulling into an *autobahn* station.

"Sounds wonderful." She bought two cups of *café au lait* from the vending machine, while Mark had the car fueled and paid the attendant.

He eased the car back onto the highway and they continued on for a while, enjoying the morning jaunt. "We need to come up with a plan," Mark said, breaking the silence. Susan agreed and waited expectantly to hear what he might suggest.

"When you interview Volar, be sure to include routine questions about the framework of his organization, the people involved, his financial support, as well as the names of his chief staff and supporters." He drummed his fingers on the steering wheel for emphasis. "Incorporate his travels, goals, and the record to date of the Center's success, as well as any problems with students, the public, and so forth."

Did he think she didn't know how to conduct an interview? She knew her handling of the Volar story was of vital importance, but she had earned her position through persistent hard work and dedication. Admittedly, a natural flair for writing had given her an edge. She wondered if Mark spoke from experience or had his family's wealth and connections given him automatic entree into the upper echelons of the business?

Perhaps Mark just thought she was out of her depth because this was a criminal investigation. She couldn't deny that but the basics of good interviewing were ingrained in her. On the other hand, she had certainly fouled up the Andersen feature, so maybe a refresher course was in order after all, especially from her boss's point of view. She swallowed her resentment, leaned back, allowing her taut nerves to unwind and soon fell into a light doze.

Bursts of radio static brought her blinking from sleep as Mark scanned the stations for news. She looked up to find him smiling at her. "Did I wake you?"

She shook her head and closed her eyes again. The BBC murmured in the background as they sped along the highway. Soon she felt the car slow as they turned off the main thoroughfare into a narrow country lane.

"Are we there?" Susan said, sitting up straight.

"Almost." Mark swung the car into Saint Abient Center's long-sweeping drive. She shivered as she glimpsed the building, positioned like a fierce, aging tyrant on a small crest overshadowing the grounds. A lingering visage of the chateau's former grandeur was all that remained. The old faded-red brick seemed to be held together by air in places where the mortar had long since worn away. Was this where they were to stay?

A dark mammoth bird swooped down and circled the veranda, then soared to the steep roof and perched, watching them with hawk-like eyes as they got out of the car, juggling their luggage. To the side were stables constructed of brick and varnished hardwood. An outmoded carriage languished nearby, neglected and abandoned.

She exchanged a wary glance with Mark as they approached the door. Above, maids shook out bed linens over small wrought-iron balconies spaced across the upper two-stories. The ordinary nature of their task helped dispel the dark sense of foreboding that seemed to hang in the air.

A quaint old woman answered their knock with a scrutiny that suggested their arrival was an intrusion. Wrinkles creased her puffy skin and strands of coarse grey hair hung limply about her face. When Mark explained they were expected, she opened the door wide enough for them to enter and introduced herself.

"I am *Madame* Retell, the housekeeper."

She led them straightaway through a large foyer and up a curving staircase.

Susan entered her drab room, feeling rather deserted as Mark set her Delsey on the hardwood floor and left. She hung her trench coat in the armoire, dropped her tote on the room's single chair and positioned her laptop on a rickety table in the corner. She flopped onto the soft-lumpy mattress and wrinkled her nose in distaste. A chill dampness pervaded the villa and its furnishings, leaving the faint odor of mildew.

The irony was that most of her friends saw her job as glamorous and were inclined to overlook the difficulties of assignments in the West or third world countries like Algeria and Sudan—places she had often traveled while working with Interaid.

True, she had also glimpsed scenes and experienced cultures others dreamed of seeing. Dinner in Venice, an evening stroll along the beach in Brisbane, rambling along the ancient Roman walls in Niems and Chester were as real to Susan as the Saturday afternoon football game was to folks back home.

With a sigh, she raised herself from the bed and examined the crumpled cotton pantsuit she wore, deciding it would have to do. A quick brush of her hair and she was ready to begin her investigation.

The curving staircase led downstairs to the foyer. To the left was a formal dining room and to the right a study. She stepped to the back of the foyer, seeing that it spilled over into two communal sitting rooms where the students read or visited. An occasional burst of laughter reminded her of her own school days. A veranda beyond overlooked wheat fields. She traced her way back to the study and knocked.

A voice called, "*Entre.*" Inside a short, rotund man sat behind an elaborate walnut desk. "*Oui?*" he said, testily.

She offered her hand. "Hi. Susan Pardue with *Random World*, here to interview Reverend Volar."

He studied her for a brief moment before rising and shaking her hand. "Bernard LeFont, Volar's assistant. Welcome to Saint Abient Center."

"Thanks." Despite the polite words, his cold manner left her keen to conclude their business quickly. "About the interview?"

He smiled disdainfully. "There is no hurry, *mademoiselle*. Today you will relax, have dinner and enjoy visiting. Tomorrow I'll arrange a tour and a few meetings with the teachers. Perhaps the next day an interview with Reverend Volar. *Tres bien?*"

She nodded in reluctant agreement, dissatisfied at having to wait so long.

"If that is everything, *mademoiselle? Bonjour.*" He returned his attention to the paperwork before him by way of dismissal.

Susan left, understanding that the Reverend's assistant meant to make her task as difficult as possible.

Mark set his luggage down, neither surprised nor perturbed by the drab room and its sparse furnishings. He was here for one reason. To see Benjamin and find out what kind of mess he had gotten himself into this time. Despite the fifteen years that separated them, his cousin was like the brother he never had. Mark had always taken an active interest in him, proud of his achievements. Then last spring without warning Benjamin left for Saint Abient.

Mark had to follow. Perhaps with his resources he should have hired a team of detectives instead. But after Julie's death, he'd felt so responsible, that he'd known he couldn't bear to sit back and leave his cousin's fate in the hands of strangers. So he came. Susan's joining him had been Jerry's idea.

Mark headed downstairs in search of food and grabbed a sandwich in the kitchen, asking about Benjamin's whereabouts while he ate.

He located the students' dorm on the second floor at the opposite end of the hall from his own room. He knocked on a caramel-colored door marked number twenty-three. When there was no response, he rapped louder. Finally, a muffled voice yelled, "Come in."

Fearful of what he might find, Mark entered. Benjamin, still groggy from sleep, lay on a narrow twin bed, dressed in jeans and a T-shirt, his face turned into the pillow.

Mark released the breath he had been holding, the normalcy of the scene reassuring. He grasped his cousin by the shoulders, and shook him. "Time to get up, sleepy head."

Eyes a deeper blue-green than his own opened in surprise. "Where did you come from?" Benjamin rubbed his eyes and sat up with a grin. "Ugh, I had a late night."

"I won't bother to ask if you were studying."

"Well—classes aren't that hard here. Anyway, they only last half a day. How are Mom and Dad?"

"Concerned they haven't heard from you. They sent their love and a few packages."

"You'd think I was still a teenager, the way everyone carries on."

"We're aware you turned twenty-one this year, but since when did ignoring your family become a sign of maturity?"

Benjamin ran his fingers through his tangled hair, flashing Mark a rueful look. "You know I don't do it on purpose. I just get busy and forget to write."

Mark shifted in his chair wondering how best to bring up the subject that worried him so. Eventually, he blundered into it. "There's been a lot of unpleasant gossip back home."

"So what else is new?" Benjamin shoved his feet into a pair of tennis shoes.

Mark stared at the tousled dark head, the face with features so much like his own. Benjamin didn't look like an addict or someone involved in anything sinister. Mark didn't know what to believe. He tried again. "Rumor has it that you're on drugs and running with the wrong crowd."

Benjamin met Mark's gaze head on. "What do you believe?"

"I don't know. Why don't you tell me what's going on, starting with the Certificates of Deposit you cashed in?"

A defensive look set in. "They were mine—an inheritance from Grandmother."

"That's it? No explanations? No attempt to ease your family's minds?"

"I'm not ready for this." Benjamin hurriedly pulled on a sweater, crossed the room and opened the door. "Let's go get some coffee. What are you doing here anyway?"

He followed his cousin down the stairs, explaining about Susan's feature on the upcoming celebrations.

"Sure, since when do you follow your writer friends about on assignment?"

"Since the two of us scheduled a holiday following this one."

"So that's the way it is."

When they reached the cafeteria and sat down with coffee, Benjamin looked hard at Mark. "I don't do drugs."

"And your friends?"

"That's their business."

"Benjamin, this is Mark. You can trust me. Is there any truth to the rumors about Volar and the Center? Are drugs involved?"

"There's nothing going on that I can't handle."

His anger flared at his cousin's naivete! "Benjamin, you can't handle the mafia. Let me help you."

"Couldn't we just relax awhile? You're coming on pretty heavy. Give me time to think about it, okay?"

"Don't wait too long. I'd hate to see you get hurt."

That evening Mark and Benjamin waited for Susan in the dining room. When she arrived Mark introduced them, ignoring his cousin's knowing grin. The fact that she was attractive made their supposed romance more believable. A soft yellow dress accented her creamy skin and shining black hair. His gaze drifted over her figure, admiring its shapeliness before he realized what he was doing.

He turned and caught Benjamin's eye. "When do we meet the illustrious John Volar?"

His cousin shrugged, his attention centered on a petite brunette approaching them at whirlwind speed. Standing, he grasped her outstretched hands, and swung her around to face them. "Everybody meet Danielle Sarb, the prettiest girl I know."

She laughed, shaking their hands, while trading cheeks, for a quick kiss of greeting, one on each side. "Welcome to France. I am very glad to meet Benjamin's friends from America. I think maybe they are nicer than some of his friends here," she said, with a charming directness.

Benjamin gave Susan and Mark a weak smile. "It seems more than one person is concerned about my friends."

"*Oui*, so we should be," Danielle said, entering into a whispered debate with him.

Mark surmised, it would be advantageous for Susan to strike up a friendship with Danielle to see what she could learn. When he whispered as much to Susan, she agreed, but warned him not to expect too much.

Obviously relieved to change the subject, Benjamin enthusiastically pointed and said, "Hey, there's Reverend Volar."

"I'd like to meet him," Susan said, starting across the dining room to where Volar stood.

Mark waved to the others and hurried to catch up. He wanted to observe the pastor's reaction firsthand, when he learned of their arrival.

10

Susan and Mark reached Reverend Volar and his assistant at about the same time.

"You could have waited for me," he whispered.

"Just doing my job," she said, in a hurried aside.

Bernard LeFont, Volar's assistant greeted her first. "*Mademoiselle,* we meet again."

She grimaced at the thought of their run-in earlier that afternoon, when she had happened into his study while searching for Volar. She had distrusted LeFont on sight; he had been cold and rude. Her gaze narrowed on Volar. The smile she pasted on her face concealed a riot of emotions, the tense questions churning within.

Volar acknowledged them with a tentative handshake, his wary blue eyes seeming to size them up in an unsettling way. "I trust *Madame* Retell has seen to it you are both comfortably settled," he said, in a somewhat stilted voice.

"Yes, thank you." Susan hoped her uneasiness didn't show. She had returned from her bout with LeFont to find the woman nosing around in her room. Even now LeFont's hard stare worried her. Had she imagined the menacing gleam, quickly veiled with blandness? She swallowed as a flash of fear caught her unaware. Fear of what? Danger? Failure? Surely, not the assistant.

Mark shifted his weight, leaning against the table, his face unreadable. "I understand Bob Chandler phoned you of our arrival."

"Actually, he didn't seem to know when you'd arrive. He did, however, indicate your interest in certain matters," Volar admitted, then hurried on to say, "Matters that I think are inappropriate to discuss now."

Mark motioned to the plates of food a student worker was placing on the table. "We've no intention of detaining you. There will be plenty of time to speak later, but we did want to meet you."

They said brief good-byes and Mark and Susan started across the room to where Benjamin and Danielle sat.

"What was that about?" she said.

"The reporter I lunched with in Paris, Bob Chandler, phoned ahead to Volar, repeating our conversation almost verbatim."

Not for the first time, she wondered, if Mark was as inexperienced at investigative reporting as she was. Susan wished she could just ask him outright but didn't feel comfortable enough with him to do so. Maybe a subtle warning would suffice. "You were wound up pretty tight back there. That's bound to put Volar more on the defensive."

Remote blue-green eyes met hers. "I don't like being second-guessed by my staff."

"And I prefer to be spoken to with courtesy and respect."

His frown relaxed a few degrees. "Sorry. I was out of line."

She drew a deep breath. "Mark, have you done much investigative reporting?"

He started to speak, then stopped, surprise flickering in his gaze. "Now that you mention it, I guess not. There was never the need before." His gaze narrowed. "If you're unhappy with the way I'm conducting this—"

"No," she backtracked. "Just curious." She guessed they were both edgy; the impromptu meeting with Volar hadn't helped. Also the notebook she kept in her purse in which she had recorded her earlier run-ins with the two strangers seemed to have vanished.

Susan couldn't help but suspect the housekeeper since she had caught her nosing around in her room. She didn't feel that she could confide in Mark about any of this with his temper so short. He'd probably just think she was being absurd. Fortunately Benjamin and Danielle were too wrapped up in each other to notice their altercation.

Mark said, "You didn't tell me you had already met LeFont."

She shrugged. "There wasn't much to it. I stumbled into his office by chance earlier." She hated the thought that a pastor on whom so many were dependent could be involved in criminal activities. Volar didn't strike her as gangster material.

"Now that we've met Volar," Mark said, "when do you plan to interview him?"

"According to LeFont, my appointment is not until the day after tomorrow. Meanwhile, I have specific orders to relax and meet the staff."

Benjamin broke into their conversation. "Yeah, that sounds like LeFont. He's really good at ordering everyone around. One of these days, he's going to go too far."

Mark cursed softly. "What's that supposed to mean? Is LeFont one of the people you're supposed to be handling?"

Benjamin looked away. "I was just letting off steam. The guy's a real jerk. That's all."

Susan suspected there was more to it. Benjamin's unreasonable outburst didn't make sense unless something was up. Maybe LeFont was part of the drug scam.

Across the room she saw a messenger hand Volar a note. He read it quickly and then rose to leave, tossing the crumpled memo beside his plate. Susan wondered, what could be so important that he'd leave his dinner unfinished?

Reverend John Volar glanced across his desk at the three men LeFont ushered into his office. His backers, the men who had helped make the Center possible. In return they asked simply that their identities remain confidential. Entries in his records listed them merely as X, Y, and Z. He and LeFont, the sole persons aware of their identity, referred to them as the three factors.

Twenty-two years ago, they had trooped into his shabby church office, offering money to assist the poor and needy throughout the city, more money than he ever dreamed possible. And then as if that weren't enough, over the years they brought more funds, for schools, training, publishing, radio work—and so the list continued, long and benevolent.

Sarb, the group's unstated leader, was a heavyset man with a brim of thinning white hair that edged the shiny, smooth crown of his head. As chief curator of the city's museums, and a man of independent wealth, he was not without influence. He opened the meeting, throwing Volar a piercing look. "We did not expect to drive down until the weekend."

Volar ran a nervous hand through his hair. He had been dreading this moment. "You three gentlemen have a large stake in the Center and its ministry. The plain truth is, I'm in a bit of a dilemma and need your advice."

Dr. Philippe Beauchamp stiffened as if in imagined affront. "It's not our place to babysit the projects we finance. You're to handle any difficulties that arise on your own."

Volar quelled his distaste. Beauchamp's nature was petty and demanding, his generosity grudging and self-serving. His practice catered to wealthy hypochondriacs, and he was a philanderer besides.

Before Volar could respond, Dominic Trudeau the third backer unwound his elegant length from the chair. "Beauchamp, that's enough." He directed a smile at Volar. "Go ahead and explain."

Volar drew a deep breath and plunged ahead. "Maybe it is nothing, but there is a rumor circulating that the Center and one of our students, Benjamin Ashley, is involved in drugs."

Beauchamp's beady eyes snapped. "You called us down here because of a rumor?"

Sarb's jaw quivered in agitation. "Let us hear what he has to say, without interruption, please. Reverend, if you will get on with it and be specific. Where did you hear this?"

"From Bob Chandler, the reporter with *US Daily*, who spearheaded our publicity campaign last year. According to him, Mark Ashley of

Random World has been asking questions. It seems his cousin, the same Benjamin Ashley, attends school here and the whole family is afraid he is on drugs."

Volar studied the men before him, somewhat reluctant to mention a U.S. investigation or Ashley's suspicions that Volar himself ran the drug ring. Beauchamp would be sure to gloat at that tidbit and Volar wasn't going to give him the chance. He continued. "The last thing we need is any adverse publicity at a time like this. We've scheduled the announcement of the South American venture for the weekend. A leak could ruin the whole affair."

Dominic spoke first, in what Volar knew was an effort to reassure him. "Rumors and publicity go hand and hand. Don't take it so much to heart. However, if a student is selling or taking drugs, he needs to be expelled. Have you talked with this young man?"

"I have a meeting set for tomorrow afternoon. I wanted to observe him first and I have seen nothing abnormal. He spends a lot of time off campus, but so do many of the students."

Beauchamp interrupted. "More important, does he come in late? Who does he associate with? Where does he go when he leaves?"

Sarb waved for silence. "Beauchamp, you investigate this. The good Reverend has his hands full," he added with a trace of sarcasm.

Beauchamp grudgingly agreed and the discussion ended.

After they left, Volar strayed to the window and gazed down upon the lawns. Benjamin wasn't his only problem. Nor were the drugs. No matter how hard he tried, he couldn't see his way out. He knew that tampering with the books could send him to prison but hindsight didn't help. At this stage, he hadn't a clue how to stop what he'd help set in motion. He clenched his fists in frustration and felt the onslaught of a migraine. He couldn't handle any more tonight.

The next morning Volar resumed his scrutiny of the accounts, searching for a path out of the chaos he'd stepped into. Three hours later, when Bernard LeFont entered his employer's office, Volar quickly moved his arm to shield the top ledger, laying open on his desk. Hunched over the stacks of papers and books, he motioned LeFont to a small desk in the corner of the room, where another pile awaited him.

He couldn't risk his assistant uncovering the appearance and disappearance of funds in the school's accounts. Several times he had almost out of necessity let LeFont in on the deal, but something within held him back. Volar lived in dread of the day he might discover the laundering and confront him. That LeFont kept the books, made it harder and harder to hide the truth from him.

Volar was also aware that someone was trying to set him up for a fall. Impossible to suspect LeFont. He searched his mind, tearing apart recent events, hunting for clues. Why had he ever thought he could get away with so much? Added to his worries was the Ashley connection. Reporters, no less, sniffing for scandal. What was he going to do?

He threw down his pen and looked across at LeFont. Instead of the expected elation over the upcoming celebration marking twenty years of successful service, Volar was worried, afraid of the outcome. The margin for error was too high. There were too many problems and the press was getting too close. He jerked at his collar. Thoughts of the scandals that had affected several American tele-evangelists haunted him. When had it begun to go wrong? Visions of disgrace at Saint Abient terrified him. His head pounded with the same questions. Where had he lost control?

Somehow, throughout the day, he managed to present a facade of obliging serenity to those about him.

Later that afternoon, he held a staff meeting and then closeted himself with his Bible and study materials until LeFont interrupted him. "Benjamin Ashley is here to see you."

"Show him in and see that we're not disturbed."

"You sent for me, sir?" Benjamin's frightened face peered at him from the doorway.

Volar waved him to a seat. "Yes, I did." Benjamin met his penetrating scrutiny with a shaky but straightforward composure. Volar eased into his questioning. "How are you doing here? Have you made many friends?"

"Some." Benjamin avoided Volar's gaze.

Volar's spirits plummeted. Until that moment he had given Benjamin the benefit of the doubt. Now he knew the youth was hiding something. He steeled himself against the young man's vulnerability. There was too much at stake to risk everything on one boy's foolishness. His voice hardened. "Information has reached me that you are selling drugs on campus. I cannot emphasize enough how serious this is. It is a criminal offence you could go to prison for."

Benjamin's face whitened. "That's a lie!" He clutched the chair arms for support. "I've never touched drugs in my life."

"How do you account for the rumors?"

A slow flush crept over Benjamin's pale face. "There's not much I can say, sir, not without incriminating friends who may be innocent." His stuck his chin out stubbornly. "You don't have a shred of evidence. It's not fair to accuse me on hearsay."

Volar walked around the desk, reluctantly admiring the young man's show of American independence. Perhaps he was innocent after all. He placed a hand on Benjamin's shoulder. "This situation reflects poorly on the school, and its ministry, as well as yourself. For the time being I'll accept your word, but I warn you, should any evidence to the contrary turn up, it will mean expulsion or at the very least suspension. Bear in mind that a man is generally judged by the company he keeps."

Benjamin's Adam's apple seemed to bulge. "Yes sir, I will and I'm sorry for the trouble this has caused you."

Volar watched him leave, unsure what to think. His thoughts of Benjamin gave way to more immediate problems. Namely, the books. Should he confess everything or wait until he was found out? It was bound to happen. Whatever way he decided, he was in deep trouble.

The breeze slammed the door shut behind her. Shivering, Susan dropped her purse and notebook on the side table in her room. Brr...it was cold for early June. She glanced at her watch: one hour until dinner. Susan kicked off her shoes and stretched out on the bed, the day's happenings chasing through her mind. Everyone had been friendly and helpful. Mark even seemed more approachable. Several times, they had shared a moment of amusement, their eyes meeting in silent appreciation of the conversation at hand.

She had not seen Volar, but one of the teachers pointed out his apartment and office. There was no reason to feel this disquiet, this sense of looming danger. But she did, perceiving subtle nuances in the atmosphere that there was no accounting for. Was she being silly? Overreacting? Or had someone been watching her today? She had nothing definite to go on besides a sensation of being under observation at certain moments. That and a barely perceptible sound of flurry whenever she paused to check. A sound she could easily have imagined.

A knuckled rap startled her. "It's Mark. May I come in?"

"The door's unlocked."

He wore grey slacks and a teal pullover that matched his eyes. "A tough day?" he said, as his gaze swept over her.

"Not particularly." She sat up and hid a smile as Mark struggled to compress his tall frame into the small wooden chair. His legs and arms extended like tentacles.

"Go ahead and laugh," he said. "When you're through you can fill me in on the latest."

"I wouldn't dream of laughing." She grinned, adjusting the pillow behind her back. "The students and teachers were an easy target. They're so proud of Volar." Susan sobered as she related the gist of her findings. "He travels frequently, and this year's trips included South America and the Middle East."

"You're sure?"

"From more than one source. The faculty broadcasts his excursions as a mark of success."

"The trips could be strictly legit."

"I hope they are. I hate the thought of him duping these people."

Mark sighed. "Our arrival here hasn't exactly helped Benjamin, either. He's in a bigger jam than ever."

"What's happened?"

"Volar is using my talk with Bob Chandler as grounds to investigate Benjamin."

"How can he do that without evidence?"

"He claims he has confidential sources."

"You met with Volar?" she said, chagrined that Mark had managed to see him when she couldn't even get in for an interview. She'd made several attempts and every one came up cold.

"Not directly. But I talked to LeFont, after I heard Benjamin's version of meeting with Volar. He's scared. But he won't tell me a thing. Did you get anywhere with Danielle?"

"Benjamin must have warned her off. Every time I tried, she managed to change the subject."

"How about the backers? Any leads there?"

He looked worried and she couldn't blame him. Susan wished she had the answers. She shook her head. "Nothing. Everyone seems to assume his projects are supported by donations."

"Well, there's one bright light on the horizon." Mark eased his length out of the small chair and held up a key. "We need to find out who the chief backers are and more about those itineraries. And to do that we need to get into Reverend Volar's office." He dropped the key into his shirt pocket. When she opened her mouth to ask how he had got it, he held up a hand. "Don't ask...there are some things you're better off not knowing."

Frustrated, she threw her pillow across the room at him.

He ducked and grinned, as it thudded against the door. "Seriously, though, I may need you for a diversion tonight. So be ready." He was gone before she could ask any questions.

Susan listened to his retreating steps. Breaking and entering? She shuddered. What next?

11

Later that evening Mark seated Susan on a secluded bench under a sycamore tree. Until now everything had been going as he planned. He had seen in a glance that the cleaning and fix-it staff were a seedy lot. No doubt a source of cheap local labor that the Center was bent on reforming. Mark locked his suitcase when he left his room and kept his cash and credit cards on his person. He was taking no chances. Earlier that day he'd obtained a key to LeFont's office with a well-placed bribe to the head handymen who for double the price told him exactly where to find a key to Volar's office and apartments as well.

Mark had dropped by LeFont's office that afternoon to find he was out. His secretary seated him inside to wait with a cup of coffee in one hand and a brochure on the Center's ministries in the other. Minutes later LeFont returned, apologizing that he had run up to Volar's office for a misplaced journal.

Mark tried to hide his elation as he watched LeFont fumble at the back of the bottom left drawer and heard a key dropping into place, just as the handyman had said. A magnetic key holder was attached to the back wall of that drawer and he was determined to get into it tonight, with or without Susan's help. It would be a lot safer with it.

Susan faced him squarely. "You agreed to level with me if I didn't act on my own."

"Can't you just follow orders?"

"This isn't simply a story. Our lives may be in jeopardy. I need to know what's at stake." She searched his face as if considering and then dug into her pocket with one hand. Susan handed him a crumpled piece of construction paper.

There was enough light for him to recognize a crude drawing of Susan. Underneath in large block letters it read:

LEAVE AMERICAN OR ELSE BANG BANG YOUR DEAD

He drew in his breath. "Is this some kind of joke? Where did you get this?"

"It was in my room, after dinner, on my bed."

"Why didn't you tell me?"

She shrugged. "There wasn't time."

He read the truth in her gaze. "You didn't plan on telling me," he said in a tight voice.

She stiffened and looked away for a moment before turning back to meet his gaze. "I was afraid you'd make me leave."

"And you wanted to stay enough to face this alone?" He held up the note.

She touched his arm in an effort to make him understand. "I feel as if my whole life is suddenly on the line and if I miss this chance, there may not be another." She seemed so small, next to him. Her hand fell to her side. "I can't expect you to understand, but don't ask me to go back. I need to do this for me and Matthew."

His hand covered hers. "This isn't the time to exorcize your guilt. Believe me, I know." A picture of his sister's youthful face rose to taunt him. "If I hadn't been so wrapped up in my life, Julie might be alive. I should have known the guy she was dating was a rat. Where was her big brother when she went to that party and took that fatal hit?"

"It's so much more than that in my case. I'm too ashamed to even speak of it."

What was she talking about? What could she have done?

"Nothing's really changed. You need my help. Let me stay."

"We both know that note changed everything. We're getting close enough to make somebody nervous." She was right about one thing. He did need her help. He was probably going to regret it, but his anger had vanished with the realization that she wasn't being difficult without cause. She had every right to be concerned after receiving that threatening note. Its message left him chilled. He nodded reluctantly and she let out a sigh of relief.

"About tonight." He quickly explained about the keys. "Volar and his secretary drove off while we were eating. I need you to be on the lookout for their return or anyone else who might happen along while I get the keys from LeFont's office and search Volar's. All right?"

She agreed and they both rose, turning at the soft scuffing of a shoe scraping stone and dirt nearby. They were startled to see Volar's doctor friend Beauchamp stealthily creeping up on them.

Mark drew Susan into his arms, his hand over her mouth stifling her protest. After a moment, she seemed to understand the need for pretense. The silence amplified the faint rustle in the bushes as the man drew nearer, spying on them.

Mark's arms tightened around Susan, his instinct warning that this was no innocent happenstance. A burst of soft laughter from the veranda floated across the lawn. Mark bent his head as if to kiss her.

She stiffened momentarily in resistance, then eased her arms around his shoulders and rested her lips against the corner of his mouth, pulling free after a moment.

"Darling," she said loud enough for the intruder to hear. "I'm so glad you're here. This assignment would be a bore without you."

Over her shoulder Mark kept a watch, feeling the heat of Beauchamp's gaze as he studied them. "You know I can't stay away from you long," he said, his fingers trailing through her hair. Apparently satisfied theirs was a lover's tryst, the man turned back to walk around the veranda toward the parking lot. Mark's grip on Susan loosened. They heard a car door slam, and then the engine revving.

Susan drew back. "What was that about?"

Mark didn't say anything. He couldn't explain his sensation that for a few minutes he'd believed their lives were in danger, but neither would he ignore it. "How about we talk later. There's a long night ahead of us still."

They walked through the side lawn to the front of the chateau. Although neither were inclined to speak Mark could almost see the thoughts racing through her mind.

Stars twinkled, and the moon lighted the path to the darkened verandah and house front. Mark guided Susan into the entry alongside him. The tick tock of a clock sounded in the quiet of the hall. He searched the foyer and what he could see of the rooms beyond. Nothing—just the rise and fall of chattering voices drifting through the closed doorways. He strode toward LeFont's office, halting once to see if they were observed and glanced at Susan. She shouldn't be here. She should be far away, on some safe assignment interviewing some woman about her favorite charity or travel spot.

He tried LeFont's door, then slipped a key into the lock. "Knock once if anyone comes near," he said, before entering the room.

A stream of moonlight filtered through the window, illuminating the intricate-wine-colored-wall tapestry behind LeFont's desk. Mark opened the bottom left drawer and felt along the back wall until his fingers found the magnetic latch.

Quickly he probed the mechanism, finding a minuscule side lever. He lost his grip as the telephone on the desk rang—once—twice, then stopped. The latch wouldn't give. His adrenalin racing, Mark reached into his pocket. With a miniature screwdriver he rotated the lever's spring, his other hand cupped to catch the two keys when they fell from their hiding place. The drawer closed. He scanned the office. The carpet showed other tracks besides his. He crossed the room and opened the door, Susan's body shielding him from view as he stepped out and locked it. He met her gaze. "We've got the key," he whispered. "Let's get to Volar's."

12

Susan tiptoed down the hall beside Mark, wondering what she'd say if somebody approached her. She clutched her shoes in one hand, the bitter chill from the wooden floor seeping through her thin nylons. By the time they reached Volar's office, she was shivering. She wanted to stop Mark from entering but she bit down on her lip, steeling herself against her own vulnerability. He was gone; the same curt command echoed in his wake. "Knock once if anyone comes."

The minutes ticked by with Susan too afraid to move. The corridor was empty, no one in sight. Gloomy shadows hovered in the corners. Her gaze scanned the area repeatedly. Mark was only a few feet away, the other side of the door. But it would be folly to depend on Mark. They lived in two different worlds and she was his employee, not friend or confidante.

Twenty-five minutes passed. Susan's nerves grew even more taut. What was taking him so long?

She made one last survey of the corridor before she eased the door open and moved inside. The room smelled of leather bound books. A shiny, teakwood desk gleamed in its center. Burgundy velvet drapes with long tassels shrouded two large windows.

"What are you doing in here?" Mark said in a low voice.

"I thought you might need some help," she whispered, reaching for a stack of files.

"Here, take these." He relinquished some of the ones he held. "I hope we don't have reason to regret this."

She accepted them wordlessly, sliding into the chair behind Volar's desk. Her attention was drawn to a green ledger on the edge of the desk. Susan reached for it, riffling through the pages. "Look at this," she called to Mark, pointing to the columns of figures totaling hundreds of thousands of dollars and the names entered to the side. "These must be the backers, except they're listed as X, Y and Z."

He peered over her shoulder and whistled softly in amazement. "I have a strong hunch what their real names are." He tapped the files in his hand. "I've found correspondence that dates back twenty years covering every major event in Volar's ministry."

"Who?" she broke off, jerking at the sound of approaching footsteps. In a flash the files were back in place and Mark was behind the drapes. Susan dropped the ledger on the corner of the desk, picked up the phone and punched the button for the international operator. Better for someone to think she'd passed by and found the door open and borrowed the phone. Anything beat being caught breaking and entering.

She realized the operator would be too slow and pressed the button to disconnect, before rapidly punching in a series of numbers. "Hello, Monroe. *Wie geht's dir?*"

"Susan, is it really you? How are you?"

"I'm fine." Susan stilled the tremor in her voice, a reflex reaction to the tender affection underlying Monroe's questions. She drew a breath and felt her world shift back into focus. "How's work?" she said.

"Nothing's changed much. I'm as madly in love with you as ever," he said, half teasing, half serious. "Are you in Vienna?"

"No. I'm in France, a small town in the middle of nowhere." She wondered if anyone was listening on the other side of the door.

"Tell me where, I'll meet you." Monroe's eagerness added yet another layer of uneasiness to her mounting anxiety. She liked him too much to trifle with his feelings.

"I'd love to see you, but I don't know when. Monroe, I've got to go or I'll be out of a job for using the director's personal phone."

"But where are you?"

"About four hours from Paris. Monroe, I have to hang up."

"Susan, don't you dare forget to call." His voice was husky. "I think of you way too often."

"I think of you too, Monroe." She had to say it. "But my feelings haven't changed."

"If you gave me half a chance, they might."

"Maybe, but I don't think so." Susan hung up the phone and edged toward the door. Although she was quaking inside, she stepped into the corridor humming a carefree tune. As far as anyone else knew, her greatest worry was her latest amour. She halted dramatically and opened her hands, palms up, mumbling aloud in complaint. "I forgot my purse." Her disgusted glance took in the entire area before she darted back to the office. "The coast is clear," she whispered to Mark as she picked up her purse. "I'll catch the lights. Meet me in my room."

She walked quickly down the hall. As she rounded the corner, she felt the impact of a hard body, then Volar's arms steadied her. "Miss Pardue."

Her heart was pounding so loud; she could hardly take in his words. She straightened her trembling knees and stepped back. "I'm sorry. I shouldn't have been rushing around the corner like that."

"Have you been visiting one of the students?" His puzzled gaze scanned the length of the hall leading to his private wing.

Susan realized she had no choice but to play the floozie. She peeked at him through fluttering lashes, then lowered her gaze in an effort to hide her apprehension. "I suppose I should confess. I needed to make a private call, one I didn't want Mr. Ashley to overhear." She hung her head in pretended embarrassment, wishing she knew where Volar stood in relation to the illegal activities. "So I used the phone in your office."

He regarded her warily. "My office is locked."

She squashed a nervous giggle. "I don't know about that. I was walking around when I noticed a light under the door. I knew it was your office from the tour. I tapped at the door, thinking perhaps you would let me use the phone. When no one answered, I went in. I'm sorry, I made a call to Vienna. I'll be glad to pay for it."

Volar frowned. "In the future, please remember my office is off limits. There is a public phone in the community room."

"Sorry."

Volar managed a weary smile. "Might I also suggest that you consider eternity?"

"Eternity?" she echoed.

"Yes, eternity." His eyes crinkled. "It's something we all must face eventually."

Susan flushed. He thought she was sleeping with one man and sneaking off to call another. She and Mark had worked hard to create that impression. She couldn't honestly blame Volar. He wasn't trying to be judgmental, but helpful. Even though such behavior was accepted as common, her own standards forbade it. She didn't sleep around.

She wanted to meet his gaze head-on and spout a few cliches of her own. She closed her lips lest her thoughts spill out and she actually spoke the words: appearances are often deceiving and don't judge a book by its cover. Instead she smiled provocatively, masking her concern. "There are some compensations though, *monsieur. Bonsoir.*"

Susan entered her room and sank down on the bed. Before her fuddled brain could sort itself out, Mark joined her.

He caught her hands. "Are you okay? Not once, but twice tonight, your life was in danger," he said, with a catch in his voice. "I don't know what to say."

Susan drew away from the solid comfort he offered, although she appreciated his kindness and concern. She gazed into the blue-green warmth of his eyes. "You didn't jeopardize my life. I accepted this assignment with my eyes wide open. So far we're not only safe, but well on our way to unraveling this enigma."

Mark rubbed the back of his neck. "Anyone see you on your way?"

"The Reverend Volar, himself."

He groaned, compressing himself into the room's one chair. "Just what we needed. What happened?"

Susan sat back down on the bed. "The thing he suspected was my virtue. It's fairly obvious he believes I'm a fallen woman."

Mark eyed her quizzically. "Making a lover's call in that office didn't exactly help."

"It wasn't a lover's call. Besides Volar couldn't have overheard. He was coming from the opposite direction." She moved to straighten her papers on the night table by the bed, and paused, mesmerized by the sudden twinkle in his eyes.

"It's hard to believe that you've managed to fade into the background the last two years at *Random World* without causing some kind of a stir. Are you always so impulsive?"

"Not nearly as much as I used to be."

He chuckled. "Life is certainly never staid with you around."

"Hey, I didn't create this situation." She returned his smile. His sense of humor cropped up at the oddest moments. He was usually so business minded that it never failed to throw her off stride. Still she was glad to note that he obviously hadn't been aware of the stir she caused with the Andersen fiasco. That particular whirlwind almost cost her job.

They discussed the evening's findings for a while. Susan thought, maybe now was the time to inform him of the men she had thought were following her and the missing notebook. She swallowed. "There's something else I've been wanting to tell you." She quickly filled him in but found he wasn't as surprised as she expected.

He gave her a wary look. "Please, don't misunderstand. I appreciate all you're doing to help Benjamin and me. However, I had be sure you were legit. People can be bought and I didn't know you from Adam back then. Consequently, I had you followed in Amsterdam and Paris."

His admission threw her. She disliked his invasion of her privacy and hated that yet another person had been following her without her knowledge. Yet on another level she understood. Susan shook her head. "I'm not sure how to respond to that."

"In your place, I'd probably be furious. My contact did mention something about you finding a package and being followed possibly as a result. But he said they looked into it and it turned out to be nothing. So you can relax on that score at least."

"Thanks. Can I also presume that I'm no longer under suspicion?"

His face gave nothing away. "You're not being followed, if that's what you're asking."

Susan held his gaze, aware that he hadn't said he trusted her. She felt an odd mixture of sympathy and resentment, realizing that he'd purposely left her to stew in Amsterdam and Paris just to see what she'd get up to. Her emotions were much too tangled to put into words. She sighed and gave up the effort, turning the subject. "About my run-in with Volar tonight.... He was so civil—almost too nice to be involved in this."

Mark arched one brow. "Don't be naive. Haven't you ever heard of wolves wearing sheep's clothing?"

"Point taken. You still haven't told me who that correspondence was from."

"Mainly, Sarb, Beauchamp and Trudeau, however, we've got some work ahead of us to prove they're Volar's major donors and that they're even involved in anything crooked."

"I would think the fact that the ledgers listed them and the correspondence linked the three definitively would be a major step toward accomplishing just that."

"We need concrete evidence. Proving they're X, Y and Z doesn't make them criminals. Though a copy of that ledger and some of those letters would sure help for starters."

"How did you get LeFont's key to begin with?"

After he explained, Mark stood. "I'd feel better if I knew who was outside that office."

"It could have been anyone." She waved her hand dismissively. "The students prowl this place."

"Maybe. Your phone call was a clever ruse. Let's hope it threw them off track." He started toward the door. "Let's call it a night. Maybe we'll wake up with some new answers."

Susan watched him walk away, a worried frown creasing his face, and felt a sense of foreboding. She closed the door behind him, quelling a sudden urge to check on Benjamin.

13

Susan glowered at the travel alarm and pressed the button to stop its persistent ring. Six o'clock. Loud raps on the door echoed the pounding in her head. She threw back the sheets.

"Who is it?"

"It's me, Danielle Sarb. I have to talk with you. Please, it's important."

Susan padded across the room, her long flannel gown billowing around her ankles. She eased the door open and motioned the puffy-eyed girl to a chair, suspecting a quarrel with Benjamin to be the reason behind the early morning visit. She sat on the edge of the bed and tried to suppress a surge of elation. An upset Danielle might let some clue to Benjamin's dilemma slip. Thus far Susan had been unable to break through her determined silence regarding Benjamin's affairs.

The girl was muttering in French, her voice rising and falling in agitation as she swallowed a broken sob.

"Take a deep breath and tell me in English what's wrong. It can't be that bad."

Danielle threw her a reproachful glance and wiped at her tears with a tissue.

Too tired to appreciate the Latin penchant for drama, Susan said, "That's enough. Are you going to tell me what's wrong or am I to guess?"

"If you knew, *mam'selle*, you would not be so calm." She sniffled. "My Benjamin is in very great danger. I fear for his life. But he makes me to promise to say nothing to anyone. So what am I to do? *Mam'selle*, it is so very awful and I am so frightened for him." She finished on a whimper.

It was impossible to resist her helpless plea. Susan gathered the weeping girl into her arms. "Danielle, you must trust me. Mark and I are here because we care. Please, won't you tell me the truth, before it's too late."

Danielle pulled away. "It is already too late. He left last night." Her amber eyes pleaded. "I promised not to tell."

Oh no, not the same thing again, Susan thought, as she squeezed the girl's hand. It was imperative that she learn from Danielle what had happened. "You must tell. Benjamin's so young—inexperienced. He can't fight this alone."

Danielle drew a trembling breath and launched into her tale.

Susan listened with growing dread, her mind racing ahead to how

Mark would accept this latest debacle. He had already suffered so much. She knew she had to be the one to tell him.

She dressed in the first outfit her hand lit upon, a soft yellow cotton dress, its sunny aspect a sharp contrast to her troubled state of mind. She gave her hair a few swift brush stokes, allowing the tousled curls to fall where they would. No time for makeup. She commanded Danielle to wait until she returned.

She found Mark in his room, awake and dressed. He sat in a rickety chair making notes. How would he react? He couldn't blame himself this time. Could he? She sat on the bed, willing him strength. "Mark, Benjamin's gone."

Something in her voice must have reached him. "He's gone?" The cautious words rang with anxiety.

She felt a curious affinity with the scarred wooden floor, stripped of its veneer. She raised her gaze to meet his. "Danielle came to my room for an early morning talk."

"And?"

She twisted her hands in her lap. "It's not so simple as that. He's on his way to Sofia. He's trying to help a friend." She was babbling. "He's not on drugs. His friend is. They've kidnapped him."

Mark crossed the room in one long stride and seized her shoulders, pulling her to her feet. "Who—who has kidnapped him?"

"Not Benjamin, his roommate Kevin." She touched his cheek. "They told Benjamin he would never see his friend alive again. They forced him to agree to pick up a drug cache in Sofia and deliver it to Bucharest for them. He's gone."

"How is he traveling?"

"I don't know. No one does."

"I'm sorry." Susan realized the words were not enough, but she needed to say something, didn't she? Words couldn't erase the terror she saw reflected in his face as destiny struck once again, unmindful of fairness. But she felt it too—almost as if Matthew was before her again and she had been given another chance.

"Who kidnapped Kevin, and who is he anyway?" he said.

"Kevin is Benjamin's roommate and Kevin's brother Frederick is Sarb's secretary. Kevin overheard a conversation between Sarb and Beauchamp. According to Kevin, Sarb is cheating Danielle's family out of their inheritance with a fraudulent will."

"What does this have to do with Benjamin?"

"I'm trying to tell you. Kevin overheard Beauchamp threatening to blackmail Sarb. Beauchamp knew about the phony trust Sarb set up."

Mark eyed her intently, and she could tell he was having trouble composing himself.

She went on. "Sarb laughed at Beauchamp's attempt to blackmail him. He said they'd both be brought up on charges if he tried that. He was in too deep."

"What kind of charges?"

"That's the catch. Danielle's not sure, but she thinks this whole thing has something to do with drugs." Mark's expression became grimmer and Susan hurried to explain. "She swears your cousin hasn't taken any. He was trying to help Kevin out of a jam. They wouldn't tell her anything about it." Susan bit her lower lip. "Instead of telling anyone, Kevin and Benjamin decided to investigate on their own."

"Let me get this straight. Did they confront Sarb?"

"No, they broke into his study, but he caught them. Afterward, they released Benjamin, on the condition he would pick up some drugs in Sofia and deliver them to their contact in Bucharest. It seems their plan is to incriminate both of them. Thus, the drug cache."

Mark shook his head. "No, it doesn't make sense. Those two are a big liability to Sarb. I'd say he found a way to separate and then get rid of them. The death of a couple of foreign students in an obscure school in France would draw the press, whereas an accident in Eastern Europe might go unnoticed. And the death of another student in France could hardly be connected to it."

Susan's throat tightened. "You don't really think that, do you?"

"What else am I to think, that Sarb would be stupid enough to chance their talking?"

"What are you going to do?"

He didn't reply; his expression remote. She waited for him to speak, say something, anything, as long it broke the silence that stretched between them. But he sat there, frozen, oblivious.

She wanted to reach out and touch him. "Say something, please. Have faith. You'll see. It'll be okay."

"You can say that after everything that's happened? Did faith save your precious Matthew or my sister Julie? Where was God then, or didn't He care?"

Susan felt the blood drain from her face but she forced herself to face the truth. "Julie and Matthew had a choice just like you and I and everyone else in this crazy universe. And they made the wrong choice, and it wasn't just once. They chose the wrong friends. The wrong parties. And God help us, the wrong death."

Mark towered over her. "You've said quite enough. You can drop the philosophical, theological jargon. I'm not interested."

"God didn't make their choices for them, any more than you or I. So you weren't there when Julie needed you. What about me? Who do you think tried drugs first in my family?" She saw the surprise flicker across his face and turned away.

The silence between them grew. Susan blinked back tears, trying to pull herself together. She avoided his gaze. "I'll send Danielle to you." Her head held high, she brushed by him. Inside, she felt hollow...empty. Why couldn't life be simple?

A hand on her arm stopped her. "Let's back up. This isn't getting us anywhere. What you did or didn't do is beside the point. This is a job and I need your help. Unless you've changed your mind about staying?"

Unable to speak, she shook her head.

"I'm sorry. This is tough enough without our ranting and raving, upsetting each other. But I don't expect to be dictated to and least of all by you."

Hurt, she lowered her gaze. He had made it clear she was an employee who had overstepped the bounds of what the job demanded. It would be the last time though, she vowed.

He stood there, his anger spent and his expression so bleak, that against her will, her heart softened. She felt a fierce urge to comfort him and when he pulled her into his arms, she didn't resist.

"Susan, first Julie and now Benjamin. Why?"

She held him, willing him strength. "I don't know why, but we have to believe it'll be okay. We'll find him before it's too late." It can't be like Julie and Matthew, she cried within. It just can't. Suddenly, her whole fight, her struggle to come to grips with life, centered upon saving Benjamin. And Kevin too. We have to save him too. Dear Lord, she prayed silently, please let us find them before it's too late. Let them be safe. Please!

14

Kevin Bartlett strode past a cool blonde on the *Rue de Nuechant*, ignoring the warmth in her gaze. He rounded the corner and ran smack into an overweight brunette. Her perusal of his lean athletic body, from the tips of his tennis shoes up to his baby blues, annoyed him. Until recently, things had always come easy to Kevin.

That morning he had skipped class and caught an early train to Paris. He dreaded this meeting with his older brother, Frederick. If it were not for his family's demands, he wouldn't be in this mess. All he had wanted was a year to travel and unwind after University and what seemed like a lifetime of school, before joining his dad's firm. But his parents insisted Saint Abient Center would be the perfect place to relax, because of the easy curriculum, and, Kevin thought glumly, the close campus environment. It was humiliating to admit how stupid he had been and how desperately he needed Frederick's help.

Kevin rang the bell to *Monsieur* Sarb's elegant townhouse, where Frederick worked as secretary. An unsmiling butler greeted him, his voice as rigid as his face. At the mention of Frederick's name, he began closing the door. "*Monsieur* has stepped out."

Not the least intimidated, Kevin wedged his foot between door and jam. "I'll wait." He pressed the disgruntled butler aside and crossed the room to perch on the edge of a lavender damask love seat in an isolated corner of the huge marble foyer. He had to see Frederick today to get enough cash to pay Reese. His own stupidity sickened him. He'd kill himself rather than work for Reese, that is, if they didn't beat him to it. Was this to be his end? Death at the hand of some second-rate lowlife?

His great prospects gone overnight, with his self-respect. What had he come to? Bad enough that he'd submerged himself in a nightmare of debts, pimps, drug pushers, but he'd brought his friend down as well. Benjamin faced possible expulsion and drug charges for helping him.

Was it a mere month ago that Benjamin had stormed into the small room they shared? "I think you owe me an explanation," he said slamming a bag of cocaine down on the study desk between their two beds.

Kevin caught it as it skidded off the smooth surface toward the floor. Ashamed of the desperate impulse that led him to hide his stash among Benjamin's things in the first place, he forced himself to meet his friend's gaze. "What are you going to do?"

Benjamin stared at him, hurt, puzzled and angry. "I don't get it—

why? I thought we were friends. Did you think the maid wouldn't go through my drawers? Or is this some kind of personal vendetta?"

"That's the problem—I just didn't think. I should have never involved you. Look, I'm sorry." They both fell silent, and finally Kevin confessed. "I thought no one would suspect you. You never used that drawer. How did you find it, anyway?"

"I didn't, the maid did."

The words echoed in his head and Kevin felt his knees go weak. "Did you tell her it wasn't yours?"

"It wouldn't have done much good. She'd never believe me. She's demanding a hundred dollars to keep quiet. I'm not stupid. I know you're in way over your head. You owe me the truth."

Kevin broke down and told him everything, how the sum total of what he wanted was out. "Help me this once. I'll do whatever you say."

"If you promise to stay completely away from cocaine. Not even a snort, or I'll tell."

Kevin released his breath. "Deal. And don't worry, I'll take care of the maid."

"No. She'll double the price if she thinks there's two of us."

"If this ever got out, you'd be expelled. Even if I confessed, they might not believe me."

Benjamin shrugged, his face noncommittal. "So pay me back. Just don't forget your promise. I'm counting on you."

"How?" Kevin's usual confidence flagged. "When I can't even pay off my gambling debts."

"Great. Maybe you'll quit."

Kevin swallowed. "Unless I buy my way out—they're after me."

In the end, Benjamin cashed in on an inheritance to loan him the money. Kevin kept his promise about the cocaine. He'd meant to give up the gambling, too. But when he went to settle his debts, he found himself coerced into one last game of chance. Rather than cause a scene, he decided he could afford to stake ten on a farewell hand. It wasn't until he lost that Reese told him the ten stood for ten thousand.

Frederick was his last hope. He stood and paced down the hall beyond the foyer, staring at the paintings lining the wall without really seeing them. He had to convince his brother to lend him the money.

Kevin halted as angry voices burst from a room to his left. He edged closer to the half-open door. Closed drapes sealed the room in near darkness. A small antique table lamp cast a faint light over Sarb and Beauchamp in heated debate.

Sarb muttered an expletive. "Get out of here. You'll not get another *franc* out of me."

"I advise you not to be so hasty, my friend." Beauchamp tapped his fingers on the table beside him. "There is a certain little matter which seems to have slipped your mind."

"Stay out of my affairs," Sarb shouted, his color rising.

"Come now, I know how you defrauded your nephew out of his inheritance to help pay for this place and your precious paintings."

Beauchamp wore a smug smile. "You're too greedy, *Monsieur*. Unfortunately, you wanted too much this time, and there isn't enough to go around. But never fear, I have confidence in your ability to appease. Or should I say deliver twelve million *francs* by Friday or else."

"Or else what?" Sarb thundered with a sneer. "One word and you sink with me."

Beauchamp's beady eyes glittered with an evil malice. "I rather doubt your willingness to fight two charges and there's not a chance it wouldn't happen if you so much as leaked a word. You can be sure I have taken care of the matter and arranged things accordingly."

Shocked and scared, Kevin's mind whirled as he hastily returned to the foyer, hoping his absence had not been noticed. They were criminals. His strait-laced brother would never believe this. And if Frederick told Sarb, the man might have them both killed. No, he couldn't trust anyone, but Benjamin. Besides, it was his girl friend's family being defrauded. Poor Danielle and Nick, duped by their own uncle. And there was more— something that could land both Sarb and Beauchamp in prison.

He forced himself to smile when Frederick finally appeared. "Why aren't you in school? Is there some holiday?" he said.

Kevin grimaced. "Has it ever occurred to you I'm twenty-two and in possession of all the schooling I want?"

Disapproval tightened the lines around Frederick's mouth. "You're right. However, you're also enrolled at Saint Abient's for some reason."

"Yeah, Mom and Dad, as if you didn't know." Kevin's shoulders drooped at his brother's unyielding demeanor. "I always wondered why you didn't join Dad's firm."

A brief flicker of sympathy lit Frederick's eyes. "I suppose they've transferred most of the pressure to you. They were just as determined when I was your age. I simply refused to cooperate."

Kevin wished he too had refused. But regrets wouldn't rescue him from the fallout of his own resentment and rebellion. Why hadn't he stood up to them like Frederick? Because it seemed impossible, that's why. They never listened, didn't even register his objections.

Kevin's heart filled with dread, despite his outer calmness. "Frederick, I need a loan— For ten-thousand dollars."

Narrowed eyes skewered him. "What for?"

59

Kevin flushed, his clammy hands clenched in an effort to brace himself. "To pay debts."

"Sell your stocks."

"I already have."

"So now you want me to cash mine in?" Frederick's scornful gaze pierced him. "Or did you think I'd have ten thousand dollars lying around here, waiting for you?"

Kevin almost lost his nerve as he stared into his brother's accusing face, but the thought of working for Reese the rest of his life brought him around. "Couldn't you take out a loan?" he said, embarrassed by the pleading in his voice.

Frederick's expression turned sour. "You want me to deprive my wife and kids to settle your debts?"

Kevin swallowed. This was worse than he had imagined. "I'll pay you back."

"When? Kate and I have been saving for years to open our own business, and we don't mean to wait until we're fifty."

"Dad would help."

"No, thank you." Frederick's voice was curt. "You're the one who had better talk with Dad. For once, take responsibility for your actions."

A black cloud settled over Kevin. "Thanks for nothing." He slammed the door as he left, hurt and anger constricting his chest. Frederick hadn't cared that his little brother might end up in a gutter dead somewhere. He'd made a halfhearted attempt to ask what Kevin needed the money for, but he hadn't cared enough to follow it up.

Now, a month later, Kevin sat at a corner table in Marcel's. The club he once thought elegant and intimate appeared dirty and gaudy in the late morning light. Waiters were cleaning up from the night before and the few woebegone drunks seated at the bar might have slept there. He wondered how much last night's play had cost them. A fortune, a home, their family? It didn't matter what, the price was too high.

He sighed. Most of his current problems could be traced to Marcel's. The extravagant friends, late night parties, girls and cocaine had consumed his allowance. When the money he borrowed from friends didn't last, Kevin found himself approaching one of the loan sharks who hung around Marcel's. Reese had been one hundred percent smiles in the beginning, but now he demanded that Kevin pay up in hard cash or work his debt off fleecing other poor suckers.

At school, Kevin learned the maid was in Reese's pay too. When she returned a second time for more money, Benjamin refused to pay and threatened Kevin with exposure if he did. Irked at the loss of revenue, she spread the story of the cocaine found in Benjamin's drawer. By the time the rumor passed from cleaning staff to teachers, no one knew where it had begun. But the harm was done. One afternoon Kevin had caught her going through that nice journalist's purse, the one dating Benjamin's cousin, but he didn't dare say anything or Benjamin would kick up a fuss. And Kevin couldn't risk another run-in with Reese. The maid seemed to be forever lurking about, a constant reminder of Reese's threats.

Since he had overheard Sarb and Beauchamp's argument the month before, Kevin had been working for Reese and his cronies. But secretly, he and Benjamin were carrying out their own investigation. Though he doubted the authorities would ever believe them if they were caught.

Not only had Reese leaked to the gendarmerie that Kevin was heavy in drug trafficking, but as insurance against any future betrayal he had compiled a dossier on Kevin's recent movements. Without proof the police would never believe Reese was blackmailing him, while masterminding the whole scenario. And without proof they'd also never believe Sarb and Beauchamp were involved as well.

As soon as Benjamin entered, Kevin strode across the club to meet him. "Let's get out of here. This place gives me the creeps." Outside, the cool night air whipped through his hair. He zipped up his jacket.

"You're sure Sarb's out?" Benjamin sounded pensive.

"Yeah. Did you bring the tools?" His long, swift stride swallowed up the distance between them and Sarb's. Benjamin tugged at the navy backpack he wore, indicating the necessary paraphernalia was inside.

Stars winked against a midnight sky and a three-quarter moon lit their way as they approached Sarb's townhouse. They crept to the back where Kevin worked to disengage the alarm system.

Benjamin followed him to the window beneath Sarb's study. "You're sure it's disconnected?" His voice cracked slightly.

"Positive." Kevin slid the window open and heaved himself in before turning back to help Benjamin. When they were both inside, he clicked on the flashlight. A walnut desk and two rust-colored wingback chairs flanked a paneled wall with built-in cabinets.

Benjamin's flashlight followed Kevin's around the room, illuminating a tall file cabinet in an adjacent corner. "Where do we start?"

Kevin slid the window shut as an extra precaution. "Try that file cabinet. I'll do the desk." He sank into the chair behind it and cursed. The drawers were locked. He would have to jimmy them open, one at a time. He set to work, finishing in disgust. There was nothing there. He rose and crossed to Benjamin. "Hand me a few of those files." Approaching footsteps in the hall started his heart racing. He whirled around as the door swung open.

15

Mark stared bleakly at the closing door. He had learned little from questioning Danielle and upset her in the process. A check of the airlines, car rental agencies and train stations had proven almost as futile. Five days remained until Volar's anniversary dinner. After that it would be difficult to contrive a reasonable excuse to extend their stay. Mark dropped his head in his hands, too weary to battle the worry tightening his chest. With Benjamin's life at stake and Susan's threatened, he felt desperate enough to confront Volar head-on with his suspicions. A gut instinct though warned him that it might do more harm than good.

He had no choice but to follow the single lead he had found. The Visis agency had rented a Volkswagen to a Bennet Asher who fit Benjamin's description. Benjamin...Bennet...Asher...Ashley. Conceivably an identity Benjamin would create under duress. Then again, there might be a real Bennet Asher.

Mark packed his bags. He and Susan would leave after breakfast. She had insisted on coming and he needed her help. He found her downstairs welcoming friends. She stood in a shaft of sunlight, her cheeks flushed from a morning walk, windblown hair tumbling around her oval face. He watched as Susan embraced Gayle.

"What a marvelous surprise," she said.

Gayle laughed, returning her hug, then greeted Mark urging Dominic forward. "I'm sure you both remember Dom."

Mark gritted his teeth and shook hands, unwilling to reveal too much too soon. The books indicated that Dominic was in tight with the drug lords and it made Mark sick to think that he could be party to Benjamin's and Kevin's disappearances as well.

Nick Sarb and Bob Chandler brought up the rear, appearing to be on close terms with Dominic. He wondered what Bob's connection to the Center was? After the stunt he had pulled calling Volar, following their confidential talk, Mark could no longer trust him.

Was he on the take? Paid to divert incriminating info from the *US Daily*? Or a partner in the drug scam? The nagging questions molded into theory. In his role as foreign correspondent, Bob traveled extensively. Who would suspect him of smuggling drugs across borders? Shock and wariness flooded through Mark. He hoped he was wrong.

He nodded to Bob and Nick, buying needed time to think things through. When the group trooped to the dining room, he managed to sit next to Susan, far enough away from Bob to avoid having to keep up a personal conversation.

Mark forced a smile and addressed the group. "Susan and I are leaving on a little vacation this morning. Naturally, we'll be back in time for the dinner Saturday."

Bob alone questioned Mark's announcement. "What about Benjamin?" he said from across the table.

Mark raised his eyebrows. "What about him?" He bit into a thick crust of French bread with butter and cherry jam.

"I mean...isn't there some kind of problem with him?"

Mark shrugged and turned to Susan, asking her if she was packed.

Bob persisted. "I know this isn't pleasant, Mark. But hasn't the school board accused him of drug abuse?"

"It's amazing how nasty gossip can get." Mark dropped his napkin with a grimace. "Benjamin is fine. What you've heard are rumors. His problems will be straightened out whether I'm here or not." He frowned at Bob. "Now, if you'll excuse us, Susan and I need to be on our way. I've made reservations in Heidelberg for tonight."

"How romantic." Gayle sighed. "German mountains and castles."

Dominic smiled at her and then looked across at Mark and Susan. "Would you two mind if Gayle and I tagged along?"

They stared at one another in dismay. The group sitting around the table laughed because they so obviously wished to be alone.

"We could drive down on our own, give you two a bit more privacy," Dom offered. "Just tell us where you'll be staying?"

Gayle said, "It'll be so much fun. I've hardly seen Susan this year."

"Selfishly, I wanted her all to myself. Away from newspapers, assignments and everything else," Mark said.

Susan blushed. "Mark and I rarely get to be alone."

"Well, it was a nice idea," Gayle said. "It would have been like old times."

Bob chimed in. "I've got it. Why don't we make up a group party to go?"

"Okay, I give up," Mark said. "Gayle and Dom may come, but I draw the line at Bob and Nick." He wrote out the name of a hotel and handed it to Dominic. After a round of goodbyes, they made their escape.

Within a quarter of an hour Susan and Mark had loaded the Mercedes and left. The road they traveled wound through small villages and cities toward the German border town of Aachen.

"Why Heidelberg?" Susan said.

"Mostly, to lose them. I've no intention of stopping there. It's a long drive, but I hope to make Munich tonight."

"Mark, have you learned anything yet or is this just guesswork?"

"One rental agency rented to an American Benjamin's age. He had dark hair, but the name was different. It's the single lead we have."

The wail of a siren split the air. Mark checked the rearview mirror. "Now what?" he said, steering the car to the side of the road. A French police van pulled to a stop behind the Mercedes. A stream of officers exited through the side door and two more from the front.

Mark stepped out of the car and spoke to the redheaded man leading the group. "Is there a problem, officer?"

The officer flashed his badge. "French Roving Border Patrol." He motioned toward Susan. "Out of the car, please. Passports."

Susan gave Mark her passport and he handed it with his own to the policeman. "What's happening?" she said, eying the policeman doubtfully.

"A routine check, I suppose."

The officer opened to their pictures and grunted. "Americans." He stared at them, matching their faces to the photos. "Your reason for visiting France?"

"I wasn't aware that one needed a reason," Mark said. "We met friends in Paris and then visited the Christian Center in Saint Abient."

"Hmmm.... You have been here four days."

Susan fished out her press card and handed it to the officer. "You see, we're journalists. We were working on a feature *Random World* is doing on the Center."

"Now we're off to Germany," Mark said.

The officer merely sniffed and pointed to their car, rattling out a volley of French. The policemen scattered and swarmed around the automobile, opening the doors and glove box.

"Now, wait a minute," Mark said. "What do you think you're doing?"

The officer tapped the car trunk. "Open."

"Not until you tell me what this is about."

The officer brought his fist down on the trunk. "Search for drugs, weapons, bombs, terrorists."

"That's ridiculous," Susan said. "Whoever heard of an American terrorist?"

The officer threw her a disdainful look. "American cities are filled with street gangs and mini terrorists." He barked out an order and one of his men removed the keys from the car ignition and unlocked the trunk. They searched the area, but found nothing aside from their luggage and a spare tire. The officer pointed to their suitcases. "Open."

Mark said, "Absolutely not."

The officer gestured to his men to begin. Mark moved to block his way and was thrust aside. One of the men swung Susan's case open first riffling the contents, his probing fingers touching every article of clothing, paper and toiletry.

Susan's cheeks reddened when he held a bra up for inspection. She turned to Mark, furious. "This is unbelievable."

"It's outrageous. But I've seen underclothes before," he said in an effort to relieve her embarrassment. The officer clicked her case shut and turned to search Mark's. "Relax," Mark said, in an attempt to calm her. "I have a feeling we're being used to train a batch of new gendarmes' recruits."

The redheaded officer snapped out another order and in response a man climbed into the trunk and examined the edges and panels. The rest of the men inspected the doors and floorboards. In the process, they knocked and measured the car's surfaces, probing for secret compartments.

"At least it shouldn't last much longer," she said as the men completed their second inspection round and reported to their chief empty-handed.

The officer's stance confirmed his authority. Haughty blue eyes peered over a long, thin, crooked nose. He pointed to his car. "Follow me."

"You can't be serious," Susan said.

"Forget it," Mark said at almost the same time.

"In order to finish the investigation, it is necessary for you to speak with our department chief," he insisted.

"As far as I'm concerned, it's finished," Mark said. "I have no wish to speak with your department head."

The officer smiled smugly and patted his pocket. "Your passports are here." He turned and led his men back to the police van. Mark had no choice but to follow. They couldn't go anywhere without passports.

They followed the van to an isolated stretch of highway where a faded building on stilts served as the police station. They parked on a concrete lot between the stilts, climbed up the side stairs and followed the officers through several rooms into the head inspector's office. A greying, slender man, he sat behind a cluttered desk flanked by a row of windows. By the time the group was seated, the large room seemed to have shrunk.

The inspector listened a few moments to his redheaded subordinate, over Mark and Susan's protests. Finally, he raised a hand to silence them. "This should not take too much of your time. A quick search of the vehicle, yourselves and a few questions to answer is all."

Mark said, "They've searched our car twice already. What do you think we're hiding?"

"This is routine procedure."

"Look, you and I both know, American tourists are not generally treated this way. I can see you're training new men. I wouldn't complain if we weren't behind schedule."

The inspector maintained a neutral but firm attitude as he gave the officer authorization to proceed. A new team was dispatched to search their car. Susan and Mark were directed to the restrooms with instructions not to flush the toilet until after the examining officer's inspection. Mark's temper blazed and one look at Susan told him she was both embarrassed and furious.

She returned to the inspector's office, her face flushed and defiant, her head held high.

The inspector motioned them to be seated. He spoke with a somber air of expectancy that caused the hairs on the back of Mark's neck to bristle. "Please *monsieur*, empty your wallet on the desk." Mark dropped his cash, a few credit and business cards and a safety deposit box key on the desk and turned the wallet upside down to show nothing remained. The inspector slowly turned to Susan, his expression grim. Alarm bells sounded in Mark's head. "*Mademoiselle*, your purse also, please."

Susan's eyes flared at the insult. "This is the first time a Western country has ever searched my purse. I could understand this if we were in Romania or India, or any other third-world country. But here in France?" Susan opened her purse. "If you think tourists will stand for this and return after such treatment, you're wrong."

The inspector shrugged. "*Mademoiselle*, I am doing my job. I have no wish to offend you. Please begin."

Susan placed her wallet on the desk. The inspector motioned her to open it and she did, showing them her driver's license, money, checks and credit cards. She pulled out a lipstick tube, a compact of blusher, a pack of tissue, a package of mints, keys, a brush, a comb and a few Nuprin. She unzipped a side flap and froze, her face a mixture of horror and disbelief.

16

Susan stared at the small bag of cocaine. A packaged disposable syringe lay beside it.

"What is this?" the inspector said, slipping on a pair of latex gloves.

"I don't know," she whispered.

He reached down and lifted the sack of snowy powder from her purse, weighing it in his hand. He turned to the gendarmes standing behind him. "Close to a quarter kilo. Worth a fortune on the streets. This is no cheap high."

"It's not mine. I don't know how it got there." She fought the urge to succumb to a sense of rising hysteria.

"This is your purse." His face was a mask of cold contempt. "We know everything about you. A phone call this morning tipped us off to the drug deal with Reese Gigot and where to find the cocaine."

She gasped. The room spun and shifted out of focus. "It's not true."

The inspector spread a handkerchief on the desk and set the bag in its center. Her mind reeled. How did coke get in her purse? Why...who would do this?

His harsh voice jerked Susan back to attention and she caught the tail end of his sentence. "... the proof we needed—before we book you."

This can't be happening she thought, raising her palms to her face in bewilderment. "Book me? But you can't!" She turned to Mark and drew back, appalled by his grim expression. Was this what came of confiding in him about her past?

Why doesn't he say something, she thought...defend me? Tell them it's not true. I'm innocent. She searched his face for some sign of reassurance. A wave of shock whipped through her, his silence louder than words. He believes I'm guilty. She panicked, the faces of the men closing in with what she imagined was pity and disdain.

Mark cleared his throat. "Inspector. There must be a logical explanation." He looked at Susan thoughtfully. "Do you have any idea how this might have got into your purse?"

She drew a deep breath, forcing the turmoil in her mind and trembling limbs to a semblance of order. He knew she didn't put that coke in her purse. How dared he question her? By nightfall she'd be in prison—and he'd be free.

A rush of determination steadied her nerves, fueling her courage as well. "Until I've made a phone call, I refuse to answer any questions.

I'm innocent." Susan motioned to the bag on the desk. "I have absolutely no idea how that, whatever it is, came to be in my purse. Maybe Mr. Ashley has some. I'm here as his assistant."

His face grew shuttered. "I'm sorry—I don't know any more about this than you do."

"You seem to think I'm capable of this." She pointed to the cocaine, forgetting everyone else in the room.

"How did you arrive at that conclusion?"

She locked eyes with him in defiance. "You didn't say one word in my defense."

The inspector pushed a buzzer on his desk and spoke in rapid French. The sergeant entered and placed the bag of cocaine into a clear container. When he left the remaining officers filed from the room as well leaving the three of them alone. The inspector broke the silence. "The lab will run tests. Meanwhile, I need a statement from both of you."

"I have nothing to say, until the test results are in." She stuck out her chin in defiance. "While you're at it, finger print my purse and that plastic bag. Someone planted it to frame me."

The inspector fixed Susan with a hostile glare, causing her to wonder if she had spoken too hastily. But no, she had to assert her rights. They weren't volunteering any for her.

"Miss Pardue, there is no reason to be difficult. It will go easier, if you cooperate."

Susan reviewed her options. She couldn't count on Mark. Her family and friends back home were too far away to help. Gayle and Dom didn't know what was happening. Of course, there was Interaid. They would stand behind her, but it would be a slow, diplomatic process. They didn't believe in pulling strings to hurry things along.

She didn't have time to wait patiently for the truth to emerge. Benjamin and Kevin were in danger this very moment. The boys came first. The people they were dealing with were ruthless. This incident with her purse more than proved it.

Mark coughed. "Inspector, I can vouch for Miss Pardue." He walked over to Susan and placed a heavy hand on her shoulder. "Don't worry, I'll get you out of this."

She stiffened. It was a bit late for the white knight routine.

The inspector claimed their attention. "That may be, *monsieur.* But who will vouch for you? Perhaps you are unaware that you are implicated as well."

"I don't understand."

"You work and travel with Miss Pardue, and I suspect you have a romantic interest. Why not a few lucrative drug deals on the side? Also, let us not forget your cousin Benjamin, who conveniently disappeared when his school was on the verge of filing drug charges."

"You appear to be well-informed, Inspector, however erroneously. Neither I, nor Miss Pardue or my cousin know anything about drug trafficking."

"Then how do you explain this note, *monsieur*?" The inspector opened his desk and drew out a letter.

Mark grabbed it and read the contents aloud.

Kevin, meet me at Henri's tonight at seven. All's clear. We're sure to get the stuff this time.

Benjamin

Mark wadded the paper and threw it down in disgust. "This doesn't prove anything. Kids call everything 'stuff' these days."

"A good try, *monsieur*, but the evidence mounts. Your cousin was arrested this morning at Sofia International Airport and charged with cocaine possession. He carried three pounds."

Mark paled and dropped heavily in the chair. He cursed softly. "What next?"

Susan turned to the inspector in concern. "What happens now?"

"*Mademoiselle*, we are charging you both with possession of cocaine."

"Without even testing it?"

"The tests are merely a formality. Yesterday, our department received an anonymous report detailing your activities. Not to mention the phone call today, telling us where to find the cocaine. The drugs are on their way to the lab. In the interim, I suggest you hire counsel."

With a dawning comprehension, Susan realized what she had to do. In the back of her mind she had known all along that she would have to call Francois. There was no other way. And truthfully, after all these years, she wanted to see him again. Francois would help her. He owed her that much and more, considering everything he'd put her through. But he wouldn't like it. "About that phone call?" she said.

The inspector stood. "As you wish." He motioned toward the phone.

Now that the moment had arrived, Susan bit her lip in agitation, assailed by doubts. Dare she call him? What if she blew his cover? But did she really have a choice? What if she couldn't find him?

"Second thoughts, *mademoiselle*?"

"I need the number. It's a Paris exchange."

The inspector made no effort to hide his displeasure at granting her the smallest assistance as he placed the Paris directory in front of him.

"The name, please?"

"Francois Rodiet. He may not be listed, though."

"Did you say Francois Rodiet?" the inspector said incredulously.

"Yes."

He pushed the phone book away and leaned back in his chair, his attention completely focused on Susan as if the concept was too much for him to take in. "It must be a different man," he muttered.

"Just a minute," Mark interrupted. "Who is Francois Rodiet anyway?"

"*Oui, mademoiselle.* Who is he?" the inspector echoed.

"An old friend. Besides, what gives either of you the right to interrogate me? Francois doesn't have anything to do with this. I simply want to speak with him. After that I'll consider answering questions." The fact that the inspector evidently knew Francois could be good or bad. Susan didn't know how to interpret his reaction.

"Humor me, *mademoiselle* and describe *Monsieur* Rodiet."

Susan realized the inspector had no intention of budging until she cooperated. In the interest of speeding up the process, she gave in. "Francois resembles a modern representation of a classical Greek statue. His face, his build, even his manners are perfect. Except he's French with black hair and chocolate eyes. And that's all I'm going to say for now."

Neither Mark nor the inspector spoke, but both of them managed to look displeased. Susan couldn't imagine how her description could be responsible for their sour expressions and she decided she didn't care. "Inspector, about that phone call?" she said.

The inspector unlocked the right-hand top drawer of his desk and drew out a small address book, flipping through the pages until he found the entry he sought. He handed Susan the telephone receiver and dialed the number.

Susan pressed the phone to her ear and glanced at her watch. It was noon. Maybe Francois would be home for lunch. What if he was away on assignment? What then? She tightened her grip on the receiver. He answered on the third ring. "Francois?"

"*Oui.*" His voice was a deep rumble. For a moment the years disappeared and Susan responded as she always had, excitement and anticipation coursing through her. She forgot Mark, the Inspector and her problems.

"Francois, it's me, Susan." She wondered if he had changed. Was his job still everything to him? Did he ever regret what might have been? Or had he completely forgotten her?

"Susan?" She heard the astonishment in his voice.

"Yes, it's really me," she said, almost in wonder. He sounded the same after all these years.

"*Cherie*, after all these years." He echoed her thoughts and she felt a thrill at the pleasure in his voice. But the sight of the inspector's face brought her back to the present with a thud. "Francois, I'm in deep trouble. I need your help desperately."

"Enough to have dinner with me?"

"This is serious, I've been arrested."

"In jail. You are joking?"

"Yes, I mean no, that is, by a French roving border patrol. Oh, Francois, it's a big mistake. I'm not sure how to get myself out of this." She quickly filled him in on the disastrous events of the morning.

He muttered a few words in French. "What station are you at?"

"Somewhere near the border to Aachen. I think the inspector, I don't even know his name, knows you."

"*Cherie*, let me speak with him. Don't worry, I will see to it."

"My boss was in the car too. I'll explain everything, but please hurry."

"Relax, put the inspector on the line. Everything will be fine."

Tears stung her eyes. "How can I ever thank you?" she said, a break in her voice.

"Never fear, something will come to mind," he said lightly. She could almost see the gleam in his eyes. "Give me your inspector now, *cherie. Au revoir.*"

Susan handed the inspector the phone and sat down.

"You and he must be close?" Mark said.

She shrugged. "Does it matter?"

Mark frowned and walked over to the window.

Her thoughts winged back to that golden summer when she and Francois spearheaded a huge relief campaign for Sudan in Southern France. Eager to make the world a better place and atone for past mistakes like Matthew, she supposed Francois felt the same, until she learned the truth.

Perhaps if he had told her himself. If she hadn't stumbled into her office that day, her hand on the connecting door before she realized he had a visitor. She hesitated, not meaning to eavesdrop, but her ears pricked up at the mention of her name.

"Have you learned anything from the girl?" A voice she didn't recognize asked.

"No." Francois' answer was curt.

"You are sure she is not getting suspicious?"

"That her fiancé's an agent? No, Susan is too naive to doubt me."

She stood there for a moment, hurt beyond measure, willing the tears not to fall. Then in a burst of angry indignation, Susan ran into the room to confront him.

The inspector's voice pulled her from the past as he hung up the phone. "Mr. Ashley, you may make your call now."

Mark stepped over to the desk and pushed in a long series of numbers which told Susan it was a long distance credit card call. She half-listened to Mark's side of the conversation. Her imagination able to guess at his friend's reaction as Mark told him their problem, ending with, "Zach, just get down here and get us out of this mess. When you meet her you'll understand, she couldn't possibly be involved." Mark hung up the phone with a harassed look of relief.

They waited hours together in the inspector's office. Late in the afternoon someone thought to bring in sandwiches and coffee. At least they weren't in jail yet and apparently, Francois' support had made the inspector more amenable.

How naive she had been when they first met. Starry eyed and in love, believing he returned her love until she learned he was an undercover French agent cultivating her friendship in the line of duty. He had denied it. Yet after discovering their whole relationship was based on a lie, she could no longer trust him. She resigned her position with Interaid and returned to America, the job with *Random World* already in hand. How ironic to find herself needing Francois for the very reasons she left him, his position and connections with the government and the international underworld.

Mark paced back and forth until the inspector finally complained. "*Monsieur*, please to be seated or stand."

"Sorry." He sat next to Susan. "Are you okay?"

"Sure. Why wouldn't I be fine? What could be more lovely than an extended vacation inside a French jail?"

"I suppose you're upset I didn't jump to your defense at the first sign of trouble."

"A few words of reassurance might have been in order."

"You got those."

"Should I smile sweetly and say thank you, better late than never?" Susan said. "Well, no thanks. Friends are there when the chips are down, not just when they feel like it." She was angry, angrier than she had been in a long, long time.

"Give me a break for trying to find a way out of this mess. Nothing I said would have swayed the inspector. At least, with me free there was a chance of getting you released."

Before she could reply, the door swung open. Her gaze met Francois' and he opened his arms wide. Susan ran straight into them.

17

"*Cherie*. A small misunderstanding has occurred. You are not to worry."

Susan wanted to believe him, but she was frightened. She had come up against tough situations before, but never anything like this. Could Francois, or Mark's friend, Zach, keep them from being charged and serving time in a French prison? Could she even be sure they were on her side?

Dear God, she didn't know whom to trust. Human strength alone was too frail an ally. Her freedom was at stake. She relaxed her grip on Francois and stepped back. She would get through this the best way she knew how—with God's help—He had never failed her yet.

She touched Francois' cheek in thanks. "I was afraid at first of compromising you."

"No, as you have discovered the inspector knows me well. We have worked together on a number of cases." He gave her hand a gentle squeeze. "I think that now we must proceed to the business at hand." As Francois led her to a chair, his tender concern conspicuous, Susan met Mark's interested gaze and the inspector's curious scrutiny. "Excuse me, while I speak with the inspector," he said, seating her.

On the other side of the room Francois confronted the inspector with a grim face. His angry voice carried. "Girard, I warn you, the situation has put me out of temper. Who gave you the authority to arrest innocent Americans? Have you no sense, man? Think what Miss Pardue has suffered today."

The inspector rose to his feet, obviously dismayed at Francois' unexpected attack. "There was cocaine in her purse. We have written and telephoned reports of her activities."

"Did it never occur to you that it might be a set up? That everything was too pat? To find out who sent the report? What do you know about these supposed sources of yours?" Francois brought his fist down on the desk. "I want her released, Girard. Today."

"Impossible." The besieged inspector stood firm in the face of Francois' determination. "Your feelings affect your judgment."

Francois sighed. "Girard, Miss Pardue is not without references. A phone call to Interaid's French director would have him here posthaste to defend her with the complete backing of the organization. The evidence may seem irrefutable but Miss Pardue is innocent, I assure you."

His staunch defense warmed Susan. The churning butterflies in her stomach lightened and she let out a relieved breath, realizing she had been holding it throughout their debate. She experienced an irrational smugness at Mark's chagrined expression.

"Nevertheless," Girard said, breaking the impasse. "The two of them are under arrest."

Francois spoke softly. "No. If I have to, I will pull rank. You have no choice, my friend. I suggest you comply, swiftly and as gracefully as possible. The charges are to be dropped, the whole case erased. A departmental mistake, you understand."

The inspector sputtered as if unable to believe he was hearing Francois right, "A departmental mistake." He sank back in his chair. The buzzer on his desk rang and he gave it an irritated push. "Yes, what is it?"

"Zach Towers is here to see Mr. Ashley."

"Send him in." Girard turned to Francois. "Let me handle this."

"Afraid not. The man is CIA."

The inspector whistled in astonishment. "Why am I always the last one to know?"

Francois shrugged.

Zach Towers, who resembled a football linebacker more than an American agent, entered. His cursory glance traveled around the room in one penetrating swoop before it landed on Mark. "Well, well." He clasped Mark on the back.

He turned to Susan. "You must be Miss Pardue. Mark's right. You don't resemble any criminal I've ever seen."

Susan laughed, as he had intended. "Thank you, sir."

Next, he sauntered over to the two Frenchmen. "Francois, I see you're in on this, too." Zach nodded toward the inspector, who appeared none too pleased to have matters slip from his control. "Inspector, let's see this cocaine you've been ranting about."

The inspector busied himself with some papers on his desk. "It has already gone to the lab."

Zach's gaze took in the long row of windows, the several shelves of books, a few chairs and the desk top scattered with an accumulation of reports, messages and file folders before he turned to the inspector. "This station has one lab pickup per day...eight A.M. Let's say my friends arrived around eleven A.M."

The inspector made as if to speak but Zach held up a hand to silence him. "I've checked. No special pickup was ordered today. You'll save everyone a lot of trouble if you just bring it in. I can easily force your hand. Interpol is behind us on this."

At Francois' nod of assent, the inspector pushed the buzzer on his desk and ordered the container brought in. While the two agents conversed in low tones, Susan watched the proceedings with avid interest. Her hopes had soared to a roller coaster high, and she feared a downward plunge remained around the bend.

"What do you think he hopes to prove?" she asked Mark.

"It's probably just a routine identification procedure. These guys go by the book."

She felt absurdly deflated.

Mark touched her arm. "We'll get out of here, one way or another."

"Then what?" she said. "Benjamin's in jail, we're fighting false charges, and his roommate Kevin is being held captive." It was all rather overwhelming.

Mark brushed a tendril of her hair back. "Still mad at me?"

"I should be."

"And I shouldn't have brought you here. The assignment was out of line. Will it help, to say I'm sorry?"

"Don't be kind." Susan blinked back tears. "Or I might cry." Why was it she could hang tough through a string of difficulties, but let someone offer a little kindness and she fell apart?

Mark patted her hand. She supposed it was his way of saying he understood. She had been so furious with him earlier, but now she felt confused. Small wonder with everything that had happened. She pursed her lips in frustration.

When the door swung open, she sat up straighter and studied the men's faces. Their gazes centered on the canister the officer set on the inspector's desk. The room grew quiet and the atmosphere became strained. Like zombies frozen in some strange time warp, no one moved or spoke until the officer left.

Susan stared at a row of large black books. What did it all mean? She felt the tension in the room increasing and wondered how much more she could stand. Like a terrified idiot she wanted to stand up and shout, what is it? What's wrong? Somebody, tell me, please. But she didn't dare move. And she didn't know why.

It was Zach who broke the tense silence which held them captive. The men shifted positions carefully, almost as if they were playing off a match with a predetermined game plan. That's ridiculous, Susan thought. Still, the feeling persisted. And somehow she felt like the pawn.

"Well inspector, are you going to open it?" Zach said.

The inspector slipped on a pair of latex gloves and slid the bag out of the canister, placing it on top of a handkerchief he had spread on the desk. "*Monsieur*?"

"Go ahead," Zach said.

The inspector removed the tie, spreading the bag wide.

Zach winked at Susan and stuck his forefinger into the bag, lifting a sampling of the fine white dust to his tongue. He smacked his lips and gave the inspector a wicked smile. "I take it you haven't given this the good old taste test. I think you had better."

Almost simultaneously the inspector and Francois reached for the bag. Francois licked his finger and then threw back his head and laughed. "Girard, you have been had this time."

The inspector tasted the powder, his eyes widening in a show of disgust.

Susan's hand closed around Mark's. Dare she believe it was true? She searched Francois' face for an answer. When their eyes met, he crossed the room and whirled her to her feet. "*Cherie*, it is powdered sugar." He gave her a happy hug, still chuckling. "Come, it is finished now."

If only it were finished, she thought, the reality of what lay ahead dampening her joy. They had to find Benjamin and Kevin.

18

At the police station the night before, Zach came through in a very practical way which never occurred to the rest of them. Who would have thought a taste test could settle things so rapidly? Within fifteen minutes Susan was in the parking lot outside the officer's bureau, her belongings in hand. She wanted to breathe in the glorious night air, take in the splendor of the moon above and the galaxy behind it. Instead, sandwiched between a possessive Francois and Mark, she was pressed to choose which of the two to accompany. Thank heaven for Zach's diplomatic suggestion that Mark drive with him to allow the two old college chums a chance to talk. That had settled the matter.

Their destination was the next point of contention. Mark, all for driving on that evening, wanted to lose no time in continuing the search for Kevin and seeing to Benjamin's release. But Zach protested. "Think, man. Are you going to drive the entire night, when a phone call or an early flight would do? Are you sure you want Benjamin free, a roving target for Sarb and his buddies? We've got to talk, Mark. I can get through to the authorities in Sofia a lot easier than you. We can call from the hotel." In the end, Mark was forced to agree.

Susan was also anxious to leave France behind and travel on to Aachen. The thought of a hotel room in Germany sounded like paradise, after her sojourn in France. But Zach had vetoed that plan as well and Francois firmly seconded him.

"*Cherie*, surely there is no sense in driving on until you decide where you are going."

How could she insult Francois and tell him she hated the thought of another night in a soft French bed? That she longed to escape from the place of her most recent ordeal into Germany's orderliness.

They had stopped at a small hotel this side of the French border. Her narrow room contained a serviceable chest and a clothes armoire. The one window overlooked a neighborhood alley.

Despite her frightening experiences the day before, Susan awoke early and throwing back the covers made a dash for the shower. The hot, steamy water oozed away the travel grime. If only her tattered emotions could be so easily set straight. She stepped into a towel, reflecting back to that first threatening message delivered to her room in Saint Abient. The note had demanded that she leave or be killed. How far were Sarb and his cronies willing to go to stop them?

From her suitcase, she chose a comfortable rose-colored suit and tied her hair back with a matching silk scarf. Next, she settled her computer on the dresser, booted up and typed in a brief report summarizing events since Benjamin's disappearance. She checked her e-mail and responded to several having to do with upcoming features she was working on that had nothing to do with this trip. She was disappointed at how seldom she found time to write after lugging her equipment across the Atlantic. Susan hoped that would change. Despite this assignment, she couldn't let her work fall behind. She gathered her trench coat, carry on bag and laptop, deciding she might as well take them down.

Downstairs the men were already eating breakfast, their table next to a set of lace-trimmed French doors leading to the veranda. Mark and Francois both rose to pull out her chair and she smothered a smile as Zach winked at her.

"*Bonjour.* You slept well?" Francois said.

"Mmm...like a log."

Mark mumbled something that sounded like good morning and poured her a cup of coffee. Understandably, he was worried about Benjamin and Kevin. Susan bit into a croissant hungrily and washed it down with a sip of coffee. She had expected the morning's discussion to be heated, if the night before were any indication. But Mark remained in a pensive mood, speaking only if spoken to. Anxious to know what their next move would be, she said, "Have you made any plans?"

"We're booked on an eleven A.M. flight to Sofia." He summoned a faint smile. "Are you up to it?"

"Sure." Susan glanced at her watch and mentally calculated the time it would take to get to the airport. It was eight o'clock. They could never make Paris or Cologne in time. If they hurried though, they could reach Brussels by ten-thirty.

Mark sliced off the top of a soft-boiled egg and picked up a spoon. "I phoned Sofia last night. They're still holding Benjamin."

Francois cut in smoothly. "Is it really necessary for Susan to accompany you?"

Mark halted the spoonful of egg midway to his mouth. "She does work for me."

"Yes—I had almost forgotten," Francois said, slowly drawing out the words. "*Cherie*, may I speak with you privately for a few moments?"

Mark dropped his spoon with a clatter, pushing his chair back before she could reply. "Please don't let me intrude." He gave Susan a shrewd glance. "Better make it snappy, if you're still coming." He didn't wait for an answer. Zach excused himself and followed him from the room.

With a sigh, Susan watched them go. The tough, aggressive Mark was back. She poured another cup of coffee and studied Francois with an objectivity she had never managed during their brief engagement. He was so attractive. The few new wrinkles jetting from the corners of his eyes and mouth gave a distinguished cast to his classical features.

He reached for her hand, resisting her effort to draw it back. "Must you go?"

"Mark is my boss," she said, feeling awkward and slightly overpowered at his persistence.

"After everything you said last night, I cannot help being anxious."

On the drive from the police station to the hotel, she had told Francois about Benjamin and Kevin's disappearance, their suspicions regarding Sarb and Volar, and the implication of funds laundered through the Center that they found when they broke into Volar's office. The things she had left out were her own conflicting emotions. "It's more than a job to me, Francois. I have to do this."

"You are still trying to make up for your brother's death. You have not yet accepted it."

"There wasn't a choice," she said, a twinge of bitterness in her voice. She struggled with the words to make him understand. "I failed with Matthew. But maybe I can help Benjamin and Kevin. It has nothing to do with blaming myself. I loved him." Emotion made her voice husky and she swallowed to get past the lump in her throat.

"If there had been someone to turn to with Matthew. Can you imagine what that would have meant to me? To Matthew? To my mother and father? He was so young and mixed up, like Kevin and Benjamin, but worse. It was a tragic waste. I can't turn my back on that as if it never happened."

"There is so little you can do," Francois said, his expression troubled. "I sympathize with what you are feeling, but this is the wrong way."

His presumption that he understood was somehow belittling. How could he know how she felt? She pushed her annoyance aside, reminding herself he merely wanted to help. There was nothing else to say. Susan rose. "I've got to hurry." She clasped his hand and leaned over to kiss his cheek.

He stood as well, pulling her closer. "What about us? Do you feel nothing for me?"

Susan gazed into his warm, chocolate eyes. Yes, she cared for him. But did she love him enough to marry him, live with him forever? Lately, her emotions were a muddle, tangled and overgrown like a rampant vine. "I can't think now. Maybe when this is over." She looked at him helplessly. Was it cruel to even give him hope? She just didn't know.

Francois sighed but made no protest, cupping her face with his hands he kissed her lightly. "*Au revoir*, Susan." He ran one finger down her cheek. "What are a few weeks compared to the last two years?" He lowered his head to kiss her again.

"You mustn't—"

His lips pressed hers, not giving her a chance to finish. The kiss filled her with a bittersweet sense of regret for what might have been, but she felt solely friendship.

When he spoke, it was as if he too sensed the change. "I have been forewarned, *cherie*. The risk is mine." He turned and quickly left. Susan watched him walk out of her life for the second time.

"How touching. I hope you've had time to pack between scenes," Mark said, from behind her.

She reeled to find Mark and Zach standing at the patio door entrance. Mark studied her with casual indifference. How much had he overheard, she wondered? Had he seen Francois kiss her? It was none of his business anyway. She raised her chin. "I packed earlier."

"Has Francois gone to get your luggage?"

"No. That's where I'm going now."

Mark tossed her a set of keys. "I'll get it. Drive the car around front, will you?" He turned to leave. "Try to remember, we're not here to play, but to find Benjamin and Kevin."

Susan gathered her belongings and fled. She mustn't let him upset her again. No one liked to be ordered around, but her response to Mark was melodramatic. She was tired of their scrimmages and the way to avoid them was to hold her emotions in check. She didn't understand why he had the power to affect her so. The good cheer she began the day with had dissipated to a general sense of despondency and she had Mark to blame. But what had he done, she thought? Nothing actually. He had been provoking, but where was her sense of humor, her perspective?

The weather was still cool and the sun bright, as she walked around back to the parking lot, unlocked the car, stashed her stuff in the trunk and got in. While driving to the front of the building, Susan took a few moments to rethink her position. Was it necessary for her to travel with Mark? Francois had a point. What could she do? A picture of a smiling Benjamin and Danielle the night before he disappeared streaked through her mind. No, she was right to go, she decided, setting aside her doubts. She might not want to go and Mark might not be the easiest boss to work for, but that wouldn't stop her.

She slid into the passenger's seat of the Mercedes, realizing there were a number of things she had overlooked in the midst of her distress and the confusion. Francois and Zach had known each other. Both were undercover agents, and neither had exhibited more than an initial surprise at the news that she and Mark were arrested and charged with cocaine possession. Nor were they unduly startled to discover the substance in the bag was powdered sugar instead of coke. Why had she neglected to question Francois? There had certainly been time. When Zach and Francois told Inspector Girard they were engaged in an international investigation, her journalistic instincts should have swung into high gear. But at the time she thought it a ruse, to secure their release. Now she wondered.

Susan watched Mark walk out of the hotel, juggling their suitcases between his briefcase, hanging bag and carry on, followed by Zach. She pushed the lever to open the trunk, her mind churning with the possibilities. Was drug trafficking the key or was it the means to accomplish a particular end? Could a political plot be the driving force behind the drug lords? Was someone else orchestrating events behind the scenes, manipulating the drug kings without their knowledge?

Susan studied Mark as he slid behind the wheel and Zach climbed into the back. She hadn't realized Zach would accompany them. But it made sense that he needed to get back to Amsterdam. Now was an opportune time to dig for the answers she needed.

Mark started the engine and eased the Mercedes into gear. "Zach is going to drop the car off in Amsterdam. It will save us time and get him home."

"Good, I have a few questions for him."

He smiled from the backseat. "Fire away, but I don't guarantee any answers."

She drew a deep breath and looked at Mark, trying to gauge his reaction to her quizzing his friend. His face was guarded but he gave her a slight nod she interpreted as a go-ahead. She decided to start with the basics, asking if he and Francois were on the case together. Zach neither confirmed nor denied her query but Susan took this as a yes and plodded on. "Is the investigation strictly narcotics?"

"You two don't give up."

Mark said, "Consider how you're going to feel when we make mincemeat of your investigation or wind up dead, because we didn't know what was going on."

"He's right," Susan said. "We could set off an entire chain of dire repercussions, making it worse for everyone."

Zach appeared to be giving their argument some consideration and Susan, encouraged, whispered a silent prayer that he would level with them. She and Mark were operating in a vacuum. They desperately needed to know what was going on.

"You're both crazy," he said. "Why do you think there are agents...professionals? To keep people like you from getting hurt. But do you care? So what if you blow our cover or get agent so-and-so killed."

"Zach, he's my cousin, like a brother to me. Julie's already dead. What would you do?"

Zach sighed. "I guess I'd do the same thing you're doing. Keep in mind, I might end up dead for doing it. You win, but I want your sworn oath, this will go no further. Is that understood?"

Mark and Susan gave him their solemn promise to tell no one.

"And that includes Francois, US agents and any provocations," he said. "To make sure we agree, repeat after me." Zach's face grew grim as Susan and Mark parroted his words. "If you had any sense you'd take your cousin and go home."

"We've been through this. Benjamin's twenty-one. He doesn't follow my orders," Mark said.

Zach said, "Crazy as it sounds, the whole thing centers around South Africa."

"South Africa?" Susan and Mark exclaimed in astonishment. Was he even on the same case, she wondered? What could South Africa have to do with Benjamin and the Christian Center in Saint Abient?

19

Mark drove along the two-lane highway toward Belgium, impatiently awaiting Zach's explanation. In the rearview mirror, he noted a dark blue sedan approaching at a dangerous speed. The next moment he felt the wrenching impact. The crunch of metal and squealing tires hammered through the air, as the automobile swerved out of control. It spun and headed for the ditch at eighty miles an hour. His body lunged forward before the seat belt clenched and rammed him back into place. Susan moaned and from the corner of his eye he saw a mass of swirling black hair as her body jerked with the vehicle.

"What the...!" Zach yelled from the back seat. A glimpse in the rearview mirror revealed him with a gun in hand.

Time stretched into eternity. Mark steered the car left and then right in a desperate attempt to straighten it and avoid the ditch. Trees flashed by at crazy angles. The car skidded downward, and slid out of a menacing spin.

"Whew!" he breathed, easing his foot off the brake. The acrid smell of burning rubber filled the air. He was reaching for Susan when the next jolt hit. She screamed as the sedan smashed into the slowing Mercedes again and again. "Hang on!" he shouted, tightening his grip on the wheel. He saw Zach take aim. The sound of gunfire and shattered glass rent the air. Susan ducked and Mark lowered his head in case of return fire. The Mercedes plunged into the ditch, as the sedan streaked past.

Mark hung onto the wheel as the tires careened, threatening to roll the car. He urged the bouncing vehicle up the steep embankment to the side of the road where it sputtered to a stop. Unable to loosen his fingers, he clutched the steering wheel in frozen relief, his knuckles white with tension. With a shudder, he turned to Susan, then Zach. "Everybody okay?" he said.

"Yes, thank heaven," Susan said.

From the back, Zach gave a thumbs up.

Mark got out and walked past the dented rear end and crumpled license plate to the passenger side of the car. He reached across to undo Susan's seat belt. "Does anything hurt?"

"I'm okay, just scared."

He slid his hands down her arms and legs, checking for broken bones. "I want you to try standing." He helped her to her feet. She seemed so fragile. What was she doing in the middle of this? He must have been crazy to consider it. How had Jerry talked him into it? His arm tightened around her, encouraging her to walk a little to be sure she was all right.

Susan insisted she was fine and trailed behind the two men as they circled the Mercedes examining the damage. Aside from the back end, and the window Zach blasted when he opened fire, the automobile wasn't in too bad shape. The insurance would cover it, but Mark didn't want to think about how they would explain the bullet holes in the glass.

"Before either of you try, let me say, it's futile to pretend that was an accident," Susan said, as they climbed back into the auto. "We all know it wasn't."

"The driver could have been plastered but I somehow doubt that he was," Mark admitted, realizing there was no dodging the truth. He glanced at Zach. "Got any idea what that was about?"

"Looks like somebody's mighty unhappy with your little private investigation. I did warn you. That was probably the end of that incident but just in case, I think we need to keep an eye out for trouble."

Mark put the car in gear. "I don't suppose anybody got a license plate number or a close enough look at the thugs to furnish a description?"

"Not me. It happened too fast," Zach said.

"It was a blur," Susan said. "Like the fast forward on a video."

"I was too busy at the wheel to catch much of anything," Mark said, turning back onto the highway. "I suppose we can look into this more, later. Zach probably caught more than he's telling and can fill us in after he's run a check. He may have seen a license plate or recognized the people inside, but as a CIA operative, he wouldn't necessarily be free to share this. We do, however, still have a plane to catch."

Mark concentrated on the road ahead. The other two seemed absorbed in their thoughts. There were no signs of the blue avenger farther down the highway. By the time they reached the small country border station, his adrenaline had slowed.

The border patrol waved them through the guard shack, not bothering to check their passports. That was the nice thing about these out-of-the-way borders, no hassle, if you discounted the traffic hazards. Mark's hand shook at the thought of how near they had come to death. He hadn't wanted to upset Susan but as she had pointed out, she was a consenting adult. He glanced over at her. "Are you okay? You haven't said anything in a while."

She gave him a piercing look. "Do you think they meant to kill us?"

Zach said, "There are a lot easier ways of doing it than risking life and limb ramming into the back of us."

"Then why did you shoot at them?"

"I couldn't take a chance, not with our lives. But I didn't shoot to kill, rather to warn them off."

Susan said, "There's a pattern emerging here. First the note, then Benjamin and Kevin's disappearance, the cocaine arrest, and now this accident."

"It may take awhile but we're going to find the answers we need," Mark promised grimly

The Belgium roadside seemed untamed after France. It reminded him in a sense of Houston. Tangled vines, overgrown weeds and bushes grew wild alongside the thoroughfare. Most of the homes were an attractive dark red brick with a definite Flemish influence. Sloping roofs marked the entryways and lace curtains hung from the windows.

"So what's this about South Africa?" Mark said. "Give us the rundown."

His friend's face sobered. "Do either of you remember when Nebut and Dower Consolidated made the headlines last year?"

"Yeah, I do," Mark said, thinking back to the incident.

"Maybe vaguely," Susan said.

Zach continued. "Our agency only has the bare bones on the story. But last year a grand jury indicted Nebut Electronics, a U.S. Corporation, and Dower Consolidated of South Africa for conspiracy. At the time the two companies held eighty percent of the $600 billion global market for industrial diamonds. We're after two of their top men, Peter Frazier and Ewald Lauter."

Susan broke in, "We met Ewald in Paris. Don't you remember, Mark? Dom introduced us."

He nodded. "Yeah, but I certainly didn't connect him with the grand jury's indictment of Nebut and Dower. That was a while back. Refresh me on what happened, Zach."

Zach hesitated. "It's a little hard to follow, but they coordinated price moves through a complex interlocking relationship which allowed the two companies to funnel illegal pricing data."

"Diamonds...drugs...where's the tie in?" Mark said, with a trace of impatience as they neared the airport.

"After the grand jury slapped their hands for price fixing, Dower decided to try another tack. By manipulating South African elections, they stood to gain control of South Africa's wealth in a way that would leave them immune to the U.S. legal system."

"I'm not sure I understand," Susan said. "Most of South Africa's businesses are privately owned. How could they gain control?"

"You're forgetting the instability factor. It's like a pot ready to boil over. All it takes is a nudge in the right direction, and poof," Zach said.

"I think I get it," Mark said. "Dower and Nebut invest in the drug trade. For a kickback, the drug lords pay out a percentage of the profits to back the company's choice candidates. No one cares if they incite a few riots and encourage a little bloodshed along the way."

"So far, so good," Zach said. "Add an innuendo campaign to discredit other candidates and you've got it."

"But we still don't know who's backing Volar. And that's what really concerns us," Susan said.

The car glided to a halt at the front entrance to the Brussels airport. Zach said, "Maybe it's a long shot but I'd say, the good Reverend's backers are tied to Ewald Lauter and Peter Frazier. That's as much as I can say. Think about it." He turned to Mark, "Are you two getting out here?"

"Let me grab the bags." Mark had to jimmy the trunk open where it was smashed in, but it finally gave. When he walked back around the car, Susan was already out and Zach in the driver's seat.

"Watch your back," Zach said, "And don't worry, I'll explain about the car." With a wave he drove off.

They both found it difficult to believe that Ewald Lauter, the debonair man they'd met in Paris, could be responsible for Benjamin's disappearance. Zach had left them much to consider as they continued their journey.

The airport was built like an old train station for utility without a thought for atmosphere and beauty. As they entered, Mark thought of how many times in the past Zach had been there for him. It was good to know some things didn't change.

They found the ticket counters in the central lobby, an enormous room with high ceilings, where sunlight filtered through old, mullion windows. Mark charged the tickets and minutes later they raced to board a Sabena aircraft scheduled to fly nonstop to Sofia.

Inside the small, sleek jet, Mark felt propelled backward by the wind force as they were airborne. "Hang on," he told Susan.

"Wow, talk about forward thrust," she said. "This is something else."

"Be glad we're on a Western airline."

She laughed. "What? You're not an Aeroflot or Balkan Air fan?"

"The lack of development in those countries doesn't encourage confidence in their mechanical prowess, does it?"

Before she could respond, a pretty, petite flight attendant handed them each a pillow and blanket. Another served them food.

"Mm, I could get used to first class," Susan said, leaning back in the lush seat. She sipped a Coke over ice and snacked on warm croissants, smoked salmon and caviar while the plane gained altitude.

"Do you always fly coach?" Mark said. "There are upgrades."

"On my salary, coach is just fine."

He frowned. "I was under the impression we paid top prices for our journalists."

"Better than most." She smiled. "I'm not complaining. I like my job."

"You've been a real trooper about everything."

"Thanks," she said, clearly disconcerted by his praise. "Wasn't it wonderful the way Francois and Zach leaped to the rescue?"

"I'm beginning to wonder if you have a knight in every country ready to ride to the rescue?"

"What do you mean?"

"I mean Jerry in Houston, that fellow Monroe in Vienna that you phoned from Volar's office, and Francois in France. Are there more?"

"They're merely friends."

"So I gathered." He liked seeing her at a loss for a change. But the role he was having to play was beginning to feel uncomfortable. They gazed into each others' eyes. For an instant, Mark forgot about Benjamin, the investigation, everything. One hand brushed her cheek and startled by the warmth of his feelings, he turned away. He opened his briefcase with a snap, his thoughts determinedly returning to his cousin's dilemma.

20

Clear skies stretched across the horizon and the Caspian mountains loomed in the distance, as the plane circled Sofia International Airport waiting for clearance to land. Susan wondered, what would they find in Sofia? How was Benjamin coping? It was terrible to imagine him locked away in some crude jail cell. What if he panicked and confessed to crimes he hadn't committed?

Mark squeezed her hand. "It won't be long now."

"What if we can't get him out?" she said, almost biting her tongue for voicing their worst fear.

"We will."

She could see his jaw line tighten.

"We have to."

Would she ever understand this man? One moment Mark was warm and reassuring, the next distant and cool. His mouth compressed into a grim line, his eyes hard. Conflicting signals, conflicting emotions, what did they mean? She reminded herself it was simply a job. Better not to forget why she was there.

From the airport, they caught a taxi to the city's center. The Bulgarian capital was struggling to recover from decades of Communist rule. The weather-beaten, sometimes cobbled streets were in poor repair and a dull, grey film clung to the buildings and cars. Vast blocks of colorless, concrete apartment buildings housing millions lined the city, the remnant of a communist era, when the authorities pushed to move the population from the villages to the cities for closer surveillance.

Susan coughed and quickly rolled up the taxi window as a jet burst of diesel fumes engulfed them. Throngs of people packed the sidewalks and the crowded streets were jammed with traffic. Russian-made Ladas and Moskviches competed for road space with old diesel buses and heavy trucks, expelling thick blasts of black smoke over the city and its occupants.

They found the police station in a block of apartment flats downtown. It bore little resemblance to an American jail. The uniformed man seated behind the wooden makeshift desk looked up when they entered. The place reeked of stale tobacco smoke; Susan wrinkled her nose in distaste. A radio blared a brassy, military march in the background.

The officer pulled a cigar from the side of his mouth. "America? USA?" His thick Bulgarian accent boomed over the scratchy music.

"That's right," Mark said. "We're here...."

"Chief," the man interrupted, thumping his chest. "Chief."

"All right, Chief," Mark said. "We'd like...."

"Moment." He shouted, "Vessy." A young man entered from a side door and the chief slapped him on the back, pointing in an effort to introduce them. "Vessy, speak English. Translate." The chief leaned back in his chair with a satisfied air puffing on his cigar before nodding at his assistant to begin.

The rather nondescript man who was to be their interpreter gave them an eager look. "You have come about the American?"

"Yes, to see my cousin, Benjamin Ashley."

He swallowed, obviously in awe to be addressing Americans, then as if to gather courage, he straightened his shoulders. "Visitors are forbidden. It is a big problem for foreigners to bring cocaine to my country."

Mark frowned. "I assure you, this is simply a misunderstanding."

"Our customs department found it in his bag."

"Maybe someone else hid it there. Maybe it's not cocaine. One of my cousin's friends might have played a joke."

With an apologetic air, the young Bulgarian pulled a report from the drawer. "The tests show it's cocaine."

Mark gave him a testy look. "Bear in mind, our ambassador to Bulgaria is a personal friend of your prime minister and if necessary I'll ask him to intervene on Benjamin's behalf."

Vessy translated this to the chief who grunted in acknowledgment.

Susan forced a smile and spoke slowly for the sake of their interpreter. "I know this is awkward. But Benjamin is incapable of doing this sort of thing." She gazed at the men beseechingly. "Please, can't we see him for a moment? So we know he's okay."

The chief shrugged uncertainly.

She sensed he was weakening and pressed her point home. "A few minutes couldn't hurt."

"Come." He stood, as if reaching a sudden decision and led them through the police station into a small back room about four feet by eight. The prisoner, an Arab with sullen bold, black eyes sat on a wooden bench.

Mark stepped back in astonishment. "He's not my cousin."

Susan exclaimed, "This man is too old. Benjamin's not anything like him." Dressed in rumpled dirty clothes, the Arab appeared to be in his late thirties.

After a few startled moments, Mark demanded to see the Arab's passport. When Vessy retrieved it, they saw the man's name and address were Benjamin's, but the picture was of the man before them. The black and white photo was clumsily attached at best and Susan, peering over Mark's shoulder, wondered how it had passed through customs. The implications were frightening. Benjamin might have lost his passport, had it stolen, or worse, been kidnapped like Kevin.

She felt sick. What if they were too late? No. Susan had to believe he and Kevin were alive. The alternative was too shattering to consider.

Mark broke the mute consternation that gripped them. "Who are you?" he said.

The Arab spat at them, then drew himself up, his lips compressed in defiant silence. The chief backhanded the prisoner, scorching him with a volley of rapid-fire Bulgarian. The man didn't react but she could see the hatred and disdain in his eyes.

Mark snapped, "We're not getting anywhere. There's no sense in waiting until that jerk chooses to talk." He turned to Vessy and the chief. "Give me his picture so we can track down this man's identity. The American Embassy can do a computer scan on him. It's possible he's wanted for other crimes. If so, it'll save us a lot of trouble tracing him."

After some haggling, he secured the photo and they caught a taxi to the embassy. There, the consulate assigned an aide to help them with the case. He led them to a small office on the second floor.

They discovered that Abdul Mehr, alias Benjamin Ashley, was wanted by US, British, and French authorities for terrorist activities. He was believed to be connected with AGAH, a group of Arab mercenaries who worked for Muslim activists to destabilize the West. The group specialized in bombs, blackmail and assassinations. But how did this fit in with Benjamin?

Nausea settled in the pit of Susan's stomach. Bombs? Terrorists? Assassins? What were they in the middle of? Maybe they should back down as Zach had suggested. What did they know about international terrorists? What if they were endangering others? She didn't know if she could handle that kind of responsibility. It was one thing to help, but a single misstep could send Benjamin or Kevin to their death—or Mark.

She glanced from him to the embassy aide. At least they weren't in this alone. The aide had been to the police station twice in an effort to assist them and made numerous calls on their behalf and the U.S.A.

As it turned out, Zach had phoned ahead to the embassy so they were readily believed and quickly assigned an agent they could trust. They had not met him yet, but she understood he was working behind the scenes. For now, denied further access to the prisoner, all they could do was wait while the authorities interrogated him.

The aide soon returned with a negative shake of his head. "You might as well go to dinner. This could take some time."

Mark said, "Have you learned anything?"

"Not about your cousin, but we've almost struck a deal. And when we do, he'll talk." A taxi was arranged to take them to the restaurant at the Hotel Sofia. "I'll let you know as soon as he breaks."

The hotel wasn't far from the station. If they had known their way around, they could have walked. The streets and stores they passed were crowded with pedestrians shopping at the end of the day. The temperature, much higher than Paris, made Susan long for a bath.

They smelled roses along the way. The Bulgarians were purported to produce seventy percent of the world's rose oil, used as a base for expensive perfumes. Tiny, carved, wooden vials of the fragrant oil sold cheaply throughout the country.

Inside the Sofia's restaurant, a red rose graced each table and in the background a string orchestra played. On the waiter's recommendation, they ordered stuffed green peppers, a Bulgarian specialty. Susan made an effort to relax but the strident rhythm of the violinist's gypsy music didn't help. She tried to ignore the smudges on the mediocre crystal, the dirty windows and the not too clean floor.

Mark, impatient for news from the embassy, looked at his food distastefully.

She swallowed a bite of seasoned cucumber and tomato sprinkled with feta from a side dish. "The salad is surprisingly good. You won't do Benjamin any good by not keeping up your strength. When we find him, he may need you more than ever and you'd better be in a good enough condition to deal with it."

"You're right. It's just so hard to believe the Benjamin I grew up with could be involved in anything like this." He took up his fork and half-heartedly began to eat.

"I guess the good news is that we're not in a French jail cell," she said, making light of the situation, and reminding them both of where they'd been the day before. She refused to speculate on how the yogurt topping the peppers and greasy meat got to be so sour.

They both chose to set aside their concerns as best they could for the duration of the meal. Despite their efforts, by the time dessert was served they had drifted into a worried silence. The frosted glasses of surprisingly delicious Peach Melba, another specialty of the house, remained for the most part untouched.

As they rose to leave, the aide strode through the doors. The Arab had broken at last. Their presence was urgently needed at the embassy. Her immediate relief was supplanted by an overpowering sensation of fear. What would they find? Lord, she prayed, help us be strong.

21

On the drive back to the embassy, the aide refused to say anything except that Wade, the agent who was to be their link with Zach, needed to speak with them. When the car halted in front of the embassy, Susan and Mark climbed the steps to Wade's office.

He rose to greet them. "I'm afraid the news is not good. We have reason to believe Benjamin is being held about one hundred kilometers south of here in the town of Plodiv."

Susan felt Mark's hand grip hers as he asked, "He's not hurt, is he?"

"We hope not. According to our informant, a group of militant Turks are holding him in an encampment west of the city. Foreigners are not generally welcome there but the police are providing escort." Wade paused. "We need you to identify the boy if he's there. I'll explain on the way." His gaze flickered over Susan. "Miss Pardue can wait here. The embassy has arranged rooms for you both at the Hotel Sofia for tonight."

"No," she insisted. "I'm coming too."

"I doubt this will be pleasant," Wade said, frowning. He handed Mark a manila envelope. "If you'll drop a spare key in there, my assistant will transfer your luggage from your car to the hotel while we're gone."

Mark sealed the envelope and gave it to Wade, then turned to Susan. "You've been through enough for one day. I want you to stay here."

He was referring to the accident that morning in Belgium. The memory had lost meaning for her and seemed long past. For his sake, she almost capitulated, but found she could not. Soon enough Mark would find out she wasn't as fragile as he supposed, but she simply said, "I'd rather be with you. I feel safer." And as insipid as it sounded, it was true. She was beginning to feel as if they were a team. There were too many foreigners at work in the embassy for her to trust its security in their harrowing race against these unknown enemies.

Wade hurried to the door. "Come along, then. But remember, I warned you it might get rough."

Mark reached out to stop her. "Susan, perhaps you should...."

"Shh," she said. "It's settled."

The unmarked police car that came for them was a shiny black 1954 Chaiko. During the course of the day it had become obvious that the government viewed Chaikos and Zils as symbols of prestige. At times whole streets were cleared for VIPs zipping past in these cars.

Geliv, the Bulgarian official who accompanied them, reminded Susan of Elvis Presley, with his casual business suit and greased back hair, a stray curl perched above one eye. His driver wore jeans, another coveted sign of affluence sold on the black market.

She crowded in the back seat between Wade and Mark, both long-legged men. On the way Wade filled them in. "The Arab's name is Abdul. He and a cohort tailed Benjamin from the car rental agency to his first fuel stop, where they knocked him over the head and stole his passport, airline ticket and car. Abdul took his place on the flight. His accomplice delivered the boy to Sarb's connections in Plodiv through a back border."

"Sarb," Mark said in consternation.

"Yes, we're getting quite a dossier on Sarb. But near as we can tell, Beauchamp does his dirty work. He's the one who paid them off."

"Did they say what they planned to do with him once they got him there?" Susan said, darting a worried glance at Mark.

"I'm afraid there's a lot we don't know," Wade said.

Susan stared out at the sunset sun. Along the highway scarf-clad women in peasant dresses hoed the fields. They often waved and Susan, touched by their smudged weary faces, waved back. Small girls with honey braids tagged behind, uprooting the weeds their mothers missed.

Susan had learned about poverty and oppression working with Interaid. Forced daily to weigh one person's need against the next, she had become jaded. Frightened by her growing insensitivity, she resigned. For a time, the need to escape haunted her. She avoided sad movies, and books crammed with meaning held no lure. She had seen enough of "reality" to want to forget its harshness, to believe in happy endings, to smell the sweet innocence of honeysuckle and rekindle the lost joy.

They reached Plodiv at twilight. The city's old quarter built by the conquering Romans centuries ago was lit by the afterglow of a rosy-orange sunset and the violet-ashen iridescence of approaching night. Tension inside the car began to mount as they passed through the narrow-winding cobblestone streets, avoiding some that were too small for a car. A mangy dog darted out almost under their wheels. The driver slammed on the brakes barely missing it. Relieved, they drove on. Susan longed for the open road. Often the upper stories of buildings cantilevered over the street, at times gracefully weaving their way to the other side. On the gentle breeze, she seemed to hear the screech of disaster.

As they neared the west end, Wade broke the silence. "We may run into trouble. In some places, hostilities between the Turks and Bulgarians have erupted into open gunfights."

"Why is that?" Susan said, startled to hear reason given to her fears.

"A crazy new law ordering the Turks to assume Bulgarian last names. But the problem goes back centuries. It started the day Turkey invaded Bulgaria."

"But that was eons ago," Susan said.

"Not to these people. They have long memories."

Susan remembered that after five-hundred years of brutal Turkish rule the Bulgarians were liberated in 1878 by the Russians. Throughout the countryside, they saw monuments erected to honor the Russians. She knew from her work with Interaid that in Communist times, Bulgaria patterned itself after Russia so well it earned the nickname Little Russia."

Before Glasnost and Perestroika reshaped Eastern Europe, changing its face forever, Bulgaria's Communist revolutionary leader Georgi Demitrov, following in Lenin's footsteps, had led the nation in a reign of terror. Bibles were forbidden, Christians persecuted and imprisoned. It was a black day for freedom. Thank God it had passed.

In the Turkish sector of the city Susan saw abject poverty; the people lived like gypsies. Families huddled around tiny campfires lit atop steel drums cooking their supper by the evening light. The children wore ragged clothing and the women wrapped long shawls about their heads, the fabric flowing over their long skirts. Gaunt, brown-skinned men hovered around the perimeter of the cooking area smoking and talking.

Finally, they came upon a sign marked "Camping Bonita" and turned onto the gravel road leading up to the reception area. To the side, one-room wooden bungalows formed a circle. Susan glimpsed some tents in the surrounding woods. The eerie beat of drums pounded through the air, sending shivers up her spine. At the sight of the Turkish men gathered at small tables outside the restaurant and on the steps of the bungalows, Mark placed a protective arm around her.

Besides drums, a few of the men strummed guitars, but most of them played with an assortment of knives ranging from long, thick, curved, glistening blades to tiny daggers with pearl-like handles that glowed in the night. Though their words were indistinguishable, the tone of underlying malice sent a frisson of alarm crawling up her spine.

Wade stepped out of the car first. The other men followed. They seemed to assume Susan would wait inside. But there was no way she was going to be left alone in this camp. She climbed out, receiving a level glare of disapproval from everyone, including Mark. No matter, she tripped forward beside Mark. The only other women in sight were a few of the loose variety, revealing flashing glimpses of breast and thigh as they draped themselves over their men.

With an Elvis-like-swagger, Geliv strode to the front and barked out orders. Abruptly, out of the surrounding darkness, armed militia men ran forward, covering the Turkish men with their rifles. It was scary standing there unable to understand a word, so Susan was grateful when Wade offered to translate.

"Geliv has inquired after your cousin. But the men are denying he's here." His translation was short on substantive detail but at least they had an idea of what was being said.

The militia collected the knives and frisked the rebels for other weapons, then marched to search the surrounding buildings and area.

A seductress with malicious dark eyes sashayed forward, swinging her hips provocatively. She flung an arm around Geliv's neck and pressed her breasts against his chest. He cursed and heaved her aside in disdain. On her way back, she stumbled and pushed Susan to the ground.

Mark helped Susan to her feet. "Are you all right?"

"I'm fine."

The woman laughed in a taunting manner and yelled to the Turkish men to join in. When Geliv snapped at her angrily, she pouted, pretending it was a mistake. The group of rebels snickered. One of them reached out as the woman passed and pulled her onto his lap for a flagrant kiss.

Susan moved to a side table and Mark followed. From where they sat she could feel the sneering looks slanted their way. The clamor of the search pierced the night. Doors slammed and boots tramped up and down the steps. Cries of outrage were met with sharp militant commands. All this played against the beat of the bongo drums and twanging guitars.

Benjamin was not found. Geliv rose from the table looking displeased. He ground out an ultimatum. The soldiers jerked two of the rebels to their feet and thrust them toward the main building. Geliv followed.

"What now?" Susan said.

Wade's face mirrored his disgust . "You don't want to know."

Stars twinkled overhead, breathtaking in a midnight sky, a reminder of God's ever presence in the midst of the chaos. From seemingly nowhere, like an evil portent, dark clouds scudded across the sky obscuring the starlight. Eyes glittering with hate seemed to surround them.

Don't be ridiculous, Susan scolded herself, wanting to dispel the sense of impending disaster. She gazed at Mark and her heart ached for him and what he must be feeling. Waiting, doing nothing was sometimes the hardest. They were at a loss, unless Geliv discovered something.

Partially remembered scriptures ran through her mind. Dear Lord, please help us, she prayed. She knew no other place to turn. Her God was a tower of strength.

When Geliv finally returned, he offered no explanation. He summoned the car and within minutes they were back on the road.

"They deny everything and we have no proof." He had a surprisingly cultured voice. Susan had not been aware that he spoke English.

"Had they heard of the American?" Wade said.

"No, and I am inclined to believe them this time."

"How can you be sure?" Mark said. "What if they've hidden him?"

"It is possible," Geliv agreed. "But I suspect the rebels back there grew suspicious of their comrades outside the country as a result of our questions." He sighed and spoke softly to Wade in Bulgarian.

When Susan heard the name Lauter, she leaned forward, exchanging a meaningful glance with Mark. That was the man Dom had introduced them to back in Paris. Zach had said Lauter and his partner Frazier were their chief suspects but she and Mark had dismissed the idea. Something about the two of them cornering the market in industrial diamonds and being indicted for price fixing. At the time, she had thought it a stretch to connect them with drugs. And even more so with Benjamin. She leaned further forward, wishing she could understand what Geliv was saying.

However, he turned to them, switching back to English. "I left men stationed in the area. They will be watching and if anything is amiss, we will soon know."

She said, hesitantly, "This man Lauter whom you spoke of.... We've met him and heard elsewhere that he might be involved in this. Can you tell us anything about him?"

Wade repeated most of what they had already heard from Zach, explaining that he too had hoped to learn something new that would connect Lauter and Frazier more concretely to their current investigation. But he too had struck out.

The drive back to Sofia passed in silence, disappointed at another defeat. She knew Mark felt it even more so. Since they had first set off to find Benjamin, they had experienced one obstacle after the other. In fact, they seemed to be going from one police station to the next lately.

Wade confirmed that the embassy had engaged rooms for them at the Hotel Sofia and transferred their baggage there earlier. When they reached the hotel, he accompanied them in, promising to book them a flight for the next day to Bucharest. According to Danielle, Sarb had ordered Benjamin to deliver the drug package he picked up in Sofia to a prearranged contact in Bucharest if he wanted to see Kevin alive again.

Susan and Mark picked up their bags at the front desk and trudged upstairs to the third floor, not wanting to wait for a slow cranky elevator.

Susan stuck the key in her door and spun around to tell Mark goodnight. There was nothing she could say to ease his burden. She wished there were. Impulsively, she kissed his cheek and turned to go.

His voice stopped her. "Do you mind if I come in for a while?"

She felt so discouraged. What else could they say? But she nodded, understanding that he didn't want to be left alone with his thoughts.

Susan flipped the light on. "I'll just be a minute," she said, crossing to the bathroom. She stepped inside, and shuddering, screamed.

22

Mark took one last look at the grim scene in the bathtub, then fled with Susan into the next room. Still stunned, she sank onto the edge of the bed. He dropped down beside her and drew a ragged breath, the horrid scene on automatic replay in his mind.

When he heard Susan scream, he had rushed into the bathroom, then horror-stricken, halted in his tracks. An unbearable anguish ripped through his chest. Dear God...No! He wanted to yell...Benjamin...not Benjamin...not bloody dead...stabbed. He fell to his knees next to the bathtub, terrified of what he'd see.

With a tremor, he peered in and then shuddered, both sickened and relieved. The corpse only resembled his cousin. It wasn't him. Mark's stomach lurched, as he caught sight of a blood-smeared note, laying nearby. It read: "Stop asking questions—you could be next."

That was when he had glanced back and saw Susan still standing there, staring at the body a greenish cast to her face. Her eyelids flickered and disturbed brown eyes met his. "Mark."

"It's okay."

"It's not...?"

"No—we don't know him." They meant Benjamin but neither dared say it, the reality was too near.

"Let's get out of here," she said, turning to leave.

That's when he had grabbed her hand and they had fled together into the next room where they sat now.

As the haze that engulfed them receded, the questions thundered, pounding relentlessly. Who? Why? Was Benjamin alive? Was he hurt? Frightened? Safe?

He looked across at Susan, thankful, that at least, she wasn't hysterical. They had enough to deal with.

She shook her head, as if in doing do she could throw off the dreadful scene. "That poor young man. Do you want me to go downstairs and tell the management what's happened?"

"No. I'd better call the police first." He reached for the phone, wondering how he would explain this? In Bulgaria of all places. Then he remembered. Zach had said they could trust Wade. He ran a hand through disheveled hair. "On second thought, maybe, I should call Wade instead."

Susan agreed. "I'd feel a lot better dealing with the American

Embassy. We don't even speak Bulgarian."

He pulled the embassy card from his shirt pocket and with an unsteady hand dialed the agent's private number. When he answered, Mark said, "Wade, there's a dead young man here in the hotel bathtub. I think you'd better get over here, fast."

There was a sharp intake of breath. "You're sure he's dead?"

"Yes. There are stab wounds in his chest."

"Can you identify the body?"

"No, but he looks American."

"Take it easy. I'll get there as fast as I can."

A surge of relief ran through Mark as he hung up the phone. He couldn't bear to think that could have been Benjamin. He found himself longing to pray. But no, he resisted. It had never mattered...never helped...not with Julie...and not now. He swallowed, taken back that he could be so callous...but the dead no longer felt, it was their mourners left behind who suffered, constrained to squeeze their fragmented lives into some semblance of shape.

Susan broke into his thoughts. "What's happening?"

"Wade is on his way with the police. They'll want to question you," he warned. The color was returning to her face and she seemed to be recovering from the shock. "Maybe you should lie down a bit before they get here."

She grimaced. "Don't worry. I'm not as fragile as I seem. So long as I don't have to go back in there." She nodded toward the bathroom. Sobered by the thought of what lay beyond the door, neither spoke for several seconds. "I don't suppose there's any chance I imagined it?" she said, a wistful cast to her face.

"I wish you had," he returned in a grim voice. "If we ever get out of this mess, I promise I'll make this up to you. Your next assignment will be a vacation in the Caribbean."

It would be so easy to drown in the softness of her eyes. To forget about Julie and Benjamin, and the dead body in the bathtub for just a few moments. Reluctantly, he turned away.

Someone was threatening them, or was it only Susan? So far, everything had been aimed at her, the note in Saint Abient, the report to the police and now this. Why? What if she would have returned to her room alone and walked in on the murderer? The thought was too appalling to contemplate. He couldn't let her stay.

Minutes later, Wade and two men from the embassy arrived with the police. They searched the bathroom for a clue to either the killer or the victim's identity, careful not to disturb anything.

The police dusted the doorknobs, and surface areas for fingerprints, examined the body and then finally released it to the coroner. A thorough inspection of the room and bath uncovered nothing. Mark hoped the fingerprint tests would reveal more. Geliv questioned the hotel staff and eventually had a team sent up to clean the bath.

Susan held up well under questioning until Geliv mentioned the note. "Can you think of any reason why someone would threaten you?" he said.

Mark interrupted, "She doesn't know anything more. Couldn't we at least spare her this?"

"She's a big girl," Wade objected. "The killer left that note as a warning to one or both of you to stop asking questions. If Susan is in danger, she needs to know it."

"He's right," Susan said. She glanced at Geliv. "I guess he—the kill—er," she stumbled over the word, "means for us to quit searching for Benjamin."

"That appears to be the case. Under the circumstances, it's a good thing Mister Ashley is already making arrangements for your departure."

Her eyes widened in sudden comprehension. "You're sending me home."

Mark winced. He had meant to tell her later. "There's no need for you to stay any longer. Frankly, with all that's been happening, your presence here complicates things unnecessarily."

"Jerry sent me here as your assistant. That much hasn't changed."

"I'm taking you off the assignment," he said sharply, wanting to end the discussion.

Her eyes flared with swiftly veiled emotion. "If there's nothing else, I'd like to get some rest."

"All right. Wait— You'll be staying in my room now."

Her lips tightened. "That's not necessary."

"This room is to be sealed off in any case," Geliv said. "Gather your belongings and go along as he says." He and Wade began to round up their men, promising to post a guard outside both rooms.

Susan thanked them gratefully. She grabbed her things and followed Mark through the hall to his room. He was relieved to see a guard already on duty outside. When the door closed behind them, Mark tried to explain he was sending her away to protect her. "I can't work if I have to worry about both you and Benjamin?"

"Credit me with being an adult capable of taking care of myself."

"Look, this has nothing to do with you. Go home. Forget about this assignment."

"Don't pretend that's all this is to me."

He forced himself to draw back, despite the sense of tenderness that engulfed him. "I don't need you here. Is that so hard to understand?"

"Stop patronizing me. If I were a man you wouldn't be taking me off the case like this."

"First of all, this assignment is off the record. Secondly, it's my responsibility to see to your safety on the job. Thirdly, I can't see that you're being here is the help we envisioned."

"If we weren't getting close enough to cause them to panic, this wouldn't be happening."

"You're tired. Get some sleep. You'll feel better tomorrow. Come on. You can clean up in my bathroom."

She gave in and showered. Although he had already gone over the room, she insisted on checking under the bed, in the clothes armoire and behind the drapes, before concluding that there was nobody there.

She sat on the edge of the bed unhappily, her freshly brushed curls falling against a long, yellow robe. "There's really no need for you to stay with me. I'm sure they have a free room so you can get a decent night's rest."

He secured the door and settled into an armchair. "I'm going to sit here all night, so you don't need to worry; whether you will or not is a mute point," he said, reaching to turn out the light.

He refused to give up until he exposed tonight's murderer. And when he did, he'd make sure the killer remained behind bars. But first he needed to find Benjamin.

23

Susan laid her robe aside and crawled into the bed, darting a quick glance at Mark, glad he had insisted on staying nearby for the remainder of the night. Truthfully, she felt safer with him there, but embarrassed at the way she had crumpled at the first sign of trouble, screaming, as if that could help anyone. No wonder Mark was sending her home. She tossed uneasily, eventually falling into a fitful sleep.

Over and over the same nightmare wove a path through her subconscious mind. *She ran uphill, struggling to catch Benjamin. Her breath came in short gasps. She was closing in, just a few more feet, when he fell with a pitiful moan. Susan dropped to her knees. Shocked, she saw it wasn't Benjamin lying there. It was her brother Matthew.*

She heard a collective sigh and twisted around to see hundreds of young men she didn't know. But wait, Benjamin and Kevin lay in a pool of blood with the others. Their eyes shadowed with death sought hers. Terrified, she stepped back. Outstretched hands pleaded with her and their voices cried, "Help, please, help."

This was followed by a sudden storm which blew furiously, sending pelting rain down upon them. Susan bent her head against its power and heard a voice thunder, "Vengeance is mine, mine, mine...I forgive and I forget."

Then she felt a stillness sweep over the land. The sun rose above the clouds obscuring its brightness. Susan's despair lifted. The cleansing rain had washed away the blood and the bodies lay in peaceful repose.

Susan awoke, feeling more tired than rested. The events of the night before crowded into her mind, along with a dim recollection of her dreams. Mark was still asleep in the chair across the room. What an uncomfortable night he must have passed. She gathered her clothes and dressed in the bathroom, swabbing her face with cotton puffs dipped in cleansing cream.

Then she remembered Mark was sending her home. The thought sent her spirits plummeting. Everything came back to Benjamin and Kevin. And try as she might to convince herself their predicament was no longer her concern—Susan cared far too much what happened to them.

The morning passed in a blur. Later, on the drive to the airport she stared out the window at people scurrying by in raincoats, carrying umbrellas. The weather had turned cooler, the overcast skies, mirroring her mood. They checked her Delsey and laptop, then walked in silence through the dingy, grey airport.

At the boarding gate, Mark handed her the tickets and she stuffed them in the pocket of her trench coat. "This should do it." He bent his head and brushed her cheek in a brief kiss. "Take care of yourself," he said, avoiding her gaze.

Susan felt the oddest pain, bittersweet and wrenching. She searched his face. "Mark, you will be careful, won't you?"

"Of course." He spoke cheerfully. "And don't worry, I won't forget to speak to Jerry about that promotion you've worked so hard for."

"As if I care about that now with Benjamin and Kevin lost."

He made an impatient grimace. "You will. Begin by writing that story on the Center." When she tried to protest, he lifted a hand to stop her and gave over her tote bag he'd been carrying. "You'd better go."

Aboard the plane, she felt as dull and grey as the pantsuit she wore, the same outfit that she had worn on the flight over from the States and a few times thereafter. How was she to write a story with the investigation pending? The magazine didn't want to encourage people to attend Saint Abient Center if Volar was corrupt. But until they knew that for sure Susan couldn't warn them away. She had no choice but to study her interview notes and piece together a feature. But that could wait until she reached Houston. Susan had checked her laptop through, thinking Mark had pulled her off the story. And he might as well have, as little as she knew.

She glanced up to see an overweight man with a mustache staring at her coldly from across the aisle. She looked away for several minutes but her gaze was drawn back to the man repeatedly, and each time it was as if his hardened gaze had never left her face. A chill started in the pit of her stomach and worked its way through her chest and upward until it was hard to swallow.

Perhaps she was overreacting but considering what had passed the night before.... She couldn't forget the threatening note that the killer had left with the dead young man in her bathtub.

Thankfully, the flight was otherwise uneventful and brief. There was a two-hour layover in Amsterdam before her connecting flight to Houston took off. She wandered through Schipol Airport, barely registering the many shops that normally had her scurrying to make quick purchases. But she did observe the heavy, mustached man. Too often, he was beside her, behind her, turning the corner after her. When he followed Susan on the escalator to the basement, fear almost paralyzed her.

Susan panicked when she reached the basement. Her steps quickened involuntarily and she streaked into the women's room. What was she going to do? In the mirror above the sink, her reflection was haggard, the result of the worst night of her life.

That man was following her. She knew it instinctively and it made her angry. Susan was tired of being buffeted about, framed, threatened and endangered. She was going to fight back, with or without Mark. Her decision made, Susan felt some of the tension drain away. She gazed once more at the pale face in the mirror and smiled as an idea struck.

She grabbed a tissue from her purse and wiped off her makeup, then removed her jewelry and placed it in her handbag for safekeeping. Next, she pulled back her hair, pinned it into a bun and covered it with a scarf tied under her chin. As a disguise it worked. The scarf hid part of her face and gave her the look of a street person.

Fortunately, her clothes and shoes were a dull shade of grey that would fade into nothingness. She slipped off her trench coat and turned it inside out. The effect was what she had hoped for. Instead of appearing to be wrong side out, the coat looked drab, ill-fitting and cheap. She surveyed herself once more wondering if she should apply dark circles to her eyes but decided that might be overdoing it and draw more attention.

Instead she slid on a pair of dark sunglasses. The face that peered back at her looked ten years older than the Susan who had first entered the ladies' room. Finally, she turned the nylon-carry-on bag inside out, replacing the articles, adding her purse to its contents. That should do it. She practiced slumping her shoulders and dragging her feet until she felt at ease with the assumed posture.

At last, prepared to put her new disguise to the test, Susan took a deep breath and steeled herself to walk through the door. Just then a red headed woman entered, gave her a brief-intense scrutiny and brushed past.

24

A drenching thunderstorm heralded Mark's arrival in Bucharest. The airport was dingy dismal and dirty. From the moment he emerged from customs, he was accosted by gypsies begging for money and hustlers who greedily eyed his belongings, while trying to convince him to trade dollars for Romanian currency. "Change, mister, change...two-hundred lei for every dollar." Bombarded with offers, he shrugged them off as best he could and hurriedly maneuvered toward the exit.

With a suitcase and brief case clutched in one hand, and an umbrella in the other, he surveyed the dilapidated cars out front that passed for taxis. Most didn't even have meters and stepping into one was taking a chance on being stranded or robbed. Nevertheless, after haggling over the price and finally agreeing to pay in dollars, he secured a ride to the Hotel Intercontinental. He settled in for the thirty-odd mile ride from the city's outskirts to downtown.

A grand boulevard in the French tradition led into the city, complete with a replica of the Paris Arch de Triomphe, reminding Mark again of the affinity between the Romanians and the French. Yet, a few feet away were peasants with little to eat, and the city, like much of the country, lay in crumbling decay. Imposing foreign embassies lined the showcase concourse once built to fool visitors as to the Romanian state. Military men in smart, olive-green jackets and trousers trimmed in red directed the flow of traffic with small-white wands through the roundabout. Decades of the disastrous reign of communist dictator Ceausescu had left the economy in shambles and the people poor. Mark wondered if milk was still a black market item, meat unknown and flour rationed?

Mark entered the hotel to find it bustling with black-marketeers, African engineering students and a very few Western businessmen. It was the single hotel in town he knew that didn't require a bribe to register. He remembered his first visit to Bucharest, when he had been repeatedly turned away from hotels supposedly full until he took the hint and slipped a folded ten-dollar bill inside his passport and handed it to the clerk. Suddenly, there were as many rooms as he could wish.

Mark shook his head. Nothing had changed since his last visit. The Romanian economy thrived on a black market currency, preferably Western, though coffee and cigarettes were commonly used as well to get automobiles repaired, children in to see the doctors, or to buy fuel when there was none.

His room on the tenth floor overlooked a plaza and grandiose opera house built at an enormous cost to the Romanians. Ceausescu had ordered whole neighborhoods demolished to make way for a canal leading to it.

Mark turned from the window and placed an overseas call to Jerry. It was almost an hour before he heard his voice at the other end. Mark had asked Susan back in St. Abient not to say anything to Jerry regarding Benjamin's disappearance.

They settled a few business matters and then Jerry said, an odd note in his voice, "I've told everyone at this end you're on vacation. And with Susan gone too...well...the tickets went through the expense accounts. Sorry but you two are an item around here."

Mark swallowed an expletive. "How is she doing?"

"I thought you knew. She stayed in Europe."

Mark cursed, hoping his suspicions were wrong. "Jerry, check with KLM and see if you can trace her destination." His stomach churned as if it were tied in knots. "Use whatever leverage it takes."

"I thought you said there were no problems."

"I didn't want to worry you. Look, I can't go into the details over the phone. I sent Susan home to keep her safe."

Mark hung up and sank back into the chair. It would be just like her to try solving this on her own. Hadn't she been frightened enough? He found himself praying—for her, for Benjamin and for himself. How long since he last prayed? Despite his jeering response to Susan's faith in God, he'd never made a conscious decision to stop praying. Somewhere along the way he got too busy. He decided to make it on his own without help. And he succeeded, proving to his father and himself that he could.

There had been a few casualties, first Julie and now Benjamin. The familiar anger and pain shot through him. Susan's words echoed in his mind as clearly as if she were standing there. "It's not your fault, Mark, not your fault. They made the wrong choices, chose the wrong friends and went to the wrong places."

If only he had been there when they needed him, instead of climbing his way to the top. But maybe, a small voice whispered, it wouldn't have made any difference. Look at Benjamin. Had his being there stopped him from taking off? His cousin hadn't trusted Mark enough to come to him when he was in trouble. That hurt. Trust was everything. Trust was something you earned and somehow he had failed to earn Benjamin's.

The minutes dragged. When the phone rang, Mark grabbed the receiver. "Jerry?"

He came straight to the point. "Susan flew from Amsterdam to Budapest. Then boarded a flight to Vienna."

"You're sure she was on board?"

"She used her ticket. Probably she's visiting that journalist with the *Washington Review* she used to date. Quit worrying."

"I hope you're right. But so much has been happening at this end, that I'd feel better if you tracked Monroe down and verified it," Mark said, feeling somehow frightened, relieved and let down at the same time. He had been so concerned for her safety. Why hadn't she mentioned traveling on to Vienna?

He hung up the phone for the second time and felt his stomach clench. Susan hadn't a clue as to what was really going on. She hadn't been there when Geliv told him that the men at the campground were not Turkish, but Arabs, a radical faction of the PLO that had broken away a few years back to form a deadly group of assassins and terrorists. They hated anything or anyone Western.

Shaken, Mark had asked, "Why don't you do something about them?"

"There is nothing we can do," Geliv said. "They all have ironclad identities."

"But they're fake."

Geliv sighed. "Bulgaria has always been close to Russia and what Russia wishes, Bulgaria does. This is not so true now as before, but still, it happens. Remember a few years back, the Bulgarian spy who shot at the pope?" He paused. "Russian orders. In Bulgaria at the time we made it a joke, because of course if Russia was right, the pope was wrong. So we said, the man was shooting in self-defense. The pope shot first." Geliv laughed seemingly pleased with the jest and went on to regale Mark with several more choice political jokes.

"Two friends were in a bar late one evening. The next day the one who slept the latest was arrested. The first one up gets to report to the police what the other let slip the night before. There were informers everywhere." Geliv shook his head, almost as if he missed those days.

Mark supposed it was good they had a sense of humor but the things they were constrained to laugh about made him shudder. He shook off his dark thoughts. Now, he needed to concentrate on finding Benjamin.

He stopped in the downstairs bar and ordered a grilled chicken and cheese sandwich, a Romanian Pepsi and potato chips. The meat took some chewing but he ate it in one of the few air-conditioned places in the country. As always a TV above the bar featured a video of "The Pink Panther." It was either a favorite or all they had. Meanwhile, he wrestled with the problem of where to begin searching for Benjamin. The bartender, eager to practice his English, told Mark of a prominent hangout for Americans in the city.

He caught a taxi at the hotel front. The rain had stopped but puddles of it mixed with oil and dirt splattered cars and pedestrians with an unwelcome brown mist that matched his mood. The humidity was high, as it often is after a rain, and the weather unseasonably warm.

The driver dropped Mark in front of a large residence. The blast of a second-rate rock band, its music punctuated with heavy-bass, reached him from the street. Several arrows pointed him around back and downstairs to the cellar.

Inside, a thick haze of smoke dimmed visibility. The Romanians, friendly and daring, were as different from the more serious-minded Bulgarians as granite from opal. The people in the club were those with enough money or power to escape a small measure of the poverty crippling the country. They sat at little round tables crammed together.

Mark felt nothing but disdain for people who squandered their meager incomes in dingy nightspots, drinking themselves into oblivion, while many in the city lacked bread and meat. This crowd was not made up of the rich and elite with money to spare. No, they were the hustlers, the needy looking for more while they spent what little they had. He had met them in Houston, Los Angeles and in like cities around the globe. They were easy to recognize and he usually managed to steer clear of them.

He picked his way through the crowd avoiding the sensuous glances of several ladies. To his mind, the word "lady," marginally described the scantily clad women, in black-translucent nylons and high heels. Ignoring their soulful, brown eyes and long dark hair, Mark noted instead the petulant discontent marring the otherwise pretty faces.

He maneuvered his way through several rooms before he came to one that looked promising. At a glance he took in the resident African students mingling with several American and European visitors. The room was quieter than the others, the people better dressed. Someone handed him a pipe that was being passed around. He pretended to take a draw, the strong odor of hashish making him feel sick.

The talk was political. Zealous activists exchanged charged rhetoric, pausing occasionally to argue spiritedly with those favoring a more laissez-faire style of government. The revolutionaries' loyalties varied and their voices rose accordingly in heated debate.

At a loss as to how to ask about Benjamin without drawing undue attention to himself, Mark saw his chance when a stoned, young American stumbled toward a closed door and handed a few dollars to a door keeper stationed just inside the room. Mark fingered a five-dollar bill in his pocket and stood to try his luck.

Inside, flickering colored lights threw kaleidoscope patterns against the darkened walls. The inhabitants sprawled about in soft lounging chairs and sofas appeared for the most part to be tripping. Mark sat next to the young man he had followed inside. "Hey, what gives here?" he said, trying to act offhand.

The youth fished two foil packets out of his pocket. "Hell. A trip to hell and back. Wanna come?" He held out a packet.

Mark shook his head. "I've never been fond of hell."

The boy gave him a morose look and with shaky hands drew out a syringe. "What's that got to do with anything? It's the big H, man, horse." He snickered, then turned thoughtful. "I never wanted to be a junkie." Almost against his will it seemed he carefully unwrapped the foil.

"Then why?"

He gave Mark a confused, half-defiant look. "Don't know." He spoke slowly, the words slurred. "Nothing left in the universe." His eyes glazed over. "They all went away...far...far...away." He smiled dreamily and clenched the packet of dope. "And now I go too. Whenever I want."

Mark shrugged. There was no reasoning with him. He was obviously loaded. "What's your name?"

"Bart, Bart from Omaha." He leaned back, closing his eyes for a moment. "Yeah, wiped out—the house, mom, dad, my brothers." He scowled at Mark. "I don't know why I'm telling you this."

Mark took in the crazed guilt in the young man's eyes. He heard himself repeating the words that had been echoing in his head the entire day. "It's not your fault."

"I was gone when they needed me." Bart's face was defiant but Mark's gaze caught the flicker of desperate hope in his eyes.

Bart fidgeted. "You don't understand. I attended Nebraska State. They were working to keep me there when the tornado hit."

Compassion softened Mark's voice. "I'm sorry. It was a tough break." The youth appeared more like a miserable adolescent than a hardened junkie. Mark doubted if he had been at this very long. "Look," he said. "Did your folks want to leave the farm?"

"No."

Mark placed a hand on his shoulder. "Your parents and brothers were right where they wanted to be, at home on the farm they loved. And they wanted you to be in school."

"Yeah, maybe. But I should have been there when they died."

How well Mark understood the anguish tearing at Bart. Hadn't he run from the same thing for years? He didn't have any words or a magic formula to ease the boy's pain but he had to try. "We can't always control the things that happen in life but we can make the best of them."

"Sure, that's easy for you to say."

Surprised Mark realized that it was easier. "You're right, but it's taken me years to get here."

Bart glared at him belligerently. "Well, I'm not interested."

"Maybe not." He studied the young man. "I bet your parents would be proud now," he prodded.

"Shut up." The youth unwrapped the foil square and poured the heroin into a metal spoon he took from his pocket. With fumbling hands he slipped a disposable syringe from its package.

"That's not going to solve anything. You can't run forever."

"Watch me." Bart dipped the needle into a glass of water and drew up enough to mix the heroin. His forehead beaded with perspiration and his hands shook.

"How long have you been on this stuff?"

"Long enough." He squirted a little water into the spoon and used a wooden matchstick to dissolve it with the heroin. Bart licked his lips, anticipation now written in every line of his face.

Mark drew a picture from his pocket. "Have you ever seen this guy?" Bart didn't even glance up. He struck the flint on his lighter and placed the spoon over the flame. "I asked you a question," Mark said.

"I said I'm not interested," Bart mumbled, intent now on cooking the heroin mixture.

The threat in Mark's voice got his attention. "You'd best change your mind, if you don't want that crap on the floor."

He peered at the picture Mark held. "Who is it?"

"My cousin."

"Never saw him before. Is he a junkie?"

"No, he was kidnapped by a worse breed, the one who supplies you with the stuff." Mark dropped a business card in Bart's pocket. "I'll be in town a few days. If you hear anything, let me know. I'm staying at the Hotel Intercontinental."

Bart closed the lighter, looking more like a kid than ever. He pulled back on the syringe, sucking the deadly nectar into its barrel. Mark thought, how do they get to this place? Bart stuck his arm out and squinted at the veins, running a finger over them until he found a strong one. He slipped the needle under the skin and pulled back on the syringe, drawing blood, then he pushed it in releasing the junk into his blood stream.

Mark felt sick. He got up and left. He had seen more than he cared to see. And he couldn't help but remember—Julie had died doing the same thing.

On the drive back, the memories rose to haunt him...a picture of pretty impulsive Julie with a needle in her arm. How had it happened? He would never know and he was beginning to realize he couldn't live the rest of his life blaming himself. Life was for the living and he'd been given a second chance.

Still he had to find Benjamin. He couldn't bear to see him hurt.

25

Once Susan had donned her disguise, she exited the ladies' room at Schipol. With trepidation she trudged by the large, mustached man who had been following her, her pulse slowing in relief when he failed to recognize her. Now what? She didn't dare fly on to Houston with him on the plane. Her only alternative was a plan that would lose him. But how?

Finally, she decided to join Mark in Bucharest and continue the search for Benjamin. Mark's idea that she would be safer returning home was a pipe dream. If she didn't see this through to the end, she might spend the rest of her life glancing over her shoulder.

That decided, to further avoid discovery, she rode the elevator up one floor and purchased a one-way ticket to Budapest. She went directly to the departure gate and spent the time until boarding in the most unobtrusive manner she could contrive, seated amid a group of Hungarians waiting for the same flight.

Ironically, her initial concern that Volar was either dealing drugs or laundering money for the mob was now the least of her worries. Susan shivered and rose as the attendant announced her flight, finding it difficult to comprehend how they had moved from a possible drug scam to international terrorism.

On the plane, she sat beside a friendly Hungarian woman who greeted Susan with a barrage of Hungarian. Her hair was dyed a burgundy shade common to Eastern Europe. On closer inspection, Susan realized she was the lady she had passed earlier in the ladies' room.

The only Hungarian word Susan recognized from her chatter was her good afternoon. "*Jonapot,*" Susan said in return, feeling silly, shrugging and shaking her head to indicate she understood little else. In fact, it was the single word she knew in that language. Besides now was a terrible time to strike up a new friendship. There were too many uncertainties, and too many risks, for her to know whom to trust.

Disappointed, the woman drew back, then her eyes lit up. "*Fraulein, sprechen sie Deutsch?*"

"*Jaa....*" Susan nodded slowly, torn between feeling pleased at the opportunity to use her Deutsch and uneasy at her seatmate's eagerness to engage her in conversation. It was not unusual that her seatmate spoke German. Hungary's ties with Austria forged during the Hapsburg's reign and later consolidated into the Austro-Hungarian Empire were still very real. It would be rude to ignore the woman, so she talked a bit and found their conversation helped take her mind off her fears.

It wasn't until they arrived in Budapest that Susan realized belatedly her luggage was by now on its way to Houston. It was time for another change in her disguise. The people pursuing her were tenacious and it would be foolish to think they could be easily routed.

In the airport boutique, she bought a nondescript dark skirt and white blouse, then changed in the ladies' room. The serviceable, black and white combo could pass for a maid, clerk or waitress uniform.

The question was what to do next? Every instinct urged her to find Mark. A direct flight to Bucharest was tempting, but she feared it would also make her an easy target to trace. And that wouldn't do. Should she make a diversionary sightseeing trip into the city?

After some reflection Susan drew out some of the emergency cash secreted away in her wallet that she carried on every trip abroad and purchased a ticket for the next flight to Vienna. If anyone checked there would be no paper trail. That was, after all, the reason she had flown to Budapest. At the gate she carefully studied the crowd, as friends, families, lovers and businessmen said their goodbyes. She zeroed in on an Austrian woman who was clearly upset. Susan moved closer.

"*Was hast du getan?*" the woman berated her teenage daughter. "*Wie kanst du dine fahrkarte verlieren? Du Böses kind!*"

Susan drew in a deep breath, thankful she understood German. Undoubtedly the two had taken an early morning flight over to shop. It was common enough practice. Goods and services were much less expensive in Hungary than Austria. But it was Susan's good fortune that the daughter had lost her return ticket. It appeared fate was going to give her the chance she needed to get rid of the ticket. It was important if anyone inquired that it seem as if she had personally used it.

She approached the woman and her daughter, praying she wasn't making a mistake, and addressed them in German. "Excuse me, I couldn't help but overhear. Perhaps I can help. I purchased a ticket to Vienna that I no longer need."

The woman eyed her suspiciously. "*Nein.* We'll buy our own."

Susan held out the ticket. "You can have this one for free."

"*Frei?*" the woman said, a gleam in her eyes.

"*Ja.*" Susan handed her the ticket. "*Gute Reise.*"

"*Danke viel mal.*" Her face split into a wide smile. "*Das ist sehr nett von ihnen.*" She bubbled over with thanks in German.

Everything was going to be okay, Susan thought as she watched them board the plane. She could almost see God's hand smoothing her path and directing her way to safety. "Thank you," she whispered.

Her last stop before leaving was to purchase Hungarian forints. Outside, the blue skies and sunshine lifted her spirits. A soft breeze ruffled her hair as she scanned the area, detecting no one suspicious. Humming, she crossed to the line of taxis waiting beyond the airport entrance. And then it happened.

The green sedan roared toward her. She stood paralyzed, too frightened to move. Horns honked and voices rose. The car didn't slow. It was almost on her. The world spun before her eyes. She was going to die. Suddenly strong arms thrust her aside and she was thrown to the ground, crushed beneath a stranger's weight.

She was alive! Somehow, she rose, thanked her rescuer and clambered into a taxi, bracing herself for the ride.

Had her near accident been happenstance? She'd probably never know. Susan leaned her head against the car window as the taxi driver pressed ahead at full throttle, not braking for red lights and turns until the last possible moment. From past trips, she theorized that Hungarian taxi drivers dealt with their inner frustrations behind the wheel. She clung to the seat in an effort to keep from flying forward or sideways.

She kept glancing back to see if they were followed as they raced through Pest's crumbling residential area and crossed the Danube into the more beautiful and ornate Buda. The green sedan was nowhere in sight. The taxi barreled up a long, winding road toward Castle town, a picturesque area of Buda that drew tourists from around the world, a place where she could easily blend in. She began to breathe easier.

The Hilton, a towering, glass complex, came into view. One of life's ironies, she thought, as the cab screeched to a halt in front of the casino, was that it was built on the ruins of an ancient monastery.

Inside, she took in the preserved, jagged rock foundations through the lobby glass on her way to the restaurant. The fragmented stone walls where monks once prayed rose in majestic defiance.

Although it was mid-afternoon she had eaten little that day. Susan ordered Chicken Paprika, a Hungarian specialty served with tiny spatzle-like dumplings smothered in sour cream, peppers and onions. As she ate, her gaze cautiously took in the people seated nearby.

Before she resumed her journey, she needed to make certain she was alone. So she strolled through the shops and market stands, trying to determine if she was being followed. It would be foolish to ignore everything that had happened. She walked down the cobbled streets to the Gothic cathedral on the corner and knelt inside for a few moments in silent prayer. If ever she needed help, it was now.

Afterward, she drifted into the art museum across the street, feeling less vulnerable where there were visible security guards. Among Old World paintings of Turkey's barbaric invasion of Hungary, she watched for anyone tailing her. But after taking in the brutal slaughter, takeover and subsequent forced march to Turkey of 10,000 Hungarians bound in chains, she left the museum more heavy-hearted than ever.

Outside, she ambled along the medieval alabaster fortress walls, climbing to a lookout tower to gaze at the Danube's murky swirling waters. She felt trapped and defeated. A few feet away, gypsies illegally peddled embroidered folk blouses and linens to passing tourists. Friendly Hungarians waved from below and Susan waved back, then made her way down the steps, unsure how safe it was to continue to Bucharest.

Back at the Hilton, she caught a taxi, still uneasy though no one appeared to be pursuing her. The cab dropped her at the train station in Northeast Pest. She bought a ticket to Szeged, a town near the Romanian border. From there she planned to rent an automobile.

Susan boarded the train with ten minutes to spare. Her first-class cabin was third-class by Western standards. Two toothless old women with handwoven baskets filled with tomatoes and green peppers sat across from her. A thin grey-haired man entered and placed a bag in the overhead space. He drew out a cigarette and stepped off the train to smoke.

She peered out the window at a curio stand. Little wonder that Budapest, often referred to as the Paris of Eastern Europe, produced goods most of the East block envied. A hand-painted porcelain plate depicting local flowers in a vibrant bouquet of colors caught her eye. It was easy to visualize it in her cheery kitchen back home.

A glance at her watch showed she could just make it. She grabbed her bag and rushed off to buy it. Happy with her purchase, she turned back to board the train, a moment too late. The whistle blew and the wheels began rolling.

She hesitated mid-step wondering what to do. A deafening roar, followed by anguished cries pierced the air. The force of the sudden blast threw her backward. As if in slow motion, she watched birds crumple and the horizon darken. She clung to the ground breathless, tasting grit in her mouth, then struggled to her feet and reached out to a young girl who had fallen beside her. She veered back toward the train car where she had sat minutes before. It was now a mass of scattered debris. Chunks of steel and wood and human bodies covered the tracks. The horror of the sight paralyzed her. She stood shakily for a moment, attempting to gather her wits. Did she dare believe this too was a coincidence?

Instinctively, she whirled and ran, not knowing where, but feeling the need to hide. Like the thunderous clamor of a warning bell, fear propelled her onward. She collided against a pair of strong arms. Susan struggled to free herself, striking out as best she could.

"Susan, stop this, it's me."

She froze. She knew that voice.

26

Susan stared at Francois' white face, unable to fathom how he came to be there. Dazed, she shook her head and felt herself crushed against his chest.

"*Cherie*, if they had hurt you."

She stilled for a moment and then drew back, squinting up at him against the sun's rays. "You think it was meant for me?" There was no reason to say the horrible words aloud—bomb—attack—they both understood too well what she meant.

Francois touched her cheek. "Why did you not go home? Away from this. It could have been avoided."

She leaned against him, drawing comfort from the strength of his arms and he responded by holding her tighter. She didn't know why he was there but she was glad. He brushed the hair back from her face as if she were a child. His soothing hands followed a gentle path down her back.

A woman near her screamed, "Petri, Petri, where are you?"

Francois placed an arm around Susan urging her forward. "We have to get you out of here."

She couldn't just leave, she realized. Susan turned and ran back to the sobbing woman. She cradled the woman to her breast, not knowing what else to do. Tears rolled down her face as she stared at the surrounding devastation. How had it happened?

Francois gripped her wrist, tearing her away. "Are you crazy? If you want to help, leave before a worse disaster strikes."

She flinched at his words but went with him because he might be right. Her presence might have caused this devastation. God, where are You in the midst of all this? A stoic silence met her inner cry but she almost heard Him whisper, just where I was when My own Son died.

They walked to the front parking lot. Francois unlocked the sedan and opened the passenger door. "Where were you going?" he said.

"To Szeged." She got in, feeling disoriented and ill, hoping she wasn't about to embarrass herself. She waited until he slid behind the wheel. "Francois, what are you doing here?"

"Following you."

"Me?" Her insides churned like sour butter in a creamer that had been stirred and left too long.

"Of course, darling. Someone has to keep you safe."

Her head felt as if it were unwinding and his running commentary didn't help. "Well, you nearly got me killed."

"Perhaps, but it was unintentional." His eyes made a bold perusal of her face and figure.

She felt the color rise in her cheeks. "Not now, please." She rolled down the window and leaned out, sick.

"Are you okay?"

She nodded and rolled up the window.

Francois passed her his handkerchief and a bottle of Perrier.

She wiped her face, took a few sips of water and felt a little better.

Assured she was okay, Francois cranked the engine and guided the car back onto the highway, pulling into a lane of traffic.

She closed her eyes for a few minutes, trying to rest but there were too many images from the train wreck flashing on the dark screen of her mind. She studied Francois for a moment, then asked, "How long have you been tailing me?"

His averted gaze fed her suspicions. "The man on the plane from Sofia to Amsterdam—was yours, wasn't he? I suppose my attempts at disguise were child's play to you professionals," she said bitterly.

"What can I say?" He gave her a look of apology. "It's their job to penetrate disguises but it helped that their female counterpart could follow you into *les toilettes.*"

So the woman on the plane she'd seen earlier in the ladies room had been a plant. She swallowed at the thought, then shook her head, unable to lightly forgive the misery and fright he'd caused. "Why? I was on my way home until your friend frightened me away."

"So that's what happened." He spoke as if he had been puzzling over her actions for some time. "It was never my intention to bring you any harm. In my own bumbling way, I was trying to protect you. Forgive me, *cherie?*"

Susan had always found that mocking smile and the roguish gleam in his eyes hard to withstand. Together they were nearly irresistible. Still she nodded reluctantly.

He reached over and squeezed her hand. *"Merci."*

"I suppose I should be grateful," she said, unable to entirely stifle her resentment at the trouble his intervention had caused.

"That would be nice. But I take it you are mad at me for interfering."

"Even you must admit you haven't been too successful." She shivered abruptly. "Those poor people in that train car blown to bits. I can't understand— It's not as if I've uncovered any incriminating evidence."

"The problem is that they do not know this to be true. You have been poking your pretty nose into their business, asking a lot of questions."

Susan opened her purse, drew out a comb and ran it through her tangled curls. She couldn't bear to think about the train explosion. "It's possible," she admitted. But she prayed they were wrong that the bomb had nothing to do with her. She brushed the dirt from her clothes. "Where are we going?"

"To the airport. You are taking the next available flight to Houston where it's safe."

"There's no safe place for me, or Benjamin, Kevin and Mark until these people are stopped and put behind bars."

His mouth tightened. "You'll certainly be better off home than here."

They drove for a few minutes in stormy silence. Susan said, "Drop me in the next town."

He studied her face for a moment and then caved in. "All right. But what's in Szeged?"

"A place to rent a car." She gave him an exasperated look. "I was trying to lose the man following me."

He sighed. "Presupposing you have a car and driver at your disposal, namely me, what has your wretched mind planned next?"

As much as she hated to admit it, she was glad of the added security of Francois' presence and tried to hide her relief at his easy acquiescence. "To join forces with Mark in Bucharest."

Francois complained as he wheeled the car in the opposite direction. "You are asking a lot. Not only will I be placing you in the middle of a dangerous situation, I will be putting you in direct contact with him."

"Him?"

"The competition."

Susan settled back. There had been little enough to smile about lately, and if Francois wished to take her mind off recent events by teasing, she was more than glad to let him. She couldn't yet think of the explosion clearly. Later, when she was alone she would face the horror of what had happened. She forced herself to relax and join in the game. "Competition? I'm afraid I don't understand."

"Don't be coy. I've seen the way you and Ashley look at each other." His words held an undertone of grimness that hit upon yet another sore spot in Susan's life. One she instinctively shied away from.

"You were always highly imaginative. Mark is my employer, end of story. You've simply to ask him. He's made that fact very clear."

He reached for her hand, covering it with his own. "Wounded, are we? I begin to see his strategy."

Susan pulled her hand free, irritated by his nonsense. "Do be serious. Are you or are you not driving me to Bucharest?"

He groaned theatrically and gave her that heart-stopping smile that used to leave her feeling weak. "We have been on the highway to Bucharest for the last ten minutes."

The road to Szeged stretched out before them like the long road to China, their progress slowed by a steady stream of slow-moving army trucks. Little East German Trabants constructed of pressed wood and Russian Ladas inched their way around the heavy trucks when oncoming traffic permitted.

"A penny for them," Francois said.

"Mmm. I was thinking about the Hungarians. How they retained their national pride even during the years of Communist occupation."

Francois shrugged, as if indifferent. "I take it you refer to the much vaunted 1956 uprising."

"Well, they did hold the Soviet military at bay for four days. Not an easy thing to do."

"To what purpose? In the end the Russian tanks crushed them into submission."

"They won the world's respect."

"True, but for all that, the world refused to help. Nobody wanted another war." Francois cleared his throat. "Not to change the subject, but has it ever occurred to you Ashley might be wrapped up in this?"

"Wrapped up how?"

"He seems to have access to a lot of inside information. His cousin had the dope."

"And you think he supplied it?" Susan laughed. "I simply don't believe it."

"You have to admit, *cherie*, someone is trying to set you up. Do not forget the phone calls and the report to the police. Not that many people in France knew your plans and had access to your purse." His voice rose in excitement. "And there was the dead body in your bathtub."

"That couldn't have been Mark. We left the hotel together and didn't even know which rooms we'd have until we returned."

"Maybe, but I find it suspicious that once again Ashley is on hand when disaster strikes."

"If that were the sole criteria, you could be considered a suspect as well. Unlike yourself, Mark was nowhere near when the train blast happened."

"Touché."

The last thing Susan needed was for Francois to fill her mind with more doubts and confusion. How could she ever consider Mark a suspect? It seemed so disloyal and impossible. Besides Mark couldn't be...could he? Susan shook her head in frustration. Was she allowing her own attraction to keep her from the truth?

She gazed out at the fields of tall sunflower plants which seemed to stretch endlessly along both sides of the highway. Susan shifted uneasily in her seat and reflected on the events of the last week and her relationship with Mark. Why bring her to Europe, if he was guilty? To set her up? As a cover for his underground business? Pressure from Jerry?

She couldn't believe it. There was something fundamentally good about Mark. She had felt it all along. He cared about people. She saw it in his eyes and heard it in his voice. That was the reason he was in Europe, because he cared about Benjamin just as he had cared for his sister Julie.

Francois, on the other hand, was primarily motivated by ambition, as she had painfully discovered in the past. The warmth in his eyes and voice might say, "I love you," but they were merely words, tools to further his objectives. It would be completely in character for him to maliciously discredit Mark to achieve his own ends. Francois had never liked being bested by anyone. Still, a small voice within whispered, Benjamin had disappeared and Julie was dead. Could Mark be responsible?

27

By the time Francois steered the sedan into a petrol station on the edge of Szeged the sun had set and the blue skies turned to a dreary drizzle. He ran inside where an old Soviet-made radio broadcast Liszt's *Hungarian Rhapsody Number Two* through the station and across the parking lot. A smile pulled at the corner of his mouth. Where else but Hungary could travelers in a backwater station expect to be serenaded so elegantly?

Francois signaled the attendant to give him a full tank of gas and then sat down to use the phone. He detested making the call but Susan had to be removed before more damage was done. He glanced around to ensure he was alone and punched the numbers in quickly. His man answered on the second ring. Francois spoke in a clipped hurried voice, his usual charm set aside. "Szeged here. Set Strauss into motion for Arad." He didn't wait for an answer, but hung up the phone and strolled into the men's room, emerging a few moments later to pay the bill.

His thoughts were grim as he got back into the car. Driving Susan to Arad had not been part of the plan, but he would have to make do. He started the engine. "Enjoy the concert?"

"Very much." She shifted and turned to face him. "Francois?" He heard the question in her voice and was glad she waited until he edged his way back onto the highway before finishing.

"How did you learn about the body in my hotel room?"

He managed to answer lightly. "*Cherie*, for shame, you dare to underrate French intelligence."

"No, not that." She glanced at him uneasily. "I had understood no one was to be told."

"Would it surprise you to learn that one of my men was on the scene? A member of the police force, in fact."

"I suppose it shouldn't," she said slowly. "Do the others know?"

"No, and I need your word that they will not hear it from you." He turned an earnest face to her. "Trust me."

"That's asking a bit much but don't worry, I'll keep your secret."

"*Merci*." He set himself to be his most entertaining as they talked along the way. A few times Susan even summoned a weak smile. He kept the conversation from drifting into any serious discussion and had the satisfaction of seeing some of the tension ease from her face. He felt more than a few pangs of guilt, sympathizing with her inner turmoil. Unfortunately, he could not oblige her with the present reprieve for long.

It was really too bad, he thought, glancing over at the lovely curve of her breast. His gaze traveled to her long shapely legs and he had to force his attention back to the road. He had dreamed of her for years. Her scent, the sweet, tender adoring looks she used to give him, promising him everything for the price of a wedding band. Circumstances had forestalled him then but what about now? His hand reached over to cover hers and he pulled her against his side into the curve of one arm. He refused to let her pull away. *"Cherie*, you will make us wreck," he warned.

She shoved against him. "Let go of me."

Francois swerved the car to the side of the road and stopped. "Try to understand. I need you, Susan."

Her eyes reproached him. "Why are you stopping? There's nothing between us, anymore. I want you to keep driving." The anger in her gaze wavered and a mixture of compassion and exasperation won out. "All I feel for you is friendship."

"Then treat me as a friend, not a stranger. Kiss me and then tell me you feel nothing."

She gasped, pushing against his chest as he attempted to draw her into his arms.

He wanted to drown in her warmth and innocence but he forced himself to keep his head. She was vulnerable; no one but a cad would press her after she had been through so much. A man after all had his pride. He had never had to force any woman. If Susan was ever to be his, he wanted her willing.

She scooted as far from him as possible against the other door. "That was inexcusable. I always thought you were a gentleman at least."

"It seems I owe you a second apology."

She gave him a stony glance, placing her jacket on the seat between them and leaned her head wearily back against the seat.

Clearly she didn't want to discuss it. He turned on the radio and Liszt's *Hungarian Rhapsody Number Six* filled the car. Eventually she slept while he drove on.

Francois woke her at the Romanian border. "Ugh, it doesn't change here, does it?" Susan said, following the long, thorough search of their car and luggage.

"Not much," he agreed. "The country though is better off without Ceausescu's brand of Communism." They endured a three-hour wait before finally receiving visas to enter Romania.

Back on the highway, Susan yawned and closed her eyes, dozing off and on. Unable to resist, Francois reached across to where she sat to brush back a few silky strands of her hair.

When they reached Arad, the sky had blackened and smoldering clouds veiled the moon and stars. The town looked dirty and deserted with the exception of several stooped peasant women sweeping the streets with bundles of straw tied together with twine.

Francois stopped the car in front of an older rundown hotel and shook Susan awake. Apprehension gripped his stomach as they climbed out of the car and up the hotel steps. The door suddenly swung open. A large muscular man blocking the entrance motioned them to leave.

"But we need a room," Susan protested as Francois turned her around.

"Come on. He is trying to tell us there are none. There must be another hotel in town." He realized the moment he feared was almost upon them. As they reached the car, a young man materialized at their side and in reasonably good English offered to direct them to a motel nearby.

Francois coasted behind the man's auto down a side road leading away from the town. They had been traveling for almost a quarter of an hour when Susan spoke up. "This is spooky. We're in the middle of nowhere. Only trees and more trees and bushes. Anything could happen."

Francois said, "There's just one of him. What could happen?"

"Plenty," she said with a worried frown. "We don't know what we'll find. Maybe...maybe he's...."

"Nonsense," he interrupted as they turned into a wooded area with a small inn.

He left Susan in the car and went inside to arrange for rooms. From within he watched the man circle the car and try to open it. Susan had locked the doors. Francois didn't want his windows broken. He muttered a curse and hurried out, calling to the man in Romanian to stop. This was not his plan.

His eyes widened as the man raised a club and slammed it against his head. Francois saw a ring of stars as he fell, crashing to the ground.

28

Left in the car alone, Susan had locked the car doors and pocketed the keys Francois had left in the ignition. Yet the strange man who led them to the inn continued to circle their vehicle as if trying to break in. She tensed as he peered into the windows and fiddled with the door handles. What was keeping Francois? She could feel the man's anger as he began to swear and kick the fenders in uncontrolled spurts of violence. Frantically, she searched the glove compartment and under the seats for a weapon, berating herself for not carrying a gun. Why had she never learned to shoot or defend herself?

The windows rattled as he struck them with his fists, pressing his face against the glass like some weirdo-monster. Finally, she discovered a small Swiss Army Knife that had at some point slipped between the seat cushions and clutching it, turned in relief to see Francois returning.

The man lifted a club as if to strike Francois. Susan screamed. Francois swung around at the sound and the Romanian seized the moment, smashing the club against Francois' head in a blow that felled the Frenchman.

Susan froze, petrified at the sight of Francois lying prone on the ground, his legs buckled beneath him. Then, she leaned against the horn, praying its deafening blare would bring help fast. The noise sent their adversary fleeing into the woods. She gathered her courage. Almost against her will her mind began to function, analyzing her options, and facing the horrible possibility that Francois might be dead and she might be next. She scanned the darkness for the attacker. Unless the inn had a back entrance, he must still be in the woods. Why hadn't the noise brought help?

Were his buddies inside? Susan shivered. She must find out if Francois was alive. She inched the door open and ran across to where he lay, still as death.

Blood oozed from his forehead. She found a faint pulse at his wrist and pressed her ear to his chest. Relief rushed through her as she picked up a slow but steady beat. Still he was out cold. She had to get Francois into the car. She dropped the Swiss knife into her pocket with the car keys, then grabbed both his arms, dragging him toward the sedan. It was slow work and her shoulders throbbed from the effort.

How would she ever lift him into the car? she wondered, trying not to panic. By the time she opened the back seat door, she was panting heavily. She knelt in the dirt and forced his upper body to a sitting position. A spare set of car keys fell from his pants pocket and she tossed them over onto the driver's seat.

The injury to his skull worried Susan as his dark head lolled against the side of the seat. She crawled across the vinyl and tugged at his arms from behind, alternately pushing and pulling until her arms ached and Francois was fully inside, stretched out across the back seat.

Relief warred with an escalating sense of panic as she slammed the back door and climbed over into the driver's seat, grabbing Francois' spare car keys. Quickly she shoved his key into the ignition and cranked the engine. It died with a shuddering sputter. Susan groaned in despair, pumping the accelerator.

The door opened and she felt the cold, steel muzzle of a gun pressed against her head. "Get out," her assailant said in a deadly voice.

Trembling, her hands fell from the ignition.

He jerked her out, keeping the gun to her head.

"*Multumesc*," he thanked her in Romanian, pointing to Francois' body. "Very good work." He grinned and smashed the gun against the back of her skull.

Pain spiraled down. She slid to the ground, darkness claiming her.

Sometime later, Susan slowly regained consciousness, feeling the steady vibrations of a moving vehicle beneath her. The strident sounds of Gershwin's *An American in Paris* bombarded her aching head and the gag tied around her mouth covered her nostrils making it difficult to breathe. Her wrists and ankles burned where the rope cut into the skin. A heavy blanket shrouded her.

She wiggled maneuvering the damp wool aside enough to see that it was still nighttime. She lay on the back seat floorboard of the sedan, alone in the car with her assailant. Where was Francois? The thick cloth wrapped against her mouth seemed to choke her.

If Mark were here.... No, she thought with a sudden rush. If I were there or if somehow we could be safe again. In her mind, she saw the scattered debris and mutilated body parts strewn across the train tracks. Would it never end?

She closed her eyes in deepening despair. Perhaps Mark was better off without her. She shivered.

And what of Francois? In trying to protect her, had he also died? She needed to hope, to believe he was alive, had managed to escape and send for help. Which is what she should've done when she had the chance. But she had feared they might kill Francois before she could return.

Self-pity and recriminations wouldn't help. If there was to be a rescue, she would have to engineer it. Her hands were bound in front. If she could just reach the knife in her pocket, it would make short work of the knots binding her.

She twisted and turned until she finally shook it loose from her pocket. It fell with a thump, the radio covering the noise. She managed to open it using her fingers but the problem was how to use it to slice the rope with her hands tied. She wedged the handle into the crack along the backside of the front passenger seat and lifted her hands, until the cord rubbed against the extended blade. The knife wobbled dangerously with the movement but it was working.

About the time the knife sliced through the last threads of rope, the car slowed. Susan stuffed the weapon back into her pocket, tossed the blanket over her head and clasped the cord tightly against her hands. She struck an unconscious pose as the car stopped.

She felt the blanket thrown back from her face and forced herself to relax, hardly daring to breathe. A rough, masculine hand slapped her cheeks and she braced herself against the sting, remaining limp. He slid his thumb to her throat and she willed her heartbeat to slow as he searched for a pulse point. She heard a grunt and felt the scratchy wool brush her face again. She didn't dare move until she heard the car door slam. Cautiously, Susan clutched the knife and cut through the twine binding her legs. She stretched for a moment and then pocketed the knife.

Susan peeked from a corner of the blanket, her heart pounding erratically. Dawn streaked across the black sky with vibrant hues of purple and pink, signaling the approach of a new day as she scrambled to her feet and crouched down.

The car was parked on a quiet, residential street lined with shade trees and old stucco homes. Across the dark avenue, a solitary light shone in the front window. He's in there, she thought. This was the chance she had been waiting for; there might not be another. She had to take it.

The back doors were locked. She climbed into the front seat and drew Francois' key chain from her pocket. She thrust the sedan key into the ignition, flinching at the sound of the engine as it turned over. She stepped on the gas pedal and glided down the street, not caring where she was going, as long as it was far away from her assailant.

At first she zigzagged from one neighborhood to the next, hoping to leave a trail impossible to follow. When she came near the main road into the city, she avoided it, fearing that would be the first place he would search. She happened upon downtown Sibiu via a side street and parked the car in a crowded lot next to an outdoor market. She stepped out of the car and reached into the back for her tote bag and purse—the only things she had left. She tossed the keys into a nearby shrub and walked away.

The bustling city, set in the hills of Romania, was one that she knew well and therefore she was not surprised when the taxi driver she hailed knew German. After all, thousands of Germans lived in Sibiu.

She scribbled the address of her friends Flora and Mircu on a torn piece of paper and handed it to him. Thank heaven, she was in a familiar place with friends nearby. Her mind grappled with a way to ensure her escape while the cab maneuvered through the noisy traffic.

Dawn's brilliant splendor had long receded, in its wake grey-shrouded skies released a fine drizzle across the city. By now Susan fully expected her assailant to be in pursuit. She had one goal, to reach Bucharest safely. Despite their disagreements, she felt it would be safer if she and Mark worked together. But he had made it quite clear he didn't want her there. Or perhaps this was an illusion fostered by her own feelings of inadequacy.

Yet, she felt the key to her present dilemma rested in Bucharest. She had tried returning to Houston and found her problems multiplied. Now she would ask Flora to help her get to Bucharest.

Traffic moved slowly, the pedestrians almost as numerous as the cars. Hunger pinched the faces of the gypsy children sitting in horse-drawn wagons. Along the roadside women swung sickles, harvesting weeds to feed their animals. She spied old men carrying huge mounds of hay on their backs, the load covering all but their legs as they walked.

People spilled onto the highway forcing the cabbie to stop. He honked but the farmers and factory workers crowded into the road, as if united in the right to use their streets, in the aftermath of losing so many other freedoms under Ceausescu's brutal dictatorship.

She remembered one fall visiting during the corn harvest to find residential streets barricaded while the military checked family cars for hidden corn kernels. Another time she and Flora were stopped by the militia for an imaginary traffic offense and charged an exorbitant fine. Instead of demanding payment, the two uniformed men pointed to their mouths and stomachs, signaling food would suffice. In the end, she scrounged a can of tuna from a sack and the two officers left happy.

Afterward Flora confided, "It breaks my heart to see my people reduced to begging. If I stop for a train or a traffic light, the children surround the car pleading for food. Milk is a black market item sold in secret by the gypsies but only to those with enough money to pay. How are our children to survive? What is to become of our nation?"

Susan shook her head sadly. The country once described as the breadbasket of Europe was in desperate shape. The winds of time had swept through tipping over the old regime, changing the very fabric of lives, but recovery was too slow and people's welfare hung in the balance.

The taxi stopped before a green stucco home with a large garden beside it. The house stood too near the main highway for comfort. At Susan's knock, Flora opened the door, surprise lighting her face before she quickly swept her inside. "Papa, Susan is here," she called, following with a volley of Romanian exclamations.

"*Pace, Pace.*" Flora planted soft kisses on Susan's cheeks as she murmured the traditional Romanian Christian greeting of peace. She drew Susan forward. "Come, you must greet Papa."

Susan looked down at her disheveled clothing. She felt an immense lightening of her spirit just being there. She smiled at Flora and told her so, with a slight catch in her voice,

Mircu, Flora's white-haired father, beamed a greeting and left it to his daughter to translate how happy they were to see her again. Though it had been two years since their last visit, it seemed like yesterday to Susan, so close did they feel to one another.

Colorful woolen tapestries decorated the walls, helping to seal out winter's chill and summer's heat. Susan sat on a worn sofa that was a reflection of the room at large, shabby but comfortable and clean. She basked in the love of her friends, grateful for this safe haven in the midst of turmoil. But she couldn't linger. Soon she must be on her way again. Never would she choose to endanger these two precious friends.

"I've come to beg a favor," she said, knowing her request would seem strange. Romanians were used to Americans arriving in powerful cars. "Can you arrange a lift to Bucharest for me?"

"Of course." Flora's smile underlined the question in her eyes. "Do you need money?" she said uncertainly.

"No," Susan rushed to assure her, knowing how little they possessed. "I have plenty but thank you. What I need is private transportation."

Flora waited expectantly for Susan to elaborate but voiced no complaint when Susan let the chance to confide slip by. "I'm not sure I understand. You want to travel in a car?"

"Yes. Though there is one minor problem." Susan shifted uneasily, hoping Flora would understand. "I need to travel incognito. No one must recognize me or know that I'm an American."

Flora's eyes widened. "You entered the country illegally?"

"No, I wouldn't dare. It's more of a personal matter but a very serious one. For your own sake, it's important that no one discover I was here."

Flora shrugged in a puzzled manner. "It shall be exactly as you say but how to get you to Bucharest?" Her eyes lit up. "I know— Our neighbor Georgi Dumbravo drives his produce to market every Thursday. Maybe he has not left yet." She shook her head abruptly. "No, better not."

"Why?"

"His wagon is slow. Uncomfortable too."

"It's perfect. I could hide in the back with the vegetables."

Flora made a wry grimace. "To be bounced and jostled and sore for days? The train would be much better."

"I don't mind the discomfort," Susan said. "The wagon is safer."

Flora's arguments were soon swept away and Georgi happily agreed to take her. In two hours time, Susan, squashed between layers of cucumbers and onions, felt every rut and rock in the road. The lingering headache from being knocked unconscious began to pound. She tried to be content but the blanket covering her smelled of horses and damp hay. Before long she realized she was ravenously hungry as well.

When Georgi stopped to water the horses, he slipped two tomatoes and a small hunk of soft-white cheese, much like the Greek feta, beneath the covers. She gratefully devoured the food and, still hungry, drew out Francois' Swiss army knife from her pocket to peel a cucumber she took from the huge pile surrounding her.

They had been traveling a few hours when one of the wheels bent and Georgi signaled her to climb out of the wagon. He flagged down a small Lada. The young family within smilingly agreed to drop Georgi in the nearest town and to carry Susan the rest of the way to Bucharest.

Susan relinquished her place in the wagon with little regret but soon learned that the back seat of the small Lada also had drawbacks. The mother and her two children were often jostled and thrown against Susan as they traveled stretches of highway which consisted mostly of gravel and boulders. By the end of the six-hour journey, Caraman and Stephen, who had become friends of sorts, insisted on seeing her safely settled at the Hotel Intercontinental. Inside, Stephen approached the reception desk to get Mark's room number. Susan, wary of being recognized, huddled in the background next to Caraman and the children.

Stephen returned with a pleased grine. "Room number four-hundred and thirty," he announced from his meager supply of English.

"*Multumesc*," Susan said, touching her heart to ensure they understood her deep gratitude for their help. She declined further escort, embracing Caraman and the children before stepping into the elevator. Stephen pressed their address and phone number into her hand and she waved a final round of thanks and goodbyes. Their faces disappeared behind the closing metal doors.

She steadied herself for the meeting with Mark. Conflicting emotions warred inside, an immense relief to have finally reached her destination and growing dread regarding Mark's reaction to her arrival.

The elevator stopped, the door opened and suddenly she found herself facing Mark.

29

Mark strode from his room to the elevator in the bleakest of moods. Nothing had gone right, or perhaps more accurately, absolutely nothing had happened. He was no closer to finding Benjamin today than a week ago. Worry for his cousin ate at him.

He pressed the button for the elevator and gaped when the door opened. "Susan? What are you doing here?"

Relief lit her face. "Oh, Mark." She almost fell into his arms.

He caught her in surprise and felt one small spring of the tightness within unwind to know she was safe. "Is everything okay? I thought you were in Vienna." He felt her stiffen and let his hands drop to his sides.

Susan glanced surreptitiously in either direction down the hall. "Let's talk in your room."

Mark nodded, wondering what had happened. He couldn't imagine what had brought her there. Had she perhaps learned something about Benjamin that was too sensitive to relate through Jerry or other channels?

He led her to his room. "Now why don't you tell me what this is about?" He eyed her critically, noticing for the first time that dark smudges marred the hollows beneath her brown eyes, stressing their uncertainty. Her clothes appeared as if she had rolled down a hillside and then slept in them for three days.

"Here, sit," he said too sharply, distressed by what he saw. He had a hunch her story would prove even more disturbing.

"Do you mind if I clean up a little first?" Susan lifted a pair of dirty hands for his inspection.

"Fine. The bathroom's over there." He gestured toward it.

She swung the tote bag onto her shoulder and crossed to the small room.

While he waited, Mark called the front desk and arranged for a room for Susan next door to his.

She returned shortly and gave him a rueful look. "I suppose you're wondering why I'm here."

He met her gaze steadily. "That will do for starters."

She caught her lower lip between her teeth, gnawing at it for a moment before she straightened and drew a deep breath. "After I left you in Sofia—" she halted.

"To fly to Houston—"

"Yes, well, the plane touched down in Amsterdam. That's when I first realized I was being followed. I had noticed the man watching me on the plane. But in the airport, everywhere I turned he was right behind me." She paused briefly, gripping the sides of the chair. "I panicked and ran into the ladies' room."

Mark reached across the small table for her hand. "He didn't hurt you?"

"No, and I don't think he would have. But I didn't know then, he was one of Francois' men."

None of this was making any sense to Mark. "Where does Francois come into this?"

She told him everything. His breath caught. While he had searched for Benjamin in relative comfort, mourning his failure to trace him, she had been nearly killed in a bomb explosion, assaulted and kidnapped. Now she sat there cool and collected as if it were the most natural thing in the world to find her way to Bucharest hidden in a wagon of cucumbers. He still quaked at the thought of the hitched ride with a couple of strangers which had followed that scenario.

Where did they go from here? Obviously, it wasn't safe to send her home. Although if Francois had never interfered she might be home, he reflected grimly.

It was disturbing how Susan was increasingly a target for their malice. Why were none of the incidents directed at him? There was the warning note, the cocaine plant, the tipoff to the police and finally the dead body in the bathtub. And the latest attempts boggled his mind.

Did they perceive Susan as a threat, an investigative reporter closing in for the kill, armed with damaging evidence that would put them away for years, or was she just an easy target? Perhaps a warning to himself and the authorities of the length they would go to protect their turf? Or maybe they simply saw her as the weak link in the chain, as Benjamin had been. An unprotected woman and a student. Mark felt more torn than ever—but one thing he knew, this was too big for the two of them to handle. He sincerely hoped Zach could make more sense out of Susan's story.

It would be foolish to say much over the telephone, especially in Bucharest where people quipped the walls were half microphones and half cement. He sighed. Francois' disappearance must be reported and Zach was the logical choice.

30

When Zach arrived the next morning, Susan and Mark discovered Francois had already briefed him on recent events. At Susan's outcry of surprise, he reassured her that Francois had escaped his captor, virtually unharmed and made it back to France. "Nothing to be concerned about. He suffered a mild concussion."

"But how? When did he escape?" Susan said.

"We gather he was left for dead. He regained consciousness in the clearing by the inn. The car was gone and the place deserted, so he hoofed it to the nearest farm and called in for help."

Susan digested the news, realizing Francois would have positioned another operative in the area, in case he ran into trouble. He was, if anything, a professional.

Zach added, "He insisted on personally notifying Interpol that you were missing before he allowed himself to be checked into the hospital."

"Under the circumstances, that was certainly thoughtful and beyond the call of duty," Susan said.

"You bet," Zach agreed. "I'd like to hear your side of what happened, if you don't mind repeating it. And as always, from the very beginning."

Susan told her story for the second time in less than twenty-four hours. She left nothing out, though she felt sure Francois had already filled Zach in on some of the details.

"Well, it's a sorry business," Zach said. "Tough break, you caught in the middle and all."

Mark said, "Why is Susan the target? Why can't these thugs torment someone their own size instead going after women and kids?"

"They know exactly what they're doing," Zach said. "Though this once, they underestimated Susan's capabilities. And it may buy us some much needed time."

Mark frowned. "We need every break we can get."

"Relax," Zach said. "You're both way too tense. In this business, you've got to hang loose."

Susan said, "That's not easy to do when you're the one being terrorized and abducted."

"And no doubt your cousins are home safe," Mark added.

Zach sighed. "Look, nothing is easy in this business. But you can't let it get to you. Lose perspective and you're lost. Judgement goes down the tubes. So unwind. By staying uptight, you're playing right into their hands. Next thing you know, they'll have you running scared."

"I am running scared," Susan said. She knew that Zach must live with constant uncertainty and danger. For them this would pass, and they'd get on with their lives, if they lived long enough that is. But for Zach, it would mean moving on to the next case. Her gaze met Mark's across the room and from the look he gave her she knew he felt the same.

Susan rested a distracted hand against her forehead, wondering what their next move should be. She felt as if there wasn't a creative bone left in her body. She was fresh out of ideas. Perhaps she and Mark had been deceiving themselves, believing they could save Benjamin and Kevin.

Mark cut into her thoughts. "Is anybody watching Beauchamp and Sarb?"

"Yeah," Zach said. "But so far, they're covering their tracks."

"What about the two South African entrepreneurs?" Mark said. "Anything there?"

"We're still waiting for the big break on that one and when it comes, Lauter and Frazier will fry." Closed lipped, Zach refused to say more. "Look, both of you, let's back up to the beginning. I want you to repeat every little detail and nuance. There's got to be something we've missed. Start with Houston."

Susan and Mark wearily agreed.

After several hours of intense questioning and going over each incident, a rap on the door startled them.

Zach waved Mark back and stationed himself behind the door. He reached inside his jacket and pulled out a pistol as he nodded a go-ahead to Mark.

"Come in," Mark called. The door swung open, revealing Bart, the youth from Omaha he'd met at the club the other night. Mark gave Zach a thumb's up and searched the youth's face. "You've been ill."

"Yes, sir." he said, taking in the three of them anxiously.

Mark motioned him to a chair and introduced the others. "They're here helping me search for my cousin."

They greeted him, doing their best to set him at ease. "So," Mark said. "I take it you have some news."

"Umm...could we talk alone?" Bart said.

"They won't do anything to harm you. You can trust them."

Bart clutched the sides of the chair. "If you're sure. I don't want any more trouble."

"I'm sure. So shoot. What's happened?"

"Well, I've been thinking about what you said. About it not being my fault and all, that my family was killed in a twister."

"I'm glad to hear that. Your parents wouldn't want you feeling guilty."

Bart's grip on the chair tightened. He lowered his head self-consciously. "I've been in the hospital. Sir, I...umm...almost OD'd." He lifted a troubled gaze to meet Mark's. "Been thinking ever since about what you said." The words came out in a rush, "Did you mean it, sir?"

Mark's features softened. "Every word." He smiled at Bart. "Your parents and brother would have been proud to see you make something of yourself."

He managed a shy grin. "Yeah, well. I've been thinking on it."

His face, that of a man-child needing approval, drew Mark's sympathy and he responded. "It's the best thing you could do to prove how much you love them and honor their memory. And it's what they would have wanted you to do."

"I suppose that's right, seeing how they tried to do just that most of the time I was growing up. But do you think if they were alive they could forgive me for messing up so bad?"

Mark clasped his shoulder. "Sure, they would. Didn't they always before?"

His face lit up. "Yeah, they sure did. Boy I've been dumb haven't I?"

"There isn't anybody who doesn't make mistakes. You were hurt. Sometimes it takes awhile to set things right. It takes a real man to admit he's wrong and go forward."

Susan listened in awe. Tears moistened her eyes to see one young life turned around. She yearned to reach out and hug Bart close, tell him God would always be his friend but Mark was doing just fine. Surely, his efforts in the youth's behalf would help heal his own hurts. It was reassuring to learn Mark wasn't quite the cynic he professed to be.

"That's one of the reasons I came," Bart finished. "I've decided to return home and go back to school."

"Wonderful. Is there anyway I can help? A loan maybe, until you get on your feet?"

Bart flushed. "Thanks, but that's not why I'm here. I thought maybe I could help. You were so nice and all. About your cousin, uh, I heard something."

Mark tensed as if ready to spring. "You did?"

"Uhuh...least ways, I think so."

"Go ahead, I'm listening."

Bart seemed to brace himself. "Well, it was like this. While I was in the hospital, they sent two guys to make sure I wouldn't rat. When they first came in they thought I was sleeping.

"I wasn't, only my eyes were closed and I heard one of them say, 'We don't want any slip ups like with the last one.'

"I knew then I better keep my eyes shut and play dead."

"Then the other one said, 'You telling me...I thought I was a goner when the boss learned the kid made it to Vienna.'

"And then the other one said, 'Well, there aren't too many Texans with a name like Ashley traveling from here, are there?'

"Then one of them told me it's time to wake up and he stuck a knife to my throat." Bart shivered, pulling his collar back to reveal a crimson welt. "They said if I ratted on anybody, they'd kill me."

"That's horrible," Susan said.

Bart shuddered. "They sure made it seem realistic like. But I wanted to let you know what I heard, in case it helped."

"Thanks. That was a brave thing to do." Mark's lips curved but Susan could see the strain around his mouth and eyes.

Bart stood. "I guess, I'll be going now."

Zach rose as well. "Not so fast." He motioned the young man back to his seat. "We're talking about criminals who've hurt a lot of people. You can't just walk out of here. This room is probably watched, and somebody's going to report back that you were here, and then what?"

"He's right," Mark said. "They'll know you were here."

Bart's eyes widened. "How come they're watching you?"

Zach placed a hand on the youth's shoulder. "Because we're trying to catch them, son." He faced him squarely. "We need your help."

"Mine?" Bart's gaze sought Mark's.

"I'm afraid so. You're one of us now. When you entered that door, as far as they're concerned you crossed to our side," Mark said.

"Man. And here I thought I was leaving my hassles behind. Just kinda freeing my conscience before I left and all." He shook his head as if to clear it. "What's it you want me to do?"

"Just tell us what you know," Zach said.

"You mean like where I got the stuff and who sold it to me?"

"Exactly."

"Butttt.... They said they'd kill me."

"Yeah and we promise to protect you," Zach said.

"Man, who would've ever thought? What are you guys anyway, the CIA? How you gonna protect me?"

"All good questions." Zach pulled a badge from his pocket and flashed it in front of Bart.

"Is this for real?" Bart touched the badge.

"You betcha."

Bart heaved a sigh of apparent acceptance. "Well, I guess if anyone can protect me you guys can."

"Just remember," Mark said. "Zach is the one with intelligence operations. The rest of us are here like you, trying to do our part."

"'Cause your cousin's missing?"

"That's a big portion of it."

"The way I see it, if they had me, I'd want some help too. So I'll do what I can. What about her?" He threw Susan a suspicious look. "Why's she here?"

Susan smiled at Bart in an attempt to reassure him. "Don't worry, I won't turn you in. I had a brother your age dealing drugs. He was murdered. I want to stop the people responsible."

A flicker of sympathy crossed his face as he shifted in the chair but his youthful optimism quickly returned. "This is better than the movies. What's next?"

Zach said, "You tell us what you know. But this is real life with live bullets flying. It's nothing like the movies, where it's a sure thing that everybody gets up and walks home at the end."

"Yeah, I get the picture. I know the score even if I did mess up. Those guys who came to my room I never saw before that night. I bought the heroin from a Nigerian student...Mewo Abaya. He wasn't any big wheel or anything like that."

"Think carefully," Zach said. "Did you ever see anybody else with him? Someone's afraid you know something. Why else would they threaten you?"

Bart tried his best to remember everything. He endured Zach's cross-examination steadily. An hour later Zach threw his hands up in disgust. "Another dead end."

"Not necessarily," Mark said. "I say we head for Vienna."

"I don't know if that's such a good idea," Zach said. "The whole thing could be a set-up. They might have seen the kid with you earlier, OD'd him on purpose and fed the information back your way to suit themselves."

"That's a lot of presupposing, Zach." Mark turned to Susan. "You haven't said much. What do you think?"

"I don't know what else we can do here except follow the Nigerian. Zach surely has men here who can do that without us."

Zach rubbed his chin. "The problem is what to do with Bart. I'm afraid we're going to have to take him into protective custody until this blows over."

"What's that mean?" Bart said.

Zach said, "It means the government foots the bill to fly you back to Amsterdam and put you up in a safe house like some VIP."

Bart gave a thumbs up. "Okay by me."

Mark clasped his shoulders. "I'll make sure you don't regret this."

"Aw, it ain't nothing," he said, embarrassed.

Susan stood and stretched. "Now that that's settled, when do we leave? I can hardly wait to set my feet on Western soil again. Good food and hotel rooms with hot water."

Mark reached for the phone and dialed the airlines. He spoke briefly, then placed his hand over the mouthpiece. "They have a one P.M. flight tomorrow. How's that?"

"Fine by me. The sooner the better," Susan said, hoping Bart's tip would lead them to Benjamin. They simply had to find him before it was too late.

31

The flight to Vienna was uneventful. They arrived at the Hotel Jesuit in the late afternoon. Susan soaked in a tub of hot water scented with rose oil, feeling positively decadent and savoring every moment of it. The hotel lay on the outskirts of the city convenient to the airport. She had first stayed there some years back with a host of network journalists and TV crews bent on interviewing the Vaschenkos, the famous "Embassy Seven" who had rushed into the American Embassy in Moscow seeking asylum. When they finally reached the West, the small unpretentious hotel had been their first stop. Impressed by its affordability, Susan had continued infrequently to utilize its facility.

She stepped from the tub refreshed. Amazing how a few amenities could soothe body and soul, she mused, tying the sash on a robe of Mark's which she'd borrowed. When she'd left Amsterdam without claiming her Delsey, the suitcase had continued on to Houston. KLM had rerouted it to Amsterdam and Zach had since arranged to have it shipped to Vienna through diplomatic channels. Susan expected it that afternoon. As for her laptop, it was lost in transit and she hoped it would soon be located and forwarded to her as well.

She wandered over to the window, gazing across the way. Cheery red and pink geraniums spilled from the window boxes of a three-story building, sweeping lawns and manicured shrubs beneath. Susan drew a deep breath, drinking in the serene beauty that washed over her like a calming balm. The Austrians were fond of saying, that God was smiling when He made their country and she could see why.

A knock on the door brought the bellboy delivering her bag that Zach had promised to send. *"Lassen sie es dort, bitte,"* she said, handing the young man a tip. *"Fur sie, Danke vielmal."*

"Bitte schön. Auf wiedersehen, Fraulein." He bowed slightly and turned to leave, clicking the door shut behind him.

It was wonderful to have clothes again. Susan rummaged through the bag, looking for something nice to wear and drew out the traveling iron as well. She was tired of looking like a maid. She placed a towel on the bed and spread out her favorite, though much worn, royal blue shirtwaist and carried on with the rather difficult task of ironing it.

She slipped it over her head and twisted to see herself in the mirror. She'd lost more weight. The dress hung loosely around her waist and hips. There was nothing she could do about it now.

Susan turned her attention to Benjamin, wondering where they should begin searching. Certainly not in the obvious places where Sarb's men had no doubt already looked.

There was the possibility of enlisting her friend Monroe's help. As a reporter in Vienna, he might be able to offer some leads on where to start looking. She felt Monroe would be willing to help but she'd have to ask Mark first. Ever since she had phoned Monroe from Volar's office, Mark had teased her about having a string of men at her command.

As if her thoughts had connected them somehow, the telephone rang. It was Mark wanting to drive into the city to look for Benjamin and grab some dinner. A quarter of an hour later she met him in the downstairs lobby and they walked out to the parking lot. "Nice color for camouflage," she quipped as she slid inside the red Audi they had rented at the airport. Mark shrugged and started the car. He had spoken little since they left Bucharest, and her heart went out to him. It was easy to see he was worried sick.

She glanced across at him as he wended his way through traffic. Working so close with him, she'd grown to admire his obvious strengths. Brave, honest, caring. Overbearing too, she reminded herself. But how wonderful to have someone like him to lean on in times of trouble. The girl who ultimately earned that right would be lucky.

Of course she would have to be "head over heels" enough not to mind when on occasion he ordered her around like she was an idiot without a brain. Susan imagined some meek spirited beauty, excusing him, grateful for the honor of presenting him with the next generation of Ashleys.

Mark drove to the city's center, circling the inner ring until he found a parking place. As they walked along the busy main street, searching for any sign of Benjamin, he remained preoccupied with his private reflections. Susan felt at home as they strode past the opulent State Opera House, Max's Theater Café and cut across to the walk plaza, a large shopping area closed to automobiles. Young artists and students often made use of the wide paved streets and tonight was no exception. She and Mark passed folk singers playing guitars and a violinist in the midst of an impromptu concert. Once Susan jerked Mark to a halt long enough to watch a pantomime drama enacted on stilts.

The longer they stayed taking in the carefree antics of the young people, the more she found herself thinking about Benjamin and Kevin. The question of how they might be spending this same night was chilling. "You did say we were driving into the city for dinner. Did you have any particular place in mind?"

"No, you go ahead and choose. I doubt that I could eat much anyway."

Susan scanned a few of the nice restaurants at hand. With regret she passed them by. On the corner, a small vendor was selling European style burgers. She bought two, then dropped onto a bench and patted the seat beside her. She handed Mark one of the hard rolls with mustard and beef, noting they had worked their way to the edge of the plaza where the majestic spires of Saint Stephen's Cathedral rose before them. Maybe the view would inspire them.

The food gave Susan a second wind. She studied Mark. He hadn't touched his food and he still seemed so distant. "We ought to discuss strategy," she said.

After a few moments, she realized that he hadn't even registered her question. She shook his arm gently to get his attention. "You need some space to work things through on your own. I'll catch a taxi back to the hotel."

Mark said, "I'm sorry. I can't seem to get past this gut feeling that something's going down tonight with Benjamin. That if I don't find him soon, it just might be too late."

Susan stared at him in sympathy. "Maybe if we could come up with a strategy for searching for him....

"I just don't know where to begin."

"Let's start with the wine cellars. It seems like the kind of place people involved in drugs might hang out."

He gave a frustrated sigh. "That's probably as likely a place as any. We're near Maria Kellner's. How about we start there?"

They walked to a dark cobbled side street and ducked into a wine cellar carved out of rough-hewn stone. Mark brought out a couple of photos handing Susan one and they began working their way through the crowd, showing the pictures and asking if anyone had seen Benjamin. "His father's very ill," Mark explained, "and we need to get word to him as soon as possible." Susan worked the opposite side of the room, spinning a similar tale to aid their search. Despite the polite interested responses they garnered, they learned nothing. Still, they moved on to the next wine cellar, desperate to uncover any clue that would lead them to Benjamin.

32

Mark leaned back in his seat at one of the plaza's sidewalk cafés where he had agreed to meet Susan. After hitting most of the nearby wine cellars, they had separated for an hour to cover more ground searching for Benjamin before leaving the plaza. He scanned the crowd and took another sip of coffee.

As far back as he could remember, from Napoleon to the present age, rumor had it that Vienna, the golden city, where Strauss first introduced the waltz, was a hotbed of spies and intrigue. For the first time he considered what that meant in modern terms. Were the men Benjamin was dealing with here? Did their controllers work out of Vienna? So many questions and no answers that Mark could find.

And it was not Benjamin alone, that he was worried about. In the last week, Susan had been abducted, hit over the head, nearly blown to bits and in general harassed. He hoped that was behind them now. They were back in the West, the land of the free. Vienna might not be America but it was a civilized nation.

Mark glanced at his watch and rose to go look for Susan. She was fifteen minutes late. Perhaps he had mistaken the café where they were to meet and she was at one down the way. He wandered the length of the plaza, taking note of his surroundings. Any other time he would have enjoyed browsing in the elegant shops lining the plaza or stopping in at one of the *Konditoreis* for *Apfel Strudel* and coffee. No one made *Strudel* like the Austrians.

As he walked, he searched through the crowds and along the benches for Benjamin and Susan. He found her exiting a cafe, looking rather despondent which told him her search had been as fruitless as his.

She turned to meet his gaze, her expressive brown eyes mirroring his own concern. "Sorry. Not a clue. I know how worried you are."

She was always so polite and kind. Her words warmed him. She didn't even have to be here. She could have refused this off the record assignment. He squeezed her arm in acknowledgment of her support.

"Where to next?" she said.

"Let's try the train stations but how about a decent dinner first." He was suddenly aware of how ravenous he was after eating so little the last few days.

Susan opened her mouth as if to comment that they'd already eaten, then closed it quickly. "That's a good idea." It probably hadn't escaped her notice that earlier he had left his burger mostly untouched.

They set out across the plaza and wandered down a few faintly lit side streets. Mark pointed out a quiet place called the Ertl. "How about this?" he said, preferring it to the crowded spots they had passed.

At Susan's nod of agreement, they entered and *Herr* Ober seated them at a corner table draped in mauve-colored linen, a vase of pink and white carnations in the center.

"Mmm." Susan breathed in the scent, waving aside the menu the waiter offered. "I know what I want. *Wiener Schnitzel und Kartoffel Petersilie, bitte.*"

"But of course," Mark said, ordering the same. "It's almost the national dish." When the food arrived, he watched Susan squeeze a slice of lemon over the breaded veal cutlet fried to a golden brown and felt his mouth water. Midway through the meal he began to feel better, realizing hunger must have played a part in his earlier abstraction. "For common fare this sure is good," he said.

Susan's fork played with the parsley topping the potatoes. "I feel sorry for the poor calves they keep from sunlight so the veal will be white."

"That's easily resolved," Mark said, wishing the situation with Benjamin could be dealt with so readily.

She wrinkled her nose. "I know, don't eat it. But I like pink veal as well as white."

Mark regarded her, amused despite his worries. "I see you have your defense well thought out."

Susan grinned. They ordered coffee and *Marillenknödel* for dessert. "Mmmm." She leaned back, satisfied. "I'd forgotten how wonderful Austrian food is. Thank you, Mark. That was a marvelous treat."

"I enjoyed it too. This must be the first decent meal I've had since we left France." He swallowed the last of his coffee. "About our plans to search the railroad stations, I think taking taxis would be best."

"That's smart. It will save time and we needn't worry about directions and parking."

"Let's check out the *Stadt Park* as well. I can't think of a more advantageous place to hide than in the woods around there."

"And it would be a cinch for someone to get lost in the crowd around where the orchestra plays too," Susan said.

"Fine. I hope you saved room for another *Nachspeise*, because the only way we'll get into that area is to order one. Of course, there's no law that says we have to eat it." Mark paid Herr Ober and they rose, feeling somewhat refreshed, and more anxious than ever to continue their search for Benjamin.

33

Benjamin watched with a measure of despair as Mark and Susan wove their way toward the park exit. If there were only some way to approach them. But he didn't dare. Not with Frazier and Lauter's thugs spying from one side of the park and Sarb's at the other.

Benjamin squatted in the darkness. A large bush concealed him from curious passersby and prying eyes. He was scared. There was no one he could trust, not without running the risk of frightening consequences. Mark and Susan were under heavy surveillance. It was impossible to go to the police or embassy people because Lauter and Frazier had well-placed minions at every level.

Then there was the suspicious guy tailing him who looked like the all-American quarterback. Benjamin didn't know who he worked for.

Mark and Susan had reached the gate. It was time to go. Benjamin faded into the night, his footsteps wearily dogging his cousin's. His spine tingled; he felt the hairs on the back of his neck rise. All week, death seemed to clutch at his heels. He had never prayed so hard. He feared he'd never see his family or Danielle again. Only a miracle could save him. He was too young to die, please God— Wasn't he?

Thoughts of home and family overpowered him as he plodded along. He wondered if Kevin was alive and prayed with a deep sense of urgency that they would meet again this side of heaven. There was so much he longed to do and see. How he wished he had confided in Mark sooner. Maybe it wasn't too late. A moment, out of time, unseen, was all he needed. Until then, like a withering vine grappling for life, Benjamin clung to the hope that he could reach his cousin in time.

He heard footsteps following and quickened his pace. His heart thudded against his chest. A rough hand covered his mouth. He kicked backward at his assailant in a desperate attempt to free himself. Then with a surge of adrenaline, he twisted his body and bit into the hand over his mouth. If only he could scream. Terror stricken he saw Mark and Susan pause in a doorway, oblivious to the drama behind them.

His body thrashed into a bulky mass of unyielding flesh. *Clunk!* The pain was blinding. He felt himself crumple. He stretched out a hand toward his cousin rapidly disappearing ahead. His mind groped for the words—help—help. *Clunk!* A searing flame slammed against his skull. Gone were the stars twinkling overhead. Gone was the beautiful night— too beautiful for him to die. Benjamin collapsed in the darkness.

34

The burly man followed Benjamin, too intent on his prey to worry about the heavy thud of leather against concrete behind him, echoing his own steps. He glanced over his shoulder. If there was a problem, he'd take care of it after the kid. He adjusted his jacket collar against the cool night; his eyes riveted ahead, a cigarette dangled from the corner of his mouth.

It was no secret where the cousin and his girl were crashing. The two of them could be dealt with later. From the snatches of conversation he'd picked up, Karl knew they were searching for the boy. It wouldn't do them any good. Orders were orders. The kid was history.

He cursed softly, tossing the cigarette on the ground. He had a personal distaste for murder. The boss had tried to warn them away. But nothing had stopped them. Consequently, they had to die. He gripped the chunk of steel in his pocket and gained on Benjamin. The dark corner ahead was deserted. Karl's gaze swept the area. He grunted, satisfied with what he saw. Karl crept closer, negating the space between them. In one move he covered the boy's mouth. Karl raised the weapon from his pocket. The steel bar crashed against Benjamin's skull again and again.

35

Zach winced when Benjamin's crumpled body hit the pavement. The youth had put up a good fight against almost insurmountable odds. His assailant gave the body a final kick before turning away. From across the street one of Zach's men gave the okay signal, a soft imitation of a cat's meow. Without checking, Zach knew one would be calling an ambulance and the other continuing the chase.

With a heavy heart, Zach approached the body and bent over Benjamin, placing his hand over the pulse point in his throat. Zach breathed a sigh of relief at finding a faint pulse. He didn't know how he could have faced Mark with the news that he had stood by and watched his young cousin clubbed to death. Gingerly, he felt the back of Benjamin's skull to assess the damage. He cursed softly as he drew back a blood-smeared hand. Zach ripped the bottom half of his shirt. Hurriedly, he folded the cloth and wrapped it tightly around the gaping wound, praying desperately the ambulance would arrive before he was saddled with a corpse. It had gone against his every instinct to remain in the background while Benjamin was beaten. But he had no choice. Too many lives were at stake. Like a game of Russian roulette, he couldn't risk them all on one play or one man.

It seemed like an eternity before he heard the sound of a siren split the air. Suddenly people were everywhere. "*Achtung! Aufpassen!*" the medics called out as they approached the scene. The small gathering crowd moved back. When the police arrived, Zach identified Benjamin, and gave Mark as next of kin, supplying the necessary information to reach him. He described the incident without revealing the deeper significance behind the attack. When the police were finally satisfied, he hitched a ride with one of them back to his hotel.

He knew he had to phone Mark before he resumed the long night ahead of him, shadowing Karl. But how was he going to break this to him? His sole hope was that Benjamin would survive. In his room he flung off his tie and sat to call Mark. He was getting too old for this and missed his wife and children besides. What he needed was a nine to five desk job. Exhausted, he dropped back onto the bed and dialed Mark's room.

36

Francois had been following Karl the entire evening. When Benjamin collapsed, Francois kept to the shadows and behind Karl. When a black sedan picked up his quarry, a flick of a button brought Francois's car to him in less than thirty seconds. He slid into the passenger's seat and typed the sedan's license plate number into a computer concealed in the dashboard. Within seconds a map of the neighborhood appeared on the screen. A flashing icon wound along the map tracking Karl's route.

Francois gave his driver a grim smile. "We've got them, Harry. Let's go."

Francois knew Karl was one of Lauter's men. What he needed was evidence to connect the two beyond a reasonable doubt. Tonight might be his lucky evening. It had galled him to sit back and watch Ashley court Susan. He was sorry about Benjamin too. But Francois' job came first. And that Susan found hard to forgive. Americans wanted everything. They were spoiled and selfish. Love and devotion. The wife always first, the job second. It goes against man's nature, he thought bitterly, to give so much. Now, the French were civilized. They handled relationships with a certain savoir-faire that Susan called indifference. But there was nothing detached about his feelings for Susan. There never had been. If he could simply make her understand.

The icon stopped moving and Harry eased the car to a stop beneath an imposing tree, its over sweeping branches hiding the Citroen in the shadows. Francois entered the address into the computer and waited for the report. When it came he learned the house was deeded in Karl's chauffeur's name. Ten minutes later, Karl emerged from the house with a small black bag in hand. Harry waited until the sedan was a city block ahead before he started the car and followed.

While they drove, Francois called in an order to search the premises. "No warrant," he said emphatically, before he hung up the phone. Francois saw that they were nearing the outskirts of Vienna and had a hunch the airport would be their next stop. He rebooted the computer to check on departing flights.

"Find anything?" Harry said.

"*Oui*. He's on his way to Brussels. Vienna Air. Flight leaves in twenty-five minutes."

"You booked?"

Francois nodded. "Take care of things here. I want his driver questioned."

"At the station?" Harry said, his voice worried.

"What is it with you people? This is an intelligence operation."

"Sorry." Harry hesitated. "But this is Vienna, we're not in France."

"*Mon Vieux*, I want some answers. And I want them tonight. Whatever it takes. Do you understand?"

"*Oui*." Harry kept his eyes on the road straight ahead.

Francois phoned for a car to meet him in Brussels. He always got tense when he was close to cracking a case and his men knew it. They also knew he had a reputation for skating near the edge on legal issues. They should be used to it by now, he thought, disgruntled at Harry's reluctance to follow orders.

At the airport, he got out and turned to Harry. "Call me as soon as you learn something." Francois watched the sedan drop Karl and pull away from the curb. He frowned at Harry. "Don't lose him."

Francois bought a ticket at the inside counter and hurried to board the plane. He sat five rows behind Karl. For a year now he'd been on the trail of Nebut Corporation and Dower Consolidated's top two executives. At first he believed smuggling diamonds was their main racket. But he soon learned their investments and interests were much broader.

South African diamonds were easily smuggled into Europe with the help of Dower's branch office in Brussels. From there it was almost child's play to unload them in Amsterdam. How they had made the leap from industrial diamonds to genuine jewels worth a fortune, Francois hadn't discovered. But he did know it involved drug pushing, namely cocaine and heroin, and major theft.

He knew the Americans suspected a political plot, whining that major cities around the world were being bought out, as Dower and Nebut greased palms to elect the candidates of their choice. Francois was too conservative to buy into a scenario that smacked of paranoia. As far as he was concerned, it was a case of pure and simple greed.

When they landed in Brussels, Francois followed Karl off the plane, through the airport and outside. Francois' new driver George was parked at the curb, waiting behind a line of taxis.

Francois slid into the passenger seat beside George.

"Good evening," he said. "Our man just stepped into the taxi directly in front of us. Follow him."

It was a short ride. Francois recognized the place. It belonged to Peter Frazier, Nebut's European manager. Frazier was also Ewald Lauter's partner in crime. Sarb's Mercedes and Lauter's BMW were parked in the drive.

This was one meeting Francois did not want to miss. His driver parked a few doors down. Francois padded his way across the lawns, as unobtrusively as possible. He found a side bathroom window unlocked. It was a bit tough squeezing through but he managed.

Inside the house, the sound of muffled voices drew him down the hall. He did a double take and came close to cursing aloud when he saw Zach Towers lurking in a small anteroom. How had he got there? He had assumed the American agent was still in Vienna, holding Ashley's hand at the hospital. Evidently, he had notified him and continued on the trail.

Zach gave him a sardonic smile and placed a finger to his lips. He inclined his head toward the room next door. Raised voices carried clearly through the walls and a space along an adjoining door provided a clear picture of what was going forth.

The authoritative tones usually associated with Sarb were in abeyance. He pleaded in a whining tone, "I've done everything you asked. You promised me the Nairobi Diamond."

Francois had first become involved when the legendary missing South African Diamond Necklace was sighted in Paris. Unfortunately, the culprit escaped with the necklace. The subsequent investigation uncovered an international drug ring operating outside of Paris. French Intelligence joined with Interpol and the Americans for reasons of their own, were in on the chase, running neck and neck with the French to see who would crack the case first. That explained Zach's presence.

Sarb was whining again. "How else am I to get enough money to refurbish my museums?"

Lauter laughed and swore softly. "Be grateful for what you've got, you swine. It's finished."

Sarb sputtered. "But I've barely begun. There is a missing Botticelli to purchase. And a Leonardo da Vinci come to light and an almost unbelievable fresco by Raphael Sanzio." His voice was a mixture of desperate greed and awestruck glee.

"Get him out of here," Lauter said, "before I puke."

Frazier shrugged apologetically. "I am afraid my partner has not explained our position very well. Our profitable association with you has by its very nature outlived its usefulness. We are no longer in need of a place to launder funds."

"What about the deals I arranged? It's suicidal to drop me without warning. You need me."

"Need you? Look at yourself, you pompous overweight fool," Lauter sneered, striking him across the face.

Sarb clutched his reddening cheek. "You promised me a share in the diamonds. A bonus." His voice lost its bravado as Lauter moved nearer. He backed away in terror. "I'm overextended," he pleaded. "You have to help me!"

Francois winced at the sound of cracking bone as Sarb squealed in pain.

"Get out, while you're still alive," Lauter said.

"You'll be sorry for this. Both of you," Sarb spat out, his face purple with rage. His voice turned panicky. "Don't you come near me." Francois heard a groan, followed by a heavy thud and then silence.

"Get him out of here, Peter, or I'll kill him right here. I've had it with fools."

Francois and Zach exchanged a meaningful glance and headed for the door. The last thing they needed was to be caught listening. This time they drew the bolt back and exited through the back door. With a wave they separated and hastened in opposite directions. When he had almost reached the car, Francois felt the hairs on the back of his neck rise. Trusting his instinct, he began to turn but not fast enough. He felt a gun dig into his back.

"Good evening, sir. Been waiting for you. Put your hands up nice and easy."

Francois raised his hands and slowly spun around, stifling a gasp when he saw it was Karl. An image of Benjamin's crumpled body as Karl had struck him down flashed before Francois. He should have known with the man's track record he would be lurking about. Where, he wondered, was his chauffeur George? A quick glance about revealed no sign of him.

"Move it," Karl snarled, shoving him toward Frazier's house. He kept the gun trained on him as they walked back up the street.

Francois paused once to try and reason with the man but the gun digging into his ribs stopped him cold.

37

Peter Frazier adjusted his metallic glasses' frames and poured two glasses of brandy. He handed one to Lauter, restraining his anger as he stared into the swirling amber liquid.

Lauter broke the silence, punctuating each word with smug satisfaction. "That takes care of Sarb, doesn't it?"

Peter clenched his jaw in an effort to keep from snapping. "Did you have to antagonize him? It's not only senseless but risky at this point to complicate things anymore than they already are."

Lauter said, "He's lucky I didn't kill him tonight. It'll have to be done though. Soon, before he decides to talk."

"What's to stop him from going straight to the police?"

"He can't lay charges against us without incriminating himself. And he hasn't reached the stage yet where he's willing to do that."

"When I joined up with Nebut and Dower, you promised me no one would be hurt."

Lauter's expression turned ugly. "Don't be stupid. We passed that turn years ago and you were more than content to look the other way as long as I handled the details and your pristine white hands stayed clean. Well, get this. I'm through shielding you. It's time you pulled your own weight." He paused. "You're in knee deep, so don't try reneging on me."

Peter didn't reply. He forced himself to meet Lauter's cold gaze, shocked by the contempt scrawled across his face. His behavior had altered terribly. Or was it, Peter wondered, that Lauter no longer felt it necessary to hold his malevolent nature in check? Had the pettiness and meanness always been there, hidden beneath the surface? Peter remembered incidents he had written off as a mere quirk or aberration in his friend's nature. He was thankful now his sister had never married him. In death, at least, she was spared that.

In light of what he'd learned in the last year, Lauter's former discrepancies had taken on an entirely different hue. As his schemes grew increasingly wilder, Peter found it harder and harder to draw back. When he tried to dissolve their business ties, Lauter went ballistic, threatening to kill him.

He couldn't stop Lauter without incriminating himself. Peter realized now that Lauter took a certain macabre pleasure in keeping him off balance. He was like a runaway freight train, impossible, unstoppable, and Peter no longer knew where they were headed. From the beginning, both men possessed a natural aptitude for high finance and equally relished the thrill of a good challenge. These attributes had lured them on to conquer the industrial diamond market. Later, they diversified, converting their profits into real gems and smuggling them for resale.

Peter had balked at the drug deals and the political maneuvers Lauter kept dragging him into. Perhaps that was when he first began to see a different Lauter. But back then he couldn't have guessed at the make-up of the unfeeling monster, lurking behind the friendly-charismatic-businessman's facade. A picture that was rapidly crumbling before his eyes. Peter shivered, struck by the sudden realization that Lauter planned for Peter to be his ultimate dupe.

A scuffle beyond the door broke into Peter's reflections, causing him to raise his gaze.

Karl held a gun in one hand. With the other he shoved an indignant dark-haired man into the room. Karl gave Lauter a worried look. "I found him sneaking around outside."

Lauter started to speak, but Peter put up a hand to silence him. "I'll handle this." The man was becoming intolerable, Peter thought angrily. Allowing his thugs to run free in his home waving guns. What if his wife and two sons had been home instead of visiting her family?

An angry flush stole up Lauter's neck, staining his cheeks. "You forget Karl works for me."

"Nevertheless, this is my home and I will thank you to treat it as such." Peter studied the man. "Who are you?"

The man bowed slightly. "Francois Rodiet, at your service, *monsieur*, however unwillingly." He smoothed the wrinkles from his jacket and turned to Karl, disdainfully deflecting the point of the gun from himself downward. He addressed Peter. "I find it easier to speak without a gun in my face."

Peter nodded his acquiescence. "You live in the neighborhood?"

"Not at all. I was searching for house number sixteen when this man," he frowned at Karl, "detained me."

Peter drew a deep breath, once again struggling to hold his temper in check. "Karl, be so good as to explain why you found it necessary to detain this man at gunpoint?"

"He was snooping around outside listening."

Peter darted a quick warning glance at Karl. From the corner of his eye, he watched for Francois' reaction but the man's face remained bland and unreadable.

Peter unhappily resumed his questioning of Karl. "You caught him in the house?"

Karl shook his head. "No, at the end of the block but he was obviously coming from here."

Peter ran a hand across the back of his neck, massaging the stiff muscles. "And you, *monsieur*, were you in my home?"

Francois gave a longsuffering sigh. "Certainly not. Let me assure you I was merely searching for my friend's address, which is not easy in the dark." He handed Peter a slip of paper. "His name and number are there. A simple remedy would be to call and ask if I am expected."

Peter took the slip of paper. He couldn't afford to ignore the possibility that this man might have been inside the house and heard everything. But if he was innocent, the repercussions of any actions they might take against him, could cause a tremendous uproar. One they could ill afford.

Peter motioned to Karl. "Search him."

Karl handed Peter a set of identification which consisted of a driver's license, two credit cards, a Euro card, three checks and an airline ticket stub. These verified that the man was Francois Rodiet, a Parisian resident, who had caught a late night flight from Paris to Brussels.

"My apologies, *monsieur*," Peter said in an attempt to smooth things over. "My guests are from South Africa. Unfortunately, recent events there have left them uneasy and unnecessarily wary." He smiled offering his hand. "You'll find number sixteen is the house on the corner." He nodded to Karl to let the man out.

Peter sighed in relief, glad to see the last of their nocturnal visitor. He frowned. There had to be some way to distance himself from Lauter before the situation blew up in his face.

38

Ewald Lauter hung up the phone and scowled across the length of the Brussels' office. Sarb was a fool, just like Peter Frazier and the rest.

That didn't bother him. He expected it. To Ewald's mind, his brain had always run circles around most of his colleagues. Superimposing his will on others was an art he had developed to perfection. His Machiavellian schemes succeeded like clockwork, one after the other.

For the moment, he must exert himself to deal with Sarb. He picked up the phone again, smiling at the thought of Sarb dead. He drew a deep sigh of satisfaction, his hands clenching, itching to do the job himself.

Which reminded him, he must set Karl straight. The man couldn't just grab someone off the street, kill him and then drop him in a bathtub because they needed to intimidate the two Americans. His rashness would land them in jail. Soon he'd have to take care of Karl. But not yet.

For now he must concern himself with Sarb. He had chosen an exciting death for Sarb. The man had lived such a dull life, thinking solely of his museums and paintings. He should appreciate Lauter's generosity in letting him go out with a bang.

His man came on the line. "Send one of Nebut's jets to pick up Sarb at twenty-one hundred. Have a bomb on board and make sure there's nothing left of Sarb or the plane. I want Nebut to get full credit. No links to Dower." He hung up the phone and leaned back in his chair, satisfied.

Peter Frazier glanced across at Lauter as the Cessna dipped over the cacao fields. An icy finger of fear shot through Peter. In his mind's eye he saw the steel prison bars clanging shut behind him. How much time could he get for this? They'd never believe he was innocent, that it was all Lauter, not after the price fixing and diamond smuggling racket he'd created. For the first time in years he considered praying. But it was too late. He'd made his choices when he said goodbye to the middle-class family who raised him. Wearily, he removed his glasses and stared at the metallic frame. There must be a way to beat Lauter at his own game.

Ewald Lauter took in the thousands of acres of potential narcotics ripe for harvest. He knew where every jungle lab was hidden, ready to destruct in less than 20 minutes should a raid occur. It had taken his unique genius to manipulate the drug cartels to political advantage, while making Peter his unknowing dupe. As Lauter's stratagems marched forward the power he craved loomed evermore within his grasp.

39

Mark and Susan had searched the *Bahnhofs* and traipsed through yet another series of wine cellars flashing Benjamin's picture to no avail. Since their return to the hotel, Mark had been restless and worried, unable to think of sleep. He tried to stifle the premonition of trouble that had been gnawing at him the entire evening. When the phone rang, he leapt to answer it.

"Mark, it's Zach."

He looked at his watch. It lacked a half-hour until midnight. Something was wrong. "What's up?"

"There's no easy way to say this." Zach hesitated on the line. "Benjamin's been hurt."

Mark clenched the receiver. "Where is he?"

"Here in Vienna. At the *Haupt* hospital."

"How bad is it?" He said in an unsteady voice.

"It's serious. You'd better hurry in case he doesn't make it. Bring Susan with you. I'll call her."

Mark hung up the phone in a shattered daze of dread and anger, only to pick it back up and call for a taxi. An awful image of his cousin's body crushed, danced before his eyes even as he willed it back, forcing himself to resist such devastating conclusions.

He smashed his fist against the table in a punishing blow that did more damage to his hand than the furniture. But it relieved some of the tension building within. If Benjamin had only listened, turned to him, this wouldn't be happening.

Mark buttoned his shirt, his fingers fumbling in their haste. Why hadn't he? Mark tried to tell him. Wasn't Julie's death warning enough? What did it take to get through to his cousin these days?

Mark pulled on his shoes. What did they want from him anyway? Hadn't he been through enough? Why was it he always felt as if it were his fault...his fault...his fault?

He thought of what this would do to his parents and his aunt and uncle. His shoulders caved in and he buried his face in his hands. "God," he cried aloud, "please—don't let it happen again. Let Benjamin live."

He had to pull himself together. He picked up a light jacket and stepped into the hall, scanning the area warily. Zach had a hunch he and Susan were slated to be the next victims. Zach had warned him to be careful and keep Susan with him.

But why? The refrain slammed through Mark's head again and

again. What had they done, besides ask a few questions? They had no knowledge that might threaten others. It made no sense. Unless Benjamin had learned something damaging and they feared he had passed it on to them.

Mark felt so powerless. Who were they—these unknown criminals capable of destroying his family on a whim?

Susan stood in front of the elevator waiting. She put her arms around him without a word and he felt the rock-hard tightness in his chest dissolve a little. Her hair smelled of roses and he rubbed his chin against the silky strands. For a few seconds he clung to her, drawing comfort from her softness, her nearness.

The arrival of the elevator ended the moment. With a visible tremor Mark released Susan and stepped inside, desperately praying that Benjamin would still be alive when they reached him.

Susan grasped his hand and he gripped hers tightly in return. He clung to it on the long ride to the hospital, welcoming the numbness and detachment that encased him. It hurt too much to feel. Susan walked beside him through the vast corridors until the nurse at ICU forced her to remain behind.

Mark drew a shuddering breath. Every semblance of his calm facade shattered at the sight of Benjamin lying unconscious in an intensive care unit. Benjamin's skin was a deathly pallor. The tube stuck down his throat was hooked to a breathing machine. A portable IV unit attached to his arm stood by the bed. His head and right shoulder were bandaged.

Heedless of the watching nurse, Mark walked up to the bed and looked into his cousin's still face. He touched Benjamin's hand, so cold and lifeless. It took all Mark's control to keep from shaking Benjamin awake.

"Why didn't you listen?" he asked the pale figure on the bed. "How many times did I warn you?" The nurse tried to stop him but he shrugged her off, his self-control shattered.

Benjamin," he said, in a half sob. "I'm so sorry. Please, don't die. God, don't take him from us. Please. Please." Mark dropped to his knees beside the bed and silently wept.

After a few moments the nurse gently led him outside the cubicle.

"Sir, the doctor will join you in the visiting area."

Mark wiped his tears as he followed the nurse. His emotions spent, blessed numbness reigned again instead. When he entered the small sitting room Susan's anxious gaze met his. He had no idea how to answer the questions he could see coming. Mark shook his head. "I don't know." His voice broke. "He looks bad."

She gave him an understanding nod and motioned him to a chair.

Susan placed a cup of black coffee in his hands and ordered him to drink it. He obeyed. It was easier to drift in a mindless haze and let her take charge. Soon they would know.

They both stood when the doctor entered.

"*Herr* Ashley?"

Mark nodded. "Doctor...is he going to...?"

The doctor raised a hand to halt Mark's question. "It is too soon to tell. But we are doing everything possible for your cousin." He signaled Mark and Susan to sit and took a seat facing them. He introduced himself and then in precise English began to explain Benjamin's condition.

"*Gott sei dank*, he lives. The single reason is the second blow to his head was deflected to his shoulder. Those broken bones with time and rest should heal nicely."

The doctor's none too subtle efforts to reassure them left Mark's fertile imagination leaping to the direst conclusions. But what about his head? a voice inside Mark cried, just as Susan asked the question.

"The head is another matter." The doctor sighed. "I'm sorry. The strike to the back of the head damaged the brain stem."

"What's that?" Mark said sharply.

"The body's breathing center located at the base of the skull, among other things. The respirator will keep his airways open and support his body's breathing mechanism." He glanced down at the chart in his hand. "The steroids should reduce the swelling."

Mark swallowed. His throat felt raw. He forced himself to speak. "I'm not sure I understand. His head is bandaged. Is there an open wound?"

"*Ah so*, *entshuldigen*. Perhaps, I must start at the beginning. Your cousin arrived here with a gaping head wound. With an MRI, we checked for internal bleeding and swelling, severe repression of the respiratory system, broken spinal column, vertebrae or bones." The doctor paused to see if they were following.

At their nod he continued. "The only broken bones were those in the shoulder. He could have sustained a broken neck or been paralyzed. The bad news is we found evidence of serious internal bleeding and swelling in the brain."

Susan's hand slipped into Mark's. "He'll be all right?"

"Again, it is too soon to know. But yes, there is reason to hope."

Mark shook the doctor's hand gratefully. "Thank you, *Herr* Doctor, for taking the time to speak with us. Is there anything we can do?"

The doctor shrugged. "Wait. Pray. We do what we can." He rose wearily. "It is time I see to my other patients. The staff will provide you blankets and pillows. *Herr* Ashley, you may visit the patient but there must be no disturbances, *bitte*."

Mark attempted a smile of appreciation, but his thoughts were so grim, his face felt frozen. "When do you expect him to wake up?" The doctor's gaze was compassionate. "You must not be too optimistic. If the bleeding continues to slow, he might regain consciousness in three days, a week or it might even be as long as a month. One never knows with a head injury."

Mark saw days, weeks stretching before him—imprisoning him in this purgatory of uncertainty. A cloud of despair engulfed him.

The doctor laid a palm on his shoulder. "If the breathing center begins to function on its own over the next forty-eight hours, it will increase his chances."

As the doctor left, Mark sank back into his chair, encouraged by the doctor's last words. Almost any information was better than the dreadful possibilities his mind conjured up. He looked at Susan. She had stood by him through so much, but this was his vigil, not hers. In the interim, as much as he hated to ask it of her, he needed her to be in St. Abient this evening.

He picked up her hand. "How can I thank you for everything? You've been wonderful." He squeezed her fingers between his own. "But I need you in Saint Abient at the anniversary celebration tonight."

"Of course, how could I have forgotten?" Susan withdrew her hand.

"Look, I know it's a lot to ask after everything you've been through but I spoke with Zach earlier and he's arranged for a couple of his agents to accompany you. They won't be obvious but they'll be there in case of trouble. I couldn't let you go back there without some protection."

"Don't worry. I'm glad to do whatever it takes. Besides I did come to cover this event. It would seem odd if one of us wasn't there."

"Precisely. I knew you'd understand." He looked anxiously toward Benjamin's room in ICU.

She paused to wipe away a stray tear. "I'll be thinking of you and Benjamin. Praying for a miracle."

He nodded bleakly. "Thanks. We both owe you big time."

She rose. "Call me if there's any change."

"Yeah, I'll do that. Better get going. You have a long day ahead." He handed her the Audi keys. "Take the car and park at the airport. I doubt I'll need transport but if I do Zach can give me a lift to pick it up."

"Okay." They said quick goodbyes and Susan turned and walked swiftly away.

Mark dropped back in his chair, feeling alone and bereft. He settled in for a long wait and found himself rehashing events. So much had occurred, he felt as if he had lived a lifetime in the last few weeks. What could he have done differently? Why were so many things beyond his control?

Over the next two days there was little change. Mark spent most of his time at Benjamin's bedside. His emotions swung the gamut. His initial terror and rage gave way to a shell-shocked acceptance that changed to a hopeful despondency at best, regarding Benjamin's precarious hold on life. Slowly, he began to pray for Benjamin. He knew nowhere else to turn but to God. At the forty-seventh hour, against reason, Mark found himself believing and praying a miracle would take place.

None did. Benjamin took a turn for the worse. His body rebelled, rejecting the help of the hospital, its machines and staff. Anger fueled Mark's chilled heart to life. How could God do this to him again? He thought of his parents' untold suffering since Julie's death. How would he ever tell his aunt and uncle that their son had died?

Mark wanted to howl against a fate that dared to mock him a second time. The rage inside him boiled. Hate for the punks who had done this consumed him. Mark paced in front of the bed, ranting and raving at his naive cousin. He didn't want to endure the anguish threatening to overtake him. He was wary of this love that spilled over and crushed, taking everything and leaving nothing but guilt and emptiness.

"Dear God," he cried. "Why aren't you listening? Can't you hear my prayers?" He knelt beside the bed and clutched Benjamin's hand. "We had some good years," he told his motionless cousin. "It won't be so bad. Julie will be there waiting for you." Mark broke down and sobbed. "If there was anything I could do, you know I'd do it." He touched his cousin's face. "You were right all along. I can see it now. I've been a selfish fool. Why didn't I listen...help when you needed it?"

Scenes from the past flooded through his mind: a ten-year-old Benjamin in a sweaty baseball jersey, grinning broadly as he clutched a trophy to his chest; a laughing boy playing chase with his dog in the park; a proud high school senior, class valedictorian; a determined young man, running to make the college track team; and finally, a zealous Benjamin, leaving for France.

Mark swallowed, admitting the truth. The single out he had offered his cousin was escape and Benjamin, too honorable to turn his back on a friend in trouble, had chosen to fight alone.

Mark looked up to heaven and asked God to forgive him for the hurtful vengeance that had been his god since Julie's death. The weapons of hate he'd carried in his heart had harmed no one but himself, alienating those he loved. Mark was not unfamiliar with the Christian faith. As a youth he attended church and Sunday school. It was in his supposed maturity and race for success that he had lost sight of God and His requirements.

He rose from the floor where he knelt and opened the top drawer of the bedside table. He gripped the Gideon Bible that lay within and opened it to the Psalms. Verses jumped out at him. "In my distress I cried unto the Lord and He heard me...I will lift up mine eyes unto the hills, from whence cometh my help. My help cometh from the Lord who made heaven and earth. He will not suffer thy foot to be moved: He that keepeth thee will not slumber." Mark read psalm after psalm, the words a healing balm, echoing the cry of his soul. He fell asleep there in the chair meditating on the words.

Later that evening, he awoke to find Benjamin in crisis. He watched the doctors do everything in their power to save Benjamin's life. With fear pumping through his veins, Mark found the strength to let go.

His cousin lay so lifeless—his inert form unmoving. On the third morning Mark prayed sincerely for God's will to be done. Now all he could do was wait, trust that if Benjamin didn't make it, he would be better off out of this life. Surprised, Mark realized that he did believe in a hereafter, a judgement, a heaven and a hell. He was glad. It gave a new meaning to life and death.

As the tiny seeds of faith and trust began to sprout in his heart, Mark felt the last vestiges of bitterness slip away, bitterness caused by a guilt which had paralyzed his spiritual growth for years. There was the guilt he felt at Julie's death, and added to it, a lifetime of shortcomings and failures. Mark's newfound peace helped him face the possibility of Benjamin's death with an equanimity he would have never believed possible.

40

Susan's flight from Vienna proved uneventful. From Paris she traveled by train to Saint Abient and caught a taxi to the center. Her brain was so numb, she didn't even try to understand the driver's French when he told her how much the fare was, but leaned forward and read the meter, counting out the francs to pay him. She stepped from the taxi, despondent and worried. The driver set her Delsey, laptop and tote bag on the graveled drive. Her laptop had arrived at the hotel just before she left.

The afternoon sun crept through the trees throwing kaleidoscope-like patterns of light across the sweeping lawn. Susan stared at the crumbling chateau with a sense of loss, her thoughts still in Vienna. She visualized Benjamin, back in that hospital, struggling for his life, and saw Mark, weary, his face drawn and anxious.

She gazed across the grassy expanse to the veranda and allowed the memories full play. Just a week ago Benjamin and Danielle, their faces shining with the exuberance of youth, had stood there holding hands. And Kevin too, she mustn't forget Kevin. Had he been nearby, laughing and groaning as usual with the other students about the Center's workload which none of them really minded?

It was too much to take in. Benjamin hurt. Kevin still missing. Mark alone with his grief and fears. If Benjamin died, who would be there for Mark? After everything she'd been through with her dad's and Matthew's deaths, her sympathy was fully aroused.

Never had it been so difficult to leave her worries in God's hands and to trust in His care and promises. She prayed that Mark would accept God's strength and that God would spare Benjamin's life.

She didn't know how long she stood beside her suitcase on the graveled drive, before Danielle Sarb burst through the door. The French girl ran forward, waving in excitement. "*Mademoiselle*, you have found him?" she said, her lower lip trembling as she waited for an answer.

"Yes, we've found him." Susan gave her a brief hug.

Danielle threw her arms around her. "I knew it."

Susan almost winced at the joyful relief enlivening Danielle's face. She braced herself to tell her the rest, dreading the dramatic reaction sure to follow. "He's critically ill, Danielle. He may not live."

A myriad of expressions crossed the girl's face, shock, disbelief, defiance. "*Non, non*! It's not true. I will never believe it." Trembling she clutched Susan's arm. "Where is he? Tell me. I must to see him."

Susan tried to calm her. "Hush, he's not here. He's in Vienna."

"*Mon Dieu.*" She turned her face heavenward in fervent appeal.

Susan felt drained. What little energy she had abruptly evaporated. What she wanted was a few minutes alone to rest and prepare for the ordeal of the long evening ahead. She began the walk up the steps.

"Wait." Danielle grabbed her hand. "You haven't told me what happened."

Susan briefly recounted Benjamin's attack but refused to divulge the name and address of the hospital. Too many people wanted to kill Benjamin. Susan had no intention of advertising his whereabouts. She fished the room key from her purse and trudged up the stairs. Tonight she would attend the celebration dinner, though it was the last thing she wanted to do. Her appearance at least, should come as a surprise. Aside from Danielle and the two incognito agents posing somewhere in the background, no one had witnessed her arrival.

The sparse little room was unchanged. With a tired groan Susan kicked off her shoes and dropped onto the bed. She had not slept the night before. She closed her eyes meaning to take a brief rest but fell at once into a troubled sleep.

A short time later she scrambled upright, wondering what had awakened her. It was then she heard the knocking at the door. She swung her legs over the edge of the bed. "Who is it?" she almost snapped.

"*Madame* Retell," the housekeeper answered.

"Oh, bother," Susan mumbled. "Danielle must have told her I'm here." She held her head groggily and squinted at the clock on the bedside table. "*Entre*," she called.

The housekeeper entered and peered about the room suspiciously.

"You wanted something?" Susan said, repulsed.

Madame Retell reluctantly handed her a folded note.

Susan scanned the contents.

It is imperative that I see you at once. Please to follow *Madame* to my apartment. I am waiting.

John Volar

Susan smoothed the wrinkles from her dress and slipped on shoes. She dug in her purse for a brush and ran it through her hair. A glance in the mirror confirmed her suspicions that she was not looking her best.

The housekeeper led the way through the long hall and up the winding staircase to Volar's apartment. This was an unexpected opportunity. Curious to know what had prompted him to send for her, Susan planned to make the most of the visit inside his inner sanctum.

Madame Retell pointed to the doorbell and left her. When Volar answered Susan stepped into the front hall, somewhat taken aback to see him dressed in casual khaki slacks and a T-shirt. She followed him into a rectangular living room, rather contemporary compared to the rest of the chateau. The outer wall, mostly glass, overlooked his private garden.

Volar motioned Susan to an overstuffed tan leather couch and sat in a matching chair opposite it. He appeared to have aged since they last met. But maybe it was the clothes. It was the first time she had seen him in anything but a suit.

He shifted nervously in the chair, his hands digging into the soft leather. "What have you learned about Benjamin?"

Susan hesitated, uncertain what to say. The men who were after Benjamin might be using Volar to find out his whereabouts so they could finish him off.

His drawn face reflected concern. "Surely, you don't doubt my regard for Benjamin? He was one of our students."

It didn't seem possible to Susan that the Reverend was a crook. She massaged her aching head. "Benjamin has everything to live for. Why can't they just leave him alone?"

Stricken, Volar said, "If I'd realized sooner what was happening none of this would have occurred."

"I'm afraid I don't understand. A mere week ago you were set on purging the Center of the likes of Benjamin Ashley. Is it any wonder I'm confused about your sincerity?"

"*Mademoiselle*, please. If you knew how much I've anguished over those two boys since their disappearance. All I'm asking is whether Benjamin and Kevin are alive?"

She lowered her eyes. "No one's heard from Kevin since he left."

He cleared his throat. "And Benjamin?"

"He's in ICU—hanging on by a thread. For all we know, Kevin may have been murdered days ago."

The Reverend leaned forward. "Thank you for that." He picked up the telephone receiver, pressed the button for an in-house line and spoke briefly in rapid French. He hung up and turned to Susan. "Dominic Trudeau and your friend, Gayle Reagan, are on their way up."

Susan's eyes widened.

He pulled a letter from inside a book on the table. "While we are waiting please to read this."

Susan took the letter wondering, what it was about? She read it slowly, trying to determine its authenticity. "How do I know this note isn't a fake?"

He pushed the phone toward her. "Call him."

Susan had no intention of falling for a phony number set-up. She dialed the operator and asked to be put through to the residence of Interaid's Director, Henry Galmiche, a man she knew she could trust.

When he answered, Susan found it reassuring to hear her former boss' voice on the line. "Henry, this is Susan. Did you write me?"

Henry quickly dispensed with the amenities and went straight to the point. "Listen carefully, Susan, John Volar is to be believed, every word."

"How can you be sure?"

"I haven't time to explain. Can you trust me?"

Susan didn't know how to respond. Of course she trusted Henry. He was above reproach. But suppose Volar had deceived him as well. "It's so hard," she finally said. "And there are so many factors involved."

"If it will help, I've been cooperating with Interpol from the beginning on this particular case. Three Interaid volunteers have been implicated. I expect they will be charged and rightly so." He paused. "I am as sure of John Volar as I am of you."

Susan bit her lip. "Okay. I'll listen to what he has to say and consider everything you said." It was the best she could offer.

She turned from the phone as Dom and Gayle entered the apartment.

The three stared at one another with Volar looking on. Then Gayle ran forward and embraced her. "I've been so worried. When we didn't find you in Heidelberg, Dom told me what's been happening. Then we heard you were arrested, and the news got worse and worse."

Susan squeezed Gayle's hand. "I'm fine but Benjamin's not and I doubt Kevin is either."

The tension in the room sharpened at her words. Gayle opened her mouth to speak but Dom shook his head. Gayle moved next to Dom, a determined light in her eyes. "Susan, there's no need to put everyone on the defensive. Try to listen with an open mind."

Volar and Dom exchanged glances that appeared to settle it between themselves that Dom would start. He leaned against the fireplace mantle, staring out at the garden, as if to gather his thoughts.

Against her will, Susan sensed an innate honesty and concern in the perceptive gaze that met hers. She braced herself against his charm and whatever else she must face.

Dom began, "For some time, Volar and I have been suspicious of our 'benevolent partners,' Sarb and Beauchamp's dealings. When the Reverend confided his fears that the books were laundered. Volar's assistant, LeFont, naturally became suspect.

"Benjamin and Kevin disappeared next, and our anxiety escalated triplefold. Too many seemingly unconnected events concerning the Center were occurring too close together for us not to be alarmed.

"As a result, we set in motion a series of private investigations, including one on the two students' disappearance, Afterwards, I received a number of threatening letters, as did Volar, who was able to trace the letters to Beauchamp. We were then able to confirm that Beauchamp was working for Sarb, mostly collecting and paying debts and having LeFont channel money through the Center for their drug racket."

"If this is true," Susan said, "why haven't they been arrested?"

"We've been working with French intelligence and Interpol who are after what you Americans call the 'big game.' Now that we are onto Sarb and his cronies, the authorities are following them in hopes of capturing their ringleaders."

Susan frowned. "Meanwhile, the rest of us remain in danger. Criminals like Sarb should be behind bars, not left free to attack innocent people. Benjamin and Kevin didn't ask to be involved."

Volar spoke up. "In a way they did. Benjamin became involved when he chose to help Kevin avoid the consequences of his drug habit."

Gayle explained. "We found out that they were also trying to uncover evidence which would negate Sarb's hold on Nick and Danielle's inheritance, and expose his involvement in the drug trade."

Susan realized Kevin and Benjamin probably never imagined their quest would lead to international terrorists. None of them had.

Apparently misunderstanding her silence, Dom said with a trace of impatience, "After what you have been through, I can understand your feelings, but putting Sarb behind bars wouldn't stop the attacks. It would merely serve to convince his yet unknown employer that you knew enough to put him there as well. You would be in more danger than ever, but worse, the authorities wouldn't have a clue as to the culprit's identity. Now they do."

Susan digested his words and nodded, unhappily agreeing with his conjecture. "What do you suggest we do next?"

Volar gave her an encouraging smile. "If you have decided to trust us, you can fill us in on what has happened since you left. It might help us piece things together better."

"Though the authorities appreciate our help, they are not exactly eager to confide their findings," Dom said.

"That's an understatement," Gayle said. "It's like pulling teeth getting anything from them."

Susan felt as if a weight had rolled off her shoulders. She wasn't here alone. She was with friends. If nothing else, there was safety in numbers, she thought, filling them in on the last five days of her life.

They stared at her incredulously. "It's unbelievable," Gayle said. "To think you were arrested, kidnapped, mugged, people dying." She shivered. "How did you stand it?"

Susan turned to Volar. "I hope you realize by now I'm not the floozie I was pretending to be. Mark and I believed if we feigned a romantic attachment to one another, people would be less guarded around us. And it did seem to work at first."

"If I was offensive, I apologize," Volar said. "I should have guessed, but at the time, I had just discovered the books were being doctored. I was petrified, until I finally applied to Dom for help and he in turn went to the authorities."

Susan said, "I just wish I knew how Benjamin and Mark are doing. I don't suppose it's safe to call him from here?"

Volar shook his head regretfully. "You might as well know. *Madame* Retell has been working hand and glove with LeFont. She's his aunt."

Susan wasn't in the least surprised; the woman had always given her the creeps. She thought back to the threatening note she received her first night there. Several times Susan had spotted the housekeeper outside her door but assumed *Madame* was cleaning. Now she wondered.

Suddenly, it dawned on her, "It must have been *Madame* who put the fake cocaine in my purse. Of all the despicable...."

Volar interrupted. "I'm so sorry but it was the maid who found the cocaine in Benjamin's drawer. She worked for Reese Gigot who ordered her at Sarb's insistence to plant the cocaine. It was done in an effort to get rid of you and Mark. Fortunately, the maid was greedy. She placed powered sugar in your purse instead. She was caught selling the cocaine and confessed everything."

Susan said, "What about that newspaper reporter with the *US Daily*? Is he involved in this?

Dom said, "Do you by any chance mean Bob Chandler?"

"Yes, he was a friend of both Mark and Pastor Volar."

Volar said, "As you Americans are fond of saying, he's clean as a whistle. Bob truly wanted to assist Mark in the matter of his cousin but the last two years working together we'd developed a fast friendship. So he was also concerned how *Monsieur* Ashley's investigation would affect me and the Center."

Once Susan had taken in their explanations, it was agreed that the four of them would attend the celebration that night, continuing to act as if they knew nothing.

Dom said, "They obviously think you know more than you do, so be careful to stay in a group. I'll escort you to and from your room."

Susan was more than willing to comply. She had no intention of being next on their hit list.

41

Susan dressed for the anniversary celebration with more anticipation than she had felt earlier. The knowledge that Volar, Dom, Gayle and her former Interaid boss were in collusion to help capture their assailants gave her new hope. They had handed the authorities concrete evidence that Sarb and Beauchamp, as well as LeFont and his aunt were guilty. Events appeared to be rapidly coming to a close. If Benjamin recovered and his roommate Kevin was found, she would be grateful for the rest of her life.

Susan twirled in front of the mirror, admiring the new pink dress. She hadn't packed anything so nice but Gayle had bought it in Paris, a gift she insisted Susan accept. She was touched and knew Gayle couldn't afford to give away gifts like this, even at bargain prices.

The soft spring color matched her rising optimism. She fastened a long strand of pearls around her neck and a pearl earring in each ear. When Dom tapped on her door, she was ready to go.

Gayle was fortunate in her choice of beau, Susan thought, gazing at the elegant man beside her. Dom was attractive and wealthy, but more important, he was kind and considerate. Susan's suspicions of him and Volar had completely receded and were fast being replaced by a growing admiration as they became better acquainted.

The banquet hall, in reality the Center's dining room, was decorated lavishly for the occasion. When they entered people were already mingling. The atmosphere sparkled with good will as the predominantly Christian crowd greeted one another.

As they joined Gayle and Nick, Susan regarded Danielle's brother with interest. She had heard so much about the deposed aristocrat-turned-bartender. From his conspiratorial wink she knew Gayle had apprised him of their earlier conversation.

"He's on our side," Gayle had confided during the afternoon's discussion. And well he should be, Susan thought, considering that Sarb stole his inheritance.

The evening seemed to drag. Beauchamp and LeFont were there but Sarb's absence was conspicuous. Dom crossed to the podium and presented Volar with a brass plaque in honor of the Center's twentieth anniversary. Volar accepted with patent humility and thanked those whose benevolence and dedication had helped make Saint Abient the success it had become, naming several of the Center's largest contributors. Volar went on to say that the Center's phenomenal growth and acceptance in Europe had encouraged him to venture into other areas where Christian influences were much needed. He was in the midst of presenting a strong case for a new Center in South America, modeled after the French one, when his speech was interrupted.

Volar's face paled as he gazed down at the note he had been handed and then up at the officials standing near the door. "Ladies and gentlemen, it is with a great deal of regret that I interrupt this presentation to acquaint you with the sad news I have just received."

A murmur of expectancy filled the hall. "*Monsieur* Sarb, a great benefactor to this Center, died this evening in a plane explosion."

A gasp went around the room. Several of the ladies shrieked. Beauchamp and LeFont whitened, causing Susan to think they were as surprised as everyone else.

Volar called the group back to order. "Once again I must ask for your cooperation as part of an official investigation is carried out here this evening."

A few rose as if to leave but were stopped as Volar introduced the Inspector who had come to stand at his side. The inspector addressed the crowd. "Please do not be alarmed. Despite this disagreeable interruption, I encourage you to enjoy the remainder of the evening. My assistant will be circulating the room, arranging brief questioning sessions. We would appreciate your utmost cooperation. Thank you."

A few of the men rumbled out complaints. "What makes us suspects?" one man called out from the back of the room.

"We weren't there," another said.

Others enjoined in agitated agreement.

The inspector raised a hand to get their attention. "You have been most generous, I understand, in supporting Pastor Volar and his Herculean efforts to assist others. For this, I commend you heartily on behalf of France. Our intention is not to cast aspersions on the character of those assembled here this evening. However, we are in hopes that one of you may inadvertently shed some light on this terrible tragedy."

The inspector stepped down from the podium and joined his assistant for a moment before settling at an out-of-the-way corner table. Plain-clothes detectives were stationed at the front exits from the building. The inspector's savoir-faire in a sticky situation was admirable. Volar was the first to be questioned and Dom soon followed. Susan wondered when her turn would come.

LeFont and Beauchamp were having what appeared to be a terse conversation, if their expressions were any indication. She edged her way toward them but they separated before she could reach them.

"Hello." The masculine voice behind Susan startled her.

She whirled around. "Nick, you frightened me."

His dark, somber gaze met hers. "There's really no need for eavesdropping. The room is wired."

"Oh," was all she could think to say to this enigmatic man.

A flicker of amusement crossed his face and for a fleeting moment he looked more like his sister Danielle. Nick tucked her arm into his. "A stroll, mademoiselle?"

"Sure." This was the first chance she'd had to speak at any length with Nick, and Susan was curious. "You don't seem overly upset at your uncle's death?"

His gaze hardened. "It might make his duplicity regarding my father's will harder to prove."

"The authorities already know what you suspect, don't they?"

"Yes, but there is a great difference between knowing and proving it as fact."

They had wandered over to the veranda door and both pulled up short at the sound of angry voices. Nick motioned for her to keep still. He crept forward, staying close to the shadows. Susan followed a few steps behind. The scene she met rounding the corner halted Susan in her tracks.

LeFont held Beauchamp by the throat with one arm, he lifted the other, smashing his fist into Beauchamp's right jaw.

Enraged, Beauchamp sneered, "Why you trumped up secretary!" With an unbelievable show of strength for one so small he hurled LeFont to the ground and began to choke him. With a curse, he said, "Where is the ledger?"

LeFont floundered helplessly struggling for breath.

"This is your last chance," Beauchamp growled, cutting off his air passages.

LeFont struggled but Beauchamp's hands tightened until the secretary's face turned blue. LeFont tried to speak but couldn't and Beauchamp's grip eased slightly.

Finally, LeFont gasped, "All right."

"Where?" Beauchamp demanded.

LeFont gulped down air like a hungry man, his voice short and raspy. "Upstairs in my room. There's a safe."

Beauchamp let go with one hand to pull a gun out of his pocket. "Go on. I'm listening."

"It's hidden. I'll— take you to it."

"Get up. And don't try anything, if you know what's good for you."

LeFont stumbled to his feet and moved toward the door. Beauchamp pushed the gun into his gut. "Not that way, the front, where no one can see us."

Susan whispered to Nick, crouched beside her. "Shouldn't we do something?"

"We'd better get back inside." Nick gestured into the distance as from seemingly nowhere, the *gendarmerie* swarmed out of the bushes, surrounding LeFont and Beauchamp. The two men were handcuffed and led away.

Susan felt shaken as she and Nick slipped inside. He placed a cool fruit drink in her hand and said, "Thankfully, we're nearing the end of this travesty."

Gayle came up beside her. "Is everything okay?"

Susan managed a weak smile. "Beauchamp and LeFont were pretty gruesome out there. However, the good news is that they've been arrested."

"Amen to that," Gayle sympathized, patting her shoulder. "It'll soon be over."

"Not soon enough for me."

"I know you're worried sick about Mark and his cousin."

Susan nodded. "I may slip into town later tonight and call them."

"Why not use your cell phone?"

"It's too risky. Someone could pick up on our frequency." She decided after a few minutes of small talk that now was a good time to turn the spotlight from herself to Gayle. Almost anything that would help her forget her problems for a while was a windfall. "What's going on between you and Dom?"

"Lately, I'm thinking he's pretty fantastic."

"And to think, back in Paris, you insisted this was a platonic relationship." Susan smiled and hugged her. "I'm happy for you."

"Hold on— I'm still not sure where this is headed."

"Yeah, life is often that way." For now though, Susan thought, they'd all be wise to concentrate on survival.

42

Mark rubbed his eyes awake and shifted in the hard chair wondering where he was until he saw his sleeping cousin. Then it came to him— the hope, frustration and pain. He felt as if he had been camping out in Benjamin's room for days. In an effort to release the tension in his shoulders, he stood with a groan, stretching his arms over his head. His glance swept the glaring, white walls of the cell-like cubicle, halting in surprise at the woman who stood in the doorway.

Susan stepped inside. "I had to come. How is he?"

Mark folded her in a crushing hug. "Benjamin knew me. He opened his eyes."

"When?"

"Shortly before dawn."

"Did he speak?"

"No, but his breathing has stabilized and the swelling is down." He pointed toward the bed. "He's off the machine."

Her face brightened. "I'm so glad. I was so afraid."

"Me, too." He swallowed past the lump in his throat. "How were the anniversary celebrations?"

"Subdued." She sank into a chair. "You heard about Sarb?"

He nodded. "Zach called."

"LeFont and Beauchamp are under arrest but refusing to talk."

"After what those thugs have done to Benjamin, they deserve to rot in prison."

"They're afraid. Whoever got to Sarb assured their silence."

He frowned. "Any more theories on who's behind it?"

"According to Interpol, Ewald Lauter and Peter Frazier, the diamond magnates. But they need more evidence to make it stick."

"We'll get it, one way or another." He mentally shifted gears, going over the possible suspects. Since Benjamin's near brush with death, Mark felt as if he had lost track of the outside world. Lately, his rocketing emotions almost overwhelmed him. Take his anger of a moment ago, all it took was the thought of Benjamin at their mercy, helpless, and he wanted to do them bodily harm. On the other hand, observing his cousin's steady progress, Mark's heart beat with thanksgiving.

He didn't speak of his newfound faith. His feelings were too recent to put into words. But if he ever did, Susan would understand. It was she who had encouraged him to lay his bitterness aside and take a leap of faith. He marveled that she had managed to trust God through the experience of her brother Matthew's death.

Though journalists were traditionally a tough breed, Susan was far from hard-boiled, certainly feminine and kind and pleasant to be around. He would see to it she got a bonus when this was over.

Benjamin continued to improve that day. By late afternoon he was conscious and able to speak. He struggled to sit up.

Susan and Mark exchanged excited glances and rushed to his assistance.

"Relax, you're not going anywhere for a while," Mark said soothingly, while Susan fluffed the pillows behind Benjamin.

He gave them a weak smile. "How long have I been here?"

"Long enough to get better." Mark's voice was gruff with emotion. His cousin's face was still pale but the deathly pallor was gone. Relief surged through Mark. Benjamin was going to make it. "How do you feel?"

"All right...Kev...in?" Benjamin strained to ask.

"We don't know anything yet. I was hoping you did." Mark frowned, wondering if he should call the nurse. He sat on the side of the bed. "Who did this to you?"

"Karl...one of Ewald Lauter's men." Benjamin shuddered. "You've got to get Kevin out before it's too late."

"Where is he?"

"I don't know...exactly. A plastics factory around Munich. Lauter uses it as a front...for his drug labs."

"Is that why they tried to kill you because you found out?" Susan said.

Benjamin's face whitened. "They held me with Kevin for a while but I escaped." He dropped back against the pillow exhausted.

Mark and Susan swapped worried looks. "He needs a nurse," she said, pressing the call button.

"No." Benjamin grasped Mark's hand. "It's...." He gasped for breath. "Too dangerous...to wait. They'll kill Kevin."

Mark squeezed his hand. "I'll find him. You worry about getting well."

Benjamin clung to his fingers. "Promise?"

"Promise," he said gruffly, sending up a silent prayer that he could keep his word.

Benjamin's grip loosened and he closed his eyes just as the nurse bustled into the room. She took in the patient's condition with a glower, setting to work. "How long has he been conscious?"

"About five minutes," Mark said.

She spared a moment from her ministrations to reprimand them. "I suppose you were questioning the boy?"

Susan looked away and Mark realized he should have notified a doctor or nurse as soon as Benjamin awakened. But apparently no harm was done.

Still, the nurse clucked in disapproval, as she checked Benjamin's vital signs. "He's better than he was," she said. "No thanks to your troubling him at a time like this." After having her say, she ordered them out. "The doctor is on his way."

A few minutes later in the visitors' room down the hall, Susan handed Mark a cup of coffee. "You seem different."

"I feel ten years older."

"No. It's not that."

His brow arched at her persistence. "It hasn't been an easy week."

"You're not pacing."

He shrugged. "I'm too tired."

"Maybe that's why you seem so—not sedate." She paused. "Serene—calm. It's not like you at all."

A frown creased his brow. Was that how she saw him? Restless? Perhaps it was true; he tended to be aggressive. His job demanded that. Susan, as an employee, naturally, saw him at his most autocratic. The situations they had faced in the last week would have tried his mother's saintly patience. "Have I been that difficult?" he said.

"Honestly?"

"I'm asking."

"Then, I have to say yes."

Mark choked on a laugh. "No one could accuse you of flattering the boss."

Her lips twitched and then her expression turned serious. "I think you've been wonderful."

He felt his face stretch into an unfamiliar grin, pleased by the sincerity he read in her gaze, but not fully understanding. "Despite my bad temper?" he risked asking. He had pulled rank more than once, reminding her who was in charge.

"Because of it, I think. You were admittedly short on patience but you were also worried and frightened for Benjamin."

"Go on," he said, intrigued at her defense of his behavior.

"It's simple, really. The same aggression that made you difficult to work with, drove you to do everything in your power to unearth Benjamin and his assailants."

"You paint a pretty picture."

She smiled. "Is it so far off?"

"Remember when you asked me to have faith?"

Her eyes widened. "Yes."

"Benjamin was dying. I knew it but I didn't know what to do or where to turn. So I prayed." He gave a short laugh. "I'd quit praying years ago. My prayers fell like empty petitions. He got worse and worse." Mark didn't know why he was telling her this. The words seemed to spill out of him. "Finally in desperation, I began to read the Psalms."

She squeezed his hand.

"Something happened. I'm not sure how or what, but I cried out and God heard me." He could hear the awe-struck tone in his voice, but that was how he felt, amazed that the God who created the heavens and earth had reached down and touched him.

"Then Benjamin got better," she said.

Mark shook his head. "No. He didn't. I realized there was no other way. With or without Benjamin, I needed the Lord in my life to make it worthwhile. I was through with bitterness and vengeance and the unhappiness they caused."

They shared a moment of comfortable silence. He realized how little he knew about her past life. Back in France, he had been shocked to learn she once dabbled in drugs. Now, for the first time, he wondered why? From what he knew of her, it seemed out of character, an aberration.

"What was it like for you when Matthew died?" he said.

She stood and moved to the window, her back to him. "I've struggled with guilt since Matthew's first encounter with drugs. And when he died." Her shoulders drooped. "You can imagine. My mother will probably never stop blaming me."

He followed her to the window and placed a comforting arm about her shoulder. "Is that why you joined Interaid, to make amends?"

"I tried so hard to make things right for Matthew. But I was so young—I didn't know how to deal with his problems." She drew a deep breath. "He left a letter. The police gave it to me with a small package of his belongings. I couldn't bring myself to open the box. But I read the letter." Her voice quivered, "What an indictment against my Christianity, my life."

He wanted to wipe the concern from her face. Mark pulled her to him and held her tight. They shared a tragic bond. "It doesn't matter. You did everything you could. He's gone." He drew back. "None of us are perfect—we were victims, too."

Her eyelids fluttered, veiling her eyes. "You're right, it was senseless to beat myself over the head."

Strange, he thought, how guilt had been the catalyst that set in motion the very events that forced them to confront their strengths and weaknesses. In the process, they had grown. Nowadays, Susan radiated a confidence and self-assurance that went a long way toward overcoming the insecurities and class-consciousness she tried to hide.

He turned and paced across the small area, giving himself space to think. Had he changed? Could others see the peace he felt within? Susan had seen it.

He looked up when the door swung open, interrupting his thoughts. "*Guten tag, Herr* Ashley, *Fraulein*," the doctor greeted them. "Your cousin's recovery *ist erstanulich.*"

Mark's heart lifted. "He's out of danger?"

"Entirely," the doctor assured them, a big smile pasted on his face. "His vital signs have improved dramatically."

"That's fantastic news," Susan said.

Incredibly relieved, Mark dropped into the nearest chair. "It's unbelievable his condition could change so rapidly."

"Such cases are not unprecedented," the doctor explained. "Especially with head injuries. Your cousin has improved remarkably but he is far from well."

"When can he go home?" Mark said.

"A week or two. One is afraid to say. We will see." The doctor rose and shook their hands before leaving.

Thoughtfully, Mark watched him walk away. He turned to Susan. "I need you to stay with Benjamin."

"You're going to Munich—to get Kevin."

"I promised."

"You'd go regardless."

He didn't bother to deny it. He may have sworn off revenge but he still believed in justice and protecting the innocent.

"If something happened, how could I defend him?" she said, anxious. "I'm willing, but I'm a woman, Mark. How can you expect me to hold off Lauter's men after everything they've done?"

She had hit on the one weak link in his plan. He hated placing her in danger. "There's no one else I trust to see this through." He took her hand. "It's asking a lot but Zach will provide backup for us both. Two special agents are already here undercover. I'll introduce you."

"If anything happens?"

He pressed her hand. "We'll know you did everything you could. That you reduced the odds of disaster considerably. And that God is in control...not me...and not you." He brushed a stray strand of hair from her face. "No matter what happens."

She hugged him. "I'll keep that in mind."

43

There was a catch in her throat as she watched Mark walk out the door. Once the doctor had Benjamin transferred from intensive care to special security, Mark made immediate arrangements to meet Zach in Munich. She hated to miss what she hoped would be remembered as the final *coup de grace* for Ewald Lauter and Peter Frazier.

"Miss Pardue, is everything okay?" Alan stuck his head around the door and Tom pushed him inside from behind. They wore blue surgical scrubs and big grins. Most of the hospital staff believed the two undercover agents were visiting interns from America, participating in an international exchange program.

Susan pointed toward the bed where Benjamin slept. "We're fine. I imagine he's out for the night."

Tom proceeded to give the room a thorough inspection, while Alan checked the connecting bath. They locked and examined the windows and returned with a thumbs up sign. "All's clear," Tom said. Susan noticed he seemed to give most of the orders. "Do you have the Beretta nearby?" he said.

She reached inside her skirt pocket. "Right here."

"Good. Remember how to use it?"

She had never fired a gun. She wasn't sure she had the courage to actually pull the trigger, but imagined if the situation was life threatening, she'd try her best to protect either herself or Benjamin.

Tom pointed to the gun. "It's a nine-millimeter automatic. You've got six shots which means you've got to be fast." He removed the weapon from her hand and replaced it with a similar model. "This one's unloaded. Let's give it a trial run. Pretend Lauter's man Karl just burst through here and he's after the kid. What do you do?"

Susan eased the pistol from her denim pocket and aimed it at the door. She slid the safety catch back in one easy movement, satisfied her coordination was going to be okay.

Tom shook his head in surprise. "Well, I'll be...."

Alan whistled. "You're a natural, lady."

She grimaced at their playful encouragement. "In the case of a real threat, I'd have to shoot."

Alan turned serious. "You'd have no choice."

Susan exchanged weapons with Tom. She didn't feel nearly so

confident, replacing the loaded gun in her pocket, though she thanked them for the lessons as they left. Just where they'd hide themselves she didn't know. But they'd promised to stay close.

She settled onto the cot that had been moved in for her to sleep on and slipped the gun under her pillow. It gave her an eerie feeling knowing it was there. After she turned out the lights, an overactive imagination played havoc with her taut nerves, causing her to spend much of the night straining to hear threatening sounds in the mostly quiet corridors beyond.

At dawn she awoke more tired than rested. She tried going back to sleep but worry for Mark kept her awake. Had he arrived in Munich yet? She wondered who would lead the raid? Interpol? The German police? What part would the US and France be expected to play?

And the most frightening question of all would plague her until she saw Mark safe again. Would anyone be hurt? Her head ached. And still more questions pushed at her brain. She finally dozed off praying but her dreams were as troubled as her thoughts.

When she awoke bright sunlight pierced the glass panes, its rays throwing crosscut patterns across the room. The traffic in the streets below roared through despite the closed window. From his bed Benjamin stared at the wall, a despondent frown on his face. Before she climbed from the bed, she offered up a quick prayer of thanksgiving that Lauter's men had not come.

Susan washed and dressed in the small connecting bath, thinking with longing of the shower back at the hotel. It might be days before she could leave the hospital. That possibility made her appreciate the dirt-proof denim skirt and wrinkle-resistant cotton top she had bought on her way back from the airport to the hospital and was now wearing.

She stepped back into the small alcove, taking in Benjamin's condition in a glance. "How's the patient this morning?"

He gave her a twisted grin. "Hi. Wondered when you'd wake up."

She began folding the blankets she had used during the night. "I didn't sleep too well. But you were out like a log."

"Yeah, I guess I got caught up. Matter of fact, I feel good enough to leave now." He placed one leg experimentally over the edge of the bed.

Susan threw him an incredulous look. "Wait a min...."

He inched his body forward. "I know what you're thinking but my head doesn't hurt."

At that moment, a redheaded, middle-aged nurse entered and exclaimed in a strong Irish brogue, "Sure and next thing you'll be swearing you're one of the wee people and no sick boy at all." An expression of disapproval on her face, she settled Benjamin back against the pillows and pointed to the IV unit attached to his arm. "And where do you suppose you'd be going with that?"

Before he could answer, she stuck a thermometer into his mouth and turned to Susan. "And what were you thinking, miss?" The woman shook her head. "Letting a patient carry on so. The call button's there for a reason. Next time, be sure and use it."

Susan didn't mind the upbraiding so great was her relief that the nurse arrived in time to keep Benjamin from harming himself. The woman reminded Susan of a few Irish teachers she had known in her youth. Quick to flare up, their anger usually dissipated just as swiftly into a sunny smile.

The nurse gave her head another shake, this one not near as ferocious as the first. "And you supposed to be taking care of the young man."

Susan flashed her a grateful smile. "You came just in the nick of time. I didn't know what to do." Some of the sternness eased from the nurse's face and Susan wondered how she came to be in Vienna. She half-suspected the woman was yet another special agent provided by the embassy.

The door opened and an orderly backed into the room rolling a stretcher. He handed the nurse a written order and she fixed Benjamin with a smug smile. "Young man, the only place you're going is for more tests."

Despite his insistence that he was okay and didn't need any more tests, Benjamin was carefully maneuvered onto the stretcher and wheeled out of the room. Reluctant to let her charge leave her sight, Susan followed alongside until a pair of double doors shut in her face. She stared at the red and white placard in disgust. *Kein Eintritt* was painted in large bold letters.

She looked in both directions down the long corridor but there wasn't a sign of Alan and Tom. Some undercover agents. Why weren't they with Benjamin now? She told herself there was no reason to worry but her anxiety grew. Her nerves were causing her to imagine problems where none existed. So much had happened and the danger was far from over and she suspected it never would be so long as Ewald Lauter ran free. Her every instinct warned that it was Lauter and not Peter Frazier who was the real threat.

She felt an urgency to burst through the closed doors and make sure Benjamin was okay. Instead she forced herself to review the events of the last week. Could there be a vital clue she had missed? The orderly...had she seen him before? Where...in the hospital? An elusive memory tugged at the back of her mind. Her head pounded from thinking. Suddenly it came to her...the *Stadt* Park...she and Mark had passed him when they had gone for a walk. Was it a coincidence? Dear Lord, she suddenly realized, that was the night Benjamin was attacked. What if...?

She didn't pause to think. She ran through the swinging doors. The room was empty. Susan rushed out the other side and down the hall, praying. A hand grabbed her from behind, covering her mouth as she tried to scream. She bit down as hard as she could.

A gun pressed into her side. "Try that again and you're dead." He hustled her down the hall and into a service elevator.

When the doors snapped, she wrenched her arm free from the big, hulking man. "What have you done with Benjamin?" She glared at him, quaking inside with the realization that any moment he might pull the trigger. She was tempted to reach for the gun in her pocket and shoot first; she couldn't; he was her single link to Benjamin.

He pulled her roughly against his chest and held her in an arm lock. "Think you can treat old Lundy any way, do you?" He slapped her face and grabbed her hair, bringing her eyes close to his. "Time you learned a lesson, girl." Repulsive lips slammed against her mouth, bruising and biting her flesh. Fright gave power to her trembling limbs. She fought his hold with what strength she could muster. He snickered and the pungent smell of garlic wurst and rotten teeth caused her to gag in disgust. She felt the bile rise in her stomach.

The elevator doors slid open and she jerked forward, but before she could escape or reach for the Beretta in her pocket, his gun dug into her side. He kept her close and she didn't dare move away. Outside in the parking lot, she knew it might be her last chance to escape. But the possibility that this man might lead her to Benjamin kept her from going for the Beretta.

He shoved her into the back of a white Mercedes delivery van. The engine started and she stumbled and fell as the vehicle drove out of the lot. She looked around desperately for Benjamin.

"Why is she here?" A menacing arm wrenched her off the floor and onto the seat.

"She was going to sound the alarm," Lundy said in a whining tone, cringing before the fury in the man's cold face. "What was I supposed to do, Karl, let her scream?"

Susan could feel the anger of the man beside her. Her stomach lurched as she took in her assailant's complete turn about. The brute she'd fought off in the elevator had wilted into a sniveling coward.

Karl released her, and grasped his friend by the shirt, and shook him. "You fool. She's one more person to worry with." He twisted Lundy's arm behind his back and then threw him against the seat. "The boss won't like this at all." He pointed to Susan. "Get rid of her. Now."

She swallowed and felt the space around her shrink to nothing. Lundy lifted the lid of the long, wooden bench where a moment before he had sat. "You don't mean...Benjamin can't be in there?" She recoiled in horror.

Lundy snickered and grabbed her arm. "Time to join your boyfriend, lady."

Karl lit a cigarette and motioned impatiently. "Get her in."

Susan tried to evade the clammy hands that wrapped around her waist. She glimpsed Benjamin's still figure and gasped. Was he dead? Panic raced through her veins. The box was like a coffin. She kicked out, flailing her arms and legs in a desperate effort to free herself. He heaved her inside on top of Benjamin. Was he alive? She sank her teeth into Lundy's hand for the second time that day with a desperation that caused him to swear loudly. She reached for her gun and he wrenched it from her grasp, tossing it aside, out of her reach.

Karl bent over the box. His face cold and hard, he held a syringe in his hand. Susan screamed and Lundy's rough hand covered her mouth again. The needle seemed to loom overhead, coming closer and closer. She watched it move slowly toward her. There was nothing she could do. She squirmed, trying to avoid it, pressing back against Benjamin's still body. Horror overwhelmed her. Her arm brushed the hypodermic. She gasped in terror as the point pierced her skin. Darkness swirled around her. Warm and grey it flew to meet her. Cold and evil it preyed upon her. She felt herself falling into a black abyss.

44

Mark picked up his bag, made his way to the plane exit and down the metal steps. A strong wind ruffled his hair, its chill penetrating the light jacket he wore. Ominous dark clouds scudded overhead in the grey sky, and prickles of rain hit his face as he rushed across the pavement to the terminal. He shivered. Germany was always like this when the sun disappeared behind the clouds. It meant snow in the mountains and cold, wet showers below in the valley. He moved swiftly through customs. The Munich airport was small and easy to negotiate.

He spotted Zach, pausing mid-step when he saw Francois beside him. He greeted Zach, then gave Francois a curt nod. "I should have guessed there would be a crowd."

"Everyone from Interpol to the German police are involved." Zach groaned. "We'll be lucky if the whole thing doesn't blow up in our faces."

Francois shook his head in amusement. "You Americans are too used to being the Lone Ranger."

Zach grimaced. "Fat chance we'd have of that here." He led them outside and across to a navy-blue BMW.

Mark climbed into the back, leaving the front seat to the agents. Fleetingly he wondered what it was about the French agent that never set right with him? Now though was not the time for speculation. Too much was at stake.

As Zach drove them toward the highway north of the city, Mark stared out at the torrent of rain. "Any luck locating the place?" he said.

"We traced one Lauter Enterprise midway between Munich and Salzburg to the town of Rattenberg, west of Highway seventeen," Zach said. "The man was pretty sure of himself, using his own name for an undercover drug lab."

After what he'd been through in the last week, Mark thought he could believe anything. "Have you uncovered any proof yet?"

Zach said, "People here don't much like his setup. Lauter's men have been running drugs and high-stakes gambling scams all over town."

"Somehow it doesn't fit," Mark said, slowly. "The man has covered his tracks amazingly well until now on every other front."

"Yeah, well, Lauter doesn't run operations here," Zach said. "Francois can fill you in."

The Frenchman turned toward the back seat. "His partner Frazier is the weak link. Lauter forced him into the drug racket. Frazier is frightened for his life. So much so that he gave evidence against Lauter and confessed to stock market manipulation and diamond smuggling. However, he swears Lauter blackmailed him into the rest."

"Which," Zach continued, "mostly included overseeing the plastics plant in Rattenberg. The deal is Frazier was too terrified to set foot in the place, said Lauter was trying to set him up and get rid of him. So he managed the plant by telephone and the operation began to fall apart."

Mark shifted in his seat. It was all becoming uncomfortably clear. "I gather as long as the drug shipments went out on time and arrived at their destinations Lauter never knew."

"That's it in a nut shell," Zach said.

"Except," Francois added, "Frazier swears Lauter's been maneuvering for political clout to further his diamond and drug empire."

Zach jumped in. "That fits in with the trail we've been following since the US versus Dower and Nebut case last year." His gaze met Mark's for a moment in the rearview mirror. "Frazier supplied us a list of the drug cartel leaders Lauter paid to buy votes for his candidates in twenty-six countries."

Francois said, "Certainly he was clever enough to start with places like Sudan and Afghanistan and South Africa that were already rife with tension."

Zach said, "Be that as it may, he's been systematically accomplishing his goals."

"I suppose," Mark said, "that's where the Arab and the former PLO factions fit in."

Francois nodded. "In some ways, they were his most valuable compatriots. They worked untiringly, among the poor spreading a militant Islam that Lauter helped fund."

Zach sighed. "The poor suckers never knew their leader was just another greedy charlatan who had joined Lauter's ranks. According to Peter Frazier the man's over the edge."

"More likely," Francois interrupted, "Frazier's in shock after catching a glimpse of the real Ewald Lauter."

Mark tried to digest the data but it was so reprehensible it hardly seemed plausible. Still he didn't doubt its validity for a moment. "How do we nail Lauter?" he said.

Zach answered. "Tomorrow. He's scheduled to meet Frazier so we can catch him red-handed with the goods."

Mark leaned back with a sense of growing reprieve. Then it hit him. "Have you heard anything about Kevin?"

"Sorry," Zach said. "Not even a sniff of his whereabouts has surfaced."

"But...."

"Look, it's been a while since Benjamin was there. A lot could have happened."

Mark winced at the apology in Zach's voice. The thought made him ill but he forced himself to ask, "You think he's dead?"

It was Francois who answered. "One step at a time, *monsieur.* Tomorrow evening we will have Lauter and his men. Soon the truth will out."

And with that Mark had to be content to wait. At least Benjamin and Susan were in safe hands, he thought, as the car turned off the highway toward Rattenberg.

At the hotel Mark settled in, not too surprised to find that Dom, Reverend Volar and Nick were there cooperating with the authorities as well. His old friend, Bob Chandler, came to mind and he was suddenly anxious as to where he fit into the scheme of things. Was he among the innocent? Or had he gone the way of the secretary LeFont, and the backers Beauchamp and Sarb, sacrificing everything honorable and worthwhile for their greed? He questioned Zach and was glad to learn that Bob was clean. He'd just been sitting on the fence between two friends, trying to help both. Dom said they had told Susan back at St. Abient but with Beauchamp's and LeFont's arrests fresh on her mind, she must have forgotten to tell him.

Once this was over, Lauter's defense attorneys would probably claim the fault lay in his madness, and Frazier's would plead that he had not willingly cooperated with the drug cartel. Yet on the shoulders of these two men, abetted by the greed and evil of others, rested the foundation of all their troubles.

45

Susan stirred in the darkness and felt the onslaught of a blinding headache. She reached for the bedside light and found nothing but air. Where was she? One hand supported her head, while the other groped for a clue. Cold concrete met her fumbling fingers. In one rushing swoop their abduction came back to her and she began to shake. She had no idea how long she had been unconscious.

"Benjamin," she whispered. When there was no answer, she screamed his name, the shrill hysterical note in her voice frightening.

She half-scooted and half-dragged herself around the edges of the chamber, fighting the rising panic. There must be a way out. If only everything wasn't pitch black. Icy despair squeezed at her chest but she pushed herself forward, continuing until she reached a door. Frantically, Susan twisted the metal knob to the left and to the right. When it refused to yield, she pounded on the door, using her fists. "Let me out! Let me out!" she yelled, her words echoing.

Dizzy and weak, she slumped to the floor. The door was locked. Discouragement set in with the torpid, relentlessness of quicksand. It was unreasonable to have expected it to open but she had.

The disasters of the last week loomed menacing before her. She reminded herself that she had survived. No matter how appalling her present circumstances, the possibility of rescue remained. She wouldn't allow Lauter to defeat her. A slow anger began to burn within, strengthening her resolve. But first, she had to find Benjamin.

Susan stepped off the length of the wall encountering no windows, guessing the chamber was about eleven foot square. She continued, feeling her way down the wall until she stumbled across a lump on the floor. Her heartbeat accelerated as she dropped to her knees. The face was warm and the pulse steady. Gingerly, she traced the bones along the jaw and forehead. It felt like Benjamin. Please, let it be him. "Benjamin, is that you?" she whispered.

He moaned. "Susan?"

Filled with relief so intense that for a moment she couldn't speak, she hugged him and sent up a silent prayer of thanks.

He groaned. "Where are we?"

"I don't know. Can you sit up?" He struggled to a sitting position and she helped him lean against the wall. "We've got to find a way to get out of here. Try to remember. Could this be the Munich factory you told us about? Anything familiar?"

"Yeah, sure, the cold concrete floor and darkness bring back memories, but we could be anywhere."

The door swung open and light flooded the room, revealing a sandy-haired man standing in the doorway. "Who are you? What are you doing here?" he demanded.

Instinctively Susan and Benjamin moved closer together. She eased her hand into her skirt pocket and realized she didn't have the gun anymore. "Just let us go and there won't be any trouble."

The man held up a transmitter. "One flick of the button and the place will be crawling with security."

Susan slid the army knife from her pocket and sprang at the man as Benjamin tackled him from the side. "Drop it or I'll use this."

Steely, grey eyes behind wirerimmed glasses met hers. He threw the device to the floor with a clatter, then twisted the knife from her grip and sent it flying as well. He pulled a pistol from his coat pocket. "Stand back, over there, both of you." As they obeyed, he said, "It's time the three of us had a little talk. Now, what are you doing here?"

Susan and Benjamin looked at each other, wondering what kind of game he was playing. Or could it be possible that this man didn't know anything about their kidnaping and the drugs Lauter and Frazier were running? But no, he had a gun and he didn't look like a security guard. He must be involved somehow. "Who are you?" she said.

"Nice try, but according to this gun, I'm the one asking the questions and I'm still waiting for an answer."

Benjamin said, "We don't know why we're here. This big dude kidnapped us and brought us."

The man paled. "How do I know you're telling the truth?"

Susan said, "Two men called Lundy and Karl forced us from the hospital in Vienna at gunpoint. We don't even know where we are."

He cursed. "You're at Lauter Enterprise, a plastics factory outside Munich. We're going to have to hide you both for now. Interpol's set up a sting here tonight to bust Lauter."

Benjamin said, "Wait, we've still got to find out if Kevin's here. This has to be the place they held us before."

How could she have forgotten Kevin? If they tried to find him now, they might never get away. But to go on without him was unthinkable. Lord, we need your help here.

The feeling was growing that she had seen this man before. In Amsterdam. The man who dropped the package. The stranger she kept running into. "Just who are you?"

"The name's Peter Frazier."

"That tears it. He's Lauter's partner."

Frazier eyed them warily. "I don't know how you're involved with Lauter but my association with him is past tense."

Susan said, "Then why were you following me in Paris and Amsterdam?"

He let out a long sigh. "Look, I did a lot of things back then that I regret. Lauter set me up to pick up some hot diamonds. It was the first time I'd ever done anything like that. Okay, so I dropped the package and along you come. I had to tail you in the beginning just to find out if you knew anything but that was it just those few days."

Susan shook her head. "I never opened that package and didn't know there were any diamonds. Except you did walk out of a jewelry store so I assumed you had bought something. Is that what this is about?"

"Right now," he said, "this is about a bust that's about to take place. You two better get out of here before it's too late. Come on, move and don't make a sound because Lauter is not in the least adverse to killing."

Susan's head spun with all that had happened. She said to Benjamin, "He was surprised to find us here. He might be telling the truth."

"It's just an act. Ask him where Kevin is."

Frazier said, "I keep telling you, I never heard of this Kevin."

"Liar. Where is he?"

"Look," Frazier said, "we've all got to get out of here fast."

"If you want us to go, then tell us the truth," Susan said.

"I've leveled with you," he said, shifting uncomfortably.

If Zach's suspicions were right, Frazier was guilty of stock market manipulation, drugs and more. She decided to start with the more. "What about the diamond smuggling?"

"I bought the jewels free and clear. Ewald took care of the rest." His eyes narrowed as he studied her. "I told you, my partner set me up for that packet you found that I dropped in Amsterdam."

"But you knew what Lauter was doing."

"It was only money." Frazier shrugged as if to say it was of no importance. "I never planned to hurt anyone."

"You helped Lauter and others suffered. People were killed."

"I'm not denying that I've done wrong, but I gave the authorities evidence against Ewald and helped set up tonight's sting. Ewald should be here any minute and if he sees you two, it will ruin everything." His words rang with a sincerity that was hard to refute.

Susan believed him. If she was wrong, she would face that later.

"Don't listen to him," Benjamin said. "They're crooks."

"If Frazier is telling the truth, Mark and Zach will be in on the sting, too. We can't chance messing things up and their getting hurt."

Benjamin raised his hands in disgust and leaped toward the door. "I'm going to look for Kevin. If he's here, I'll find him," he yelled, slamming the door behind him.

"Wait." Susan turned to follow. But before she knew what was happening, Frazier grabbed her from behind and held her back.

"I'm not going to hurt you," he said, keeping a viselike hold on her. "Once you've seen reason I'll let go."

She rubbed her arm. "Why did you do that? I said I believed you."

"So, you did. But I wasn't sure how far." Frazier glanced at his watch. "Ewald may already be here. It's too dangerous for you on your own out there." He urged her out the door. "Follow me and keep quiet."

Susan trailed behind Frazier, her heart pounding. Had she made a mistake in trusting him? What if she were walking into a trap?

Frazier stopped and Susan slammed into his back. His hand covered her mouth, a warning to keep silent. "Ewald Lauter," he mouthed.

The room was like a chapel. Candelabra cast flickering shadows against the wall. Frazier put a finger to his lips.

Ewald Lauter appeared so evil and sinister, that she was too terrified to do anything, but stand there and gape. He held a black cat, his long, effeminate hands stroking the fur in a way that set her nerves on edge. She shuddered and moved back but not so far away she couldn't see.

Ewald Lauter had entered the building early. He needed time to himself before his meeting with Peter Frazier. His plans were so near fruition and he couldn't help gloating over his successes. He picked up one of the black cats he kept around the factory. The power was within his grasp. His drug and diamond empire encompassed so much of his life's work that it had become a mirror extension of himself. Like the Internet, it ran fast and sleek, its vast neutrons shooting out networks that, though undetectable, consolidated his wealth. He would never feel helpless again.

Lauter squeezed the cat in his arms. For so long he had kept up the facade of the generous philanthropist, while consumed with a rage that had been lit in his youth. A rage that began, when one evening his drunk father had blinded his mother. Ewald vowed then that once he reached maturity, he would never be powerless again.

Though he was merely eight years old, he'd known what to do. He'd stretched the wire across the stairway late one evening after his drunk father had gone to bed. He sat in a corner of the upstairs hall and waited through the long night, watching to be sure. The next morning his dad stumbled over the first step and fell headlong down the stairs. He died with a broken neck. Ewald calmly untied the wire and went back to bed. Justice had been executed.

He'd thought his rage finished then. But the unfairness of Diane's death, the sole woman he had ever loved, brought it back triplefold.

And now Peter's bumbling cowardliness and the Americans' determination to foil the control he'd worked his entire life to gain was pushing him over the edge again. He felt it. Felt the need to place his hands around his enemy's throat and squeeze until there was no breath left, just a beckoning call to death's hollow grave.

Killing had never been difficult, until Diane. If she'd never found out, he wouldn't have needed to silence her. Once she threatened to go to the authorities, her fate was sealed. He'd never blamed her. Like his mother she was too pure to understand his need to control.

Victory was so close with Sarb dead and Peter next and no one to know, except for Karl, and he needn't worry about Karl. Lauter felt the high lift him, allowing his anger to take him deep within to that other self that gained him the control he sought.

The cat slipped from his grip and he cursed, reminded of how everything he'd worked for might be slipping away because of two Americans. In a rage he grabbed the cat back. Small, helpless and trusting, the cat nuzzled the hand that clutched it.

The next moment he heard a commotion at the door and the cat leapt from his arms. Lauter took a deep breath, struggling for his other face. "Peter, is that you?"

Suddenly the room was filled with people. Who were they? His business was with Peter, and of course, Karl, when the time arrived. Lauter, used to being in command, addressed the group at large. "Don't just stand there. Get back to work, the lot of you."

Strangely, no one moved.

Before he could repeat his orders, several more men rushed into the room. A field of semiautomatics was leveled at him.

"All right Lauter. It's over. Put your hands in the air." The speech was reiterated in German and French.

The truth hit Lauter with the force of a sledgehammer pounding into his skull. Frazier set him up. He'd pay. Maybe not today but one day they would all pay. He took a moment to memorize their faces. Frazier stood next to the Pardue girl and Ashley who'd come with the police. Trudeau and the airline girl were in on it too. His foot located the button under the edge of the table and he positioned himself.

For a spilt-second the room seemed to spin as the floor opened beneath him. The outraged cries of disbelief that followed this deed furnished him an exorbitant sense of satisfaction. When his feet touched solid ground on the floor below, he headed for the back stairs. He had to reach the laboratories—destroy the evidence before it was too late.

46

Lauter threw the circuit breakers for the top two floors and made his way swiftly down the cellar stairs. In a matter of minutes, Frazier would realize where he was headed and lead the authorities below to the concealed labs. Lauter was counting on the darkness to slow them.

He ran through the storeroom, fleeing past stacked metal drums of chemicals used to make cocaine and heroin. Anger exploded anew at the thought of destroying the precious ether. The contents of the fifty-five gallon barrels mixed with the cocaine base in the final process cost $500 a barrel. In Columbia a barrel sold for $12,000. His one consolation was that Frazier and the rest would blow up with them and in the end he would win.

He tilted one of the drums on its side and opened the bunghole, allowing the ether to gush across the floor. The metal rumbled as he rolled it into the production lab. The unique barbecue to follow might have cheered him if it were not for the millions he would lose in the process. The loss of the refined cocaine stored in the next room alone was a fortune. Survival, however, meant cutting his losses, and Lauter was a survivor.

For a brief moment he hesitated, taking in the huge vats and containers of coca paste, gasoline, ammonia, acetone and ether joined by tubes and various paraphernalia to form a sophisticated cocaine-producing lab. The complexity of the operation was breathtaking. His was no jungle lab to be dismantled in twenty minutes, he thought with pride. But curse them all—he probably had minutes at the most, despite the breakers shut-down.

Lauter dipped a handkerchief in the acetone vat and drew out a match. He rushed for the door and turned back to light the fire. Footsteps thundered down the hall. They were closing in. His only chance to escape was the hidden passage. He clutched the match, darting across the room.

Susan and Mark raced down the hall trailing the authorities. She sniffed. What was that smell? The men began to spread out in different directions but Mark pulled her forward. She gasped and drew him back, peering inside the room they'd just passed. She'd found the lab and Lauter. He was trying to escape. She thought, he's going to blow us up. Susan saw her life vanish in an instant and knew she didn't want to die.

"Stop! You'll kill us all."

She rushed forward but Lauter shoved her aside.

Some sixth sense sent her gaze in a slow search around the room until she saw what looked like a body in the corner.

"Get back!" Lauter yelled, reaching to stop her as she ran toward it. She ducked, eluding his grasp and made it to the corner.

Lauter whirled on her and stumbled, striking his head on a metal file cabinet as he fell.

Mark ran into the room. "Susan--"

"It's Kevin," she called.

In a moment, he was beside her, helping to untie Kevin. Between them they half-carried, half-dragged him to the door, where Mark took over.

On their way out, Susan glanced back and saw that Lauter had risen. The match—he held the match as if ready to strike it, his eyes daring her to move. Mark and Kevin's retreating steps echoed down the hall.

The seconds dragged into years, her heart pounding as if it would burst. The faint scraping of match head on metal reached her ears and she gasped as the tempest rocked her.

Lauter stood in the midst of the fire. Small explosions erupted along the length of the room. There was no way to reach him. The flames appeared to engulf him.

He shouted above the tumult, "You can't destroy me!" A frenzied laugh rang out in the chamber, followed by a last frantic shout, and Lauter disappeared.

Susan watched, feeling as if time were frozen and somehow she'd wake up, the nightmare ended. She couldn't be sorry that a man so evil would die.

She felt Mark tugging on her arm, trying to pull her away.

"It's not safe," he yelled.

Uncomprehending, she dragged her feet, gazing back at the flames, mesmerized. He shook her roughly.

"We've got to get out of here. The whole place is going to blow."

Suddenly coming to her senses, Susan swallowed in terror and ran beside him. She flew up the stairs and outside. Then it hit her.

"Benjamin and Kevin. Mark, they're in there."

The harsh planes in his face softened. "Relax." He turned her around and she saw Kevin and Benjamin huddled under a tree. Astonishingly, Gayle and Dom were with them.

She spotted Zach and Francois among the authorities and breathed a sigh of relief and a prayer of thanksgiving. They were all safe.

Mark held her in the circle of his arms and together they watched the building detonate into an angry inferno. Passionate bursts of red, orange and torrid yellow lit the night; the ferocious flames, fanning higher and higher in the sky, appeared almost to reach out and ignite the sliver of moon overhead. It was a horrible moment, and, just then, she could feel no remorse at Lauter's certain death.

Susan shivered and Mark drew her closer. She closed her eyes, wanting to erase the memory of what she'd just lived through.

Tomorrow, she thought. Somehow, they'd pick up the pieces and go on. Somehow, they'd forget the horror they'd experienced this night.

The gift of tomorrow beckoned, a token promise for the future.